Praise for Jon Loomis

MATING SEASON

"A poet and a college professor with an ear for comedy . . . Loomis heaps up the bodies in this peaceful, playful beach town."　　　　—National Public Radio

"A black comedy full of raunchy vocabulary and kinky sexuality. He's definitely a writer to watch, given his knack for illuminating human nature."
　　　　　　　　　　　　　　　—*Publishers Weekly*

"Homicide fiction doesn't get much sexier—literally and figuratively . . . The locals and the local color are artfully presented here . . . The dialogue—as perfectly juicy and salty as a fresh, expertly prepared clam roll—also serves as an enormous enticement to indulge in this mystery. The action is pleasingly paced, while the story remains simple, yet well-constructed . . . Prepare to have your buttons pushed, and expect to like it."　　　　　　　　　　　　—*Shine*

"This sequel to *High Season* features quirky characters and witty repartee."　　　　　　　—*Library Journal*

HIGH SEASON

"[Frank] Coffin is an enormously appealing invention . . . P-town proves a plum setting for lighthearted crime . . . With his honed sense of humor and keen *mise en scène*, Loomis is a keeper, and so is Coffin."
　　　　　　　　　　—*The Washington Post Book World*

Also by Jon Loomis

High Season

Vanitas Motel

The Pleasure Principle

MATING SEASON

JON LOOMIS

St. Martin's Paperbacks

This is a work of fiction. All of the characters, organizations, and events portrayed in this novel are either products of the author's imagination or are used fictitiously.

MATING SEASON

Copyright © 2009 by Jon Loomis.

Cover photos: of house by Susie Cushner / Graphistock / Jupiterimages; of wood by istockphoto.com / NYCShooter; of sky by istockphoto.com / CGlade.

For information address St. Martin's Press, 175 Fifth Avenue, New York, NY 10010.

Library of Congress Catalog Card Number: 2009003614

EAN: 978-0-312-94440-7

Printed in the United States of America

Minotaur edition / May 2009
St. Martin's Paperbacks edition / May 2010

St. Martin's Paperbacks are published by St. Martin's Press, 175 Fifth Avenue, New York, NY 10010.

10 9 8 7 6 5 4 3 2 1

For Allyson and Mrs. Lizard

AUTHOR'S NOTE

ONE

Detective Frank Coffin stood in the sun-streaked living room that had, until sometime the day before, belonged to Kenji Sole. It was a very nice living room indeed: spacious and airy, furnished in an eclectic mix of antiques and Eames-era modern, with several excellent abstract paintings hung on the white walls. Coffin recognized a door-sized Rothko in violet and umber, and what might have been an early de Kooning in black and white. Tall windows ran along the living room's south side overlooking Provincetown Harbor, which sparked in the bright morning sunlight. A massive stone fireplace dominated the opposite wall. The floor, made of wide oak planks, was mostly covered by an enormous Persian rug, patterned in watery blues and greens, which would have been quite beautiful if Kenji Sole's dead body had not been lying on it in the middle of a large and complicated bloodstain.

"Looks like a stabbing," said the policeman standing next to Coffin. His big belly strained against his uniform shirt. He was Coffin's cousin Tony Santos.

Coffin looked at him, then back at the eight-inch chef's knife protruding from Kenji Sole's chest. "You think?" he said.

Sergeant Lola Winters tapped Tony on the shoulder.

"Maybe you'd better go outside and keep a lid on traffic," she said.

"I don't see any traffic," Tony said, looking out the north window at the steep, narrow road leading up to Mayflower Heights from Route 6A.

"Then it'll be easy," Coffin said.

"Okay." Tony sighed. "Fine. I get it. I could use a smoke anyway."

Coffin held up a finger. "Crime scene. No cigarette butts."

"Right, no worries," Tony said, trotting down the open staircase.

Coffin rubbed his temples. He felt dizzy; a high-pitched whine sang faintly in his left ear. Kenji Sole had been a beautiful young woman. Asian or part Asian, she had almond-shaped eyes, an oval face, a strong nose that hinted at some European genetics. She had long, shag-cut hair dyed honey blond. It was hard to say how old she was: early thirties, maybe. Slender and small-breasted, she'd kept her pubic hair trimmed to a neat, dark strip. She was nude except for a sheer baby-doll nightgown and an ankle bracelet made of tiny shells, which glowed pale in the sunlight against her skin. Coffin looked away, feeling queasy, then looked again. She had been stabbed at least five times and was covered in drying blood.

"Frank?" Lola said. "You want to go outside? Get some air?"

"Yeah," Coffin said. "Just for a minute. Sorry."

Coffin sat on the back steps. He felt better; the buzzing sound in his head had subsided, and his peripheral vision seemed almost normal. Lola fanned him slowly with her uniform hat.

"I'm okay now," Coffin said. "You can stop with the fanning."

"You still don't look so good, Frank."

A car passed below them on 6A, heading toward Provincetown. A pair of grackles waddled across the narrow lawn.

"I'm fine," Coffin said. "Let's check out the rest of the house. Then we'll go talk to the cleaning ladies."

The house was a big seventies modern, two stories, newly remodeled. There was a detached three-car garage with an upstairs carriage house.

The kitchen was well designed and almost pathologically neat. Sparkling crystal wine goblets hung, globes down, from an overhead rack; the six-burner Wolf range was spotless, as though it had never been used. There were gleaming black granite countertops and cherry cabinets so perfectly finished they seemed to glow from within. A sliding glass door opened onto a broad deck that faced southeast, toward Truro. The built-in stainless steel refrigerator was big enough to hang a body in. The thought gave Coffin a quick shiver. He resisted the urge to open the refrigerator door. There was an antique ship's clock on the wall. Coffin glanced at his watch: The clock was nine minutes fast.

"Check it out, Frank."

Coffin turned. Lola was squinting at Kenji Sole's collection of kitchen knives, stored in a slotted oak block.

"Shun," Lola said. "Japanese. The fancy set." She pointed to an empty slot in the block. "Our killer found his weapon here, instead of bringing his own."

"Indicating what?" Coffin said.

Lola cocked an eyebrow. "What is this, a quiz?"

"Sorry," Coffin said, smoothing his mustache. "Just thinking out loud."

"You could plan to kill someone and still improvise

the weapon," Lola said. "You go to their house intending to strangle them and then decide you like the look of the chain saw out in the garage, or the fireplace poker."

The kitchen's southeast wall was made almost entirely of glass. Coffin stood for a moment looking at the small waves slopping into the curve of lion-colored beach, out past the treetops and the North Truro tourist motels. "I wonder what's upstairs," Coffin said.

"Holy crap," Lola said, standing next to Coffin in the master bedroom. "It's like a bomb went off. I wonder what they were looking for." Clothes and jewelry lay scattered everywhere. Most of the books had been pulled from the floor-to-ceiling shelves. The closet had been turned inside out, the mattress slashed, the dresser drawers dumped on the floor. Two small paintings had been torn from the wall and flung across the room. One lay facedown; the other was a black-and-white abstract that might have been a portrait of a nude woman. One print still hung on the wall: a dune-and-sunset picture with an idealized lighthouse in the middle distance. It seemed oddly out of place among all the abstract-expressionist and color-field pieces—some of which, Coffin thought, were probably worth a lot of money.

He opened the door to the bathroom. The walls and floor were green marble. The shower and the Jacuzzi were enormous and outfitted with gold fixtures. "Jesus," Coffin said, his voice echoing softly off the marble walls. "You could throw a party in here. It's bigger than my living room."

There were three smaller bedrooms and two additional baths. All were as neat as the kitchen, thoroughly dusted, tucked, and straightened—tasteful and impersonal.

The study had been tossed as thoroughly as the master bedroom. The drawers of the carved antique desk had been yanked out and dumped onto the floor. Pens, pencils, legal pads, CDs, paper clips, and Post-it Notes were everywhere. The Aeron chair lay on its side. There was a printer on a wooden stand, and a computer keyboard had been flung into the corner.

"Keyboard, printer," Coffin said, pointing.

"No computer," Lola said.

"I hope this isn't going to be about technology," Coffin said. "I hate technology."

"I'm guessing it's about sex," Lola said. She scratched her belly. She had a long scar that ran from below her right breast to her left hipbone; sometimes it itched. "They only searched her personal space. Not the guest rooms, not the kitchen or the living room. Weird."

"Like they knew where to look," Coffin said. "Or got scared off. Or found whatever it was and left."

The bedrooms all opened onto a wraparound deck, suspended over a steep bluff that dropped sixty feet straight down to the edge of the old highway. The trees below had been trimmed so that the view of the harbor and Cape Cod Bay were unobstructed. Coffin stood on the deck for a long moment and watched a red sailboat noodling around on the water. The sun glinted; the sailboat fluoresced. Coffin wanted a cigarette, but his girlfriend, Jamie, had thrown away his last pack and ordered him to quit again.

"I wonder what's keeping Mancini and the boys?" Lola said, standing in the sliding glass door. Mancini was the Cape and Islands district attorney; he and his team of state police detectives were on their way from Barnstable, driving up Route 6 in Mancini's big Lexus.

Coffin looked at his watch. It was almost 8:45. "They'll

be here any minute," he said. "We'd better have a talk with the cleaning ladies."

In the past few years there had been an enormous influx of Eastern Europeans—mostly girls in their late teens and early twenties—into Provincetown's summer labor force. They came with student visas and worked mostly illegally, waiting tables or cleaning toilets or running cash registers at the A&P. No job was too menial, no living conditions too squalid. Coffin had ridden along on more than one nuisance call to the older North Truro motels that now served as cheap living spaces for seasonal workers and found as many as twelve Eastern Europeans living in a room, sleeping in shifts, three to a bed. They came from poor countries, mostly: Serbia, Bulgaria, Croatia. They needed money to pay for school, and the rest they sent back home to their families, at least until they got caught up in the American consumer frenzy and decided to keep it for themselves. Some of them, unsurprisingly, fell into drug use or prostitution, though there wasn't much demand for female prostitutes in Provincetown.

Kenji Sole's cleaning ladies were young Eastern European women who worked for a service called Maid to Order. Their car, a ten-year-old Honda Civic with a trunk full of vacuums and cleaning supplies, was parked in the drive between the house and the garage. Both girls were very pretty: a tanned, big-breasted blonde named Minka and a slim brunette named Zelenka. They were sitting on the steps to the carriage house and smoking. Coffin didn't bother checking their IDs.

"So you got here at what time?" Coffin asked them.

"A little after eight," Minka said, her hand shaking as she took a drag from her cigarette. "We went in kitchen door and right away start to work. Zelenka saw her first."

"The door was unlocked?" Lola said.

Minka shrugged. "Is P'town," she said. "Who locks their door?"

"Was that normal?" Coffin asked. "You'd just show up at 8:00 A.M., let yourselves in, and get to work?"

The brunette, Zelenka, nodded. "It was normal," she said. Her eyes were bright blue and almond-shaped, her hair cut short. "She always leaves money on the counter—cash, two hundred dollars. Sometimes she comes downstairs for coffee, but mostly we don't see her."

Coffin nodded. Their accents made his heart leap in his chest. "If you didn't see her, where would she be? Out?"

Minka shrugged. "I don't know. Out, sure. Not in the house, or we would see her."

"Two hundred dollars?" Lola said. "Isn't that kind of a lot?"

"Is big house," Minka said. "We clean everything."

"So," Coffin said. "Zelenka, you saw her first?"

"Yes." Zelenka's hair bobbed a little when she nodded her head. "I am going into living room to vacuum, and she is there. So much blood! I feel very frightened when I see her."

"Did you touch her? Or touch anything in the living room?"

Zelenka shook her head vigorously. "No. I don't touch nothing."

"She screams very loud," Minka said. " 'What is going on?' I say. She runs outside, screaming, screaming. So I am afraid. I go outside, too. She says Miss Kenji is dead."

"You knew she was dead?" Coffin asked.

"Yes," Zelenka said, taking a last hit from her cigarette, then lighting a new one from the butt. "I see dead people before, in my country. Many times. She is dead."

"So then what did you do?"

"Minka calls our boss on her cell phone. Boss calls police." She pointed to the carriage house. "Also, the man who lives there comes outside to help us. He is nice man, I think."

"He helped you? How?"

"He checks in house, to make sure is safe."

"Safe?"

"He makes sure whoever stabs Miss Kenji is gone," Zelenka said. "He is very brave."

"How long was he in there?" Coffin said.

Minka shrugged. "I don't know. It seems like long time. Ten minutes maybe? Long time. I start to worry something happens to him. Then he comes out."

The carriage house apartment was a large studio, well appointed but messy. It had a fireplace, a small kitchen, and high, wide windows overlooking Route 6A and the harbor. Coffin wondered what it rented for.

"What time did you hear Zelenka scream?" Lola said, pen poised above her notebook.

"Right around eight o'clock. I was in bed, and when I heard her screaming I threw some clothes on and went outside." Bobby Cavalo was a tall, muscular man in his early thirties, remarkably handsome, with square white teeth and a mass of dark, curly hair that made Coffin think *poodle*.

"Like what, a minute after you heard her scream? Less?"

"A little more, I think. I sleep naked, and I'd been out late. It took a minute or two to get my bearings, find clothes, put them on."

"So you got your bearings, got dressed, went downstairs," Coffin said. "Then what?"

"One of the girls was on her cell, calling her boss. The other one was standing there with her hands over her mouth, pale as a ghost. They told me what had happened. I said they could come upstairs if they wanted, but they wouldn't."

"Why not?"

"Maybe they were scared."

"Scared?" Coffin said. "Of you?"

Cavalo shrugged. "They don't know me," he said. "I guess it makes sense, given what happened to Kenji."

"So then you went inside the house?" Coffin said. "What for?"

"I thought that if Kenji was still alive, I might be able to help her," Cavalo said. "You know, mouth-to-mouth or something."

Lola met Coffin's eyes, then looked down at her notebook.

Coffin rubbed his chin. "That's not what Minka said. She said you went in to make sure whoever killed her was gone."

"She must have misunderstood," Cavalo said. "The language thing, I guess."

"Weren't you worried that they might still be in there?" Lola said. "I would be."

"Sure, I thought about it. That's why I came back up and got my gun."

Coffin's eyebrows went up. "You have a gun?" he said.

"Sure," Cavalo said. "It's just a little .22. I keep it for protection. Want to see it?"

"Protection from what?" Coffin said.

Cavalo looked out the window and nodded toward Kenji Sole's house. "From what happened to Kenji," he said. "Among other things."

"Among other things like what?"

Cavalo lowered his voice a little. "Let's just say some people I don't want to see may decide to come looking for me," he said. "Old grudges, that kind of thing. That's all I can say about it."

"Fair enough," Coffin said. "So you went in."

"I went in and she was definitely dead; nothing I could do. I looked around a little just to make sure no one else was in there. I had my gun, but I was still pretty spooked. I didn't stay very long."

"How long would you say?"

"Three, four minutes, tops. Probably less. The hair on my neck was standing up the whole time."

"You didn't see anyone? Hear anything?"

"No."

"Did you touch anything?"

"I don't think so, but my fingerprints are probably all over the house already, if that's what you're thinking."

"I'm more interested in whether you moved anything or took anything."

"No. I didn't."

"So your fingerprints are all over?" Lola said. "You hung out there a lot, is what you're saying?"

"Not a lot, no. We had drinks together sometimes. You know, cocktails. She invited me over for dinner every now and then. She's a great cook. Was."

"Was that it?" Lola said. "The whole relationship? Drinks and the occasional dinner?"

"You mean, did we sleep together?" Cavalo asked, tossing his dark curls.

"Right," Lola said.

"Sure," Cavalo said. "Once in a while. Kenji liked sex a lot."

"If she liked it so much," Coffin said, "why just once in a while?"

"She was pretty busy," Cavalo said. "With other men, I mean. She kind of slept around, I guess you could say."

"Did that bother you?" Coffin said.

"Nah. I liked Kenji and all, but I'm really more into guys."

"When was the last time you saw Ms. Sole alive?" Coffin said.

"Day before yesterday, I think," Cavalo said. "I stopped by on my way into town. I had a DVD I wanted to give her."

"She liked movies?" Lola said.

Cavalo laughed. "She *loved* movies. She collected them. She wrote about film, you know, for a living."

"What," Coffin said, "like a critic?"

"Academic," Cavalo said. "She's written a couple of books on film theory, and she taught at BU, part-time."

"What kind of films?" Lola said.

Cavalo bit his lip. "Mostly adult."

"Adult?" Lola said. "As in porn?"

"Right. She was interested in porn from a cultural studies perspective. She wrote her dissertation on it."

"Cultural studies," Coffin said.

"You made porn, she studied it," Lola said, tapping her pen on her notebook. "Funny how that worked out."

"We had that connection, yeah," Cavalo said.

Coffin scratched his earlobe. "Hundreds of DVDs? I didn't see any DVDs in there."

"You must have missed the screening room," Cavalo said. "It's downstairs, off the living room. If you didn't know it was there, you'd think it was a broom closet. It's got the big-screen HDTV, surround sound and everything."

Coffin looked at Lola. "Surround sound and everything," he said.

"Some house," Lola said. "For an academic."

Cavalo lowered his voice. "Trust fund," he said. "From her grandfather. He was, like, *stinkin'* rich. Left her millions. If she wanted it, she could buy it." He pointed at the floor, the garage below it. "Range Rover for winter, Porsche convertible for summer. She also owns a boat, but I think it's being repaired. And an apartment in the West Village. And a place in Key West."

"Any other family that you know of?" Coffin asked. "Parents still alive? Siblings?"

Cavalo frowned. "No siblings. Mother's dead, but her father's still very much alive."

"You say that like it's a bad thing," Coffin said.

"Her father is J. Hedrick Sole—he's about eighty and maybe a little bit senile. Senior partner at a big Boston law firm, Scrooby, Sammitch, and Sole. Semiretired now. Very rich and very . . . difficult. He and Kenji had a *complicated* relationship."

Lola wrote in her notebook. "How so?" she said.

"J. Hedrick has a girlfriend. She's young enough to be his granddaughter—twenty-five, maybe. She's costing him a fortune. Fancy condo, fancy car, jewelry, clothes, use of a private jet, the whole enchilada. Kenji hired a private eye to have her checked out."

"Let me guess," Coffin said. "She's a hooker."

"Nah," Cavalo said, grinning. "It's better than that. She's a performance artist."

Cavalo's teeth were perfectly white and perfectly straight. *Dentures?* Coffin wondered. Then he thought, *Veneers, maybe. Everybody's got veneers these days.*

"Uh-oh," Lola said.

Cavalo nodded. "She's all about shock on a grand scale: lots of very public nudity, even public sex. Her last performance was in the middle of Vatican Square, if you can believe that, with a bunch of guys dressed up like nuns. She almost started a riot. She has a full camera crew to document her performances, and a fancy lawyer on call for when she gets arrested."

"And Kenji didn't think she was a suitable companion for good old Dad," Coffin said. He squinted out at the harbor, which was just visible through the screen of trees.

"Kenji hated her—thought she was a gold digger and a fraud. She was very upset."

"Daddy was squandering the inheritance," Coffin said.

"Exactly. Last time we talked about it she was looking into having him declared incompetent. She wanted power of attorney."

"What were you doing last night?" Lola said. "After six, say?"

"I was out. Went to the A-House until closing, then to an after-hours party until around 5:00 A.M. Then I came home and went straight to bed."

"You didn't see or hear anything unusual before you went out, or when you came home?"

"No. Except that a lot of Kenji's lights were still on."

"Was that unusual?"

"Enough that I noticed it, I guess."

"Any idea who might have killed her?"

"No."

"Any idea why they might have searched the place?"

"No. Sorry."

Coffin smoothed his mustache. "What was the DVD?"

Cavalo looked confused.

"The one you gave her the day before yesterday," Coffin said. "What was it?"

"It was a porn thing," Cavalo said, blushing a little. "One of mine."

"One of yours?" Lola asked. "You mean, one from *your* collection?"

"No," Cavalo said. "I mean one I'm in. That's what I do for a living. I'm a porn actor." He stood up, crossed the room, and took a DVD from a small wooden rack next to the TV. "Here. This is the one. Hot off the presses." He handed it to Coffin.

The DVD was called *Daddy Knows Best*, and Cavalo's picture was on the cover. He was wearing nothing but motorcycle boots, a leather cap, and a pair of black leather chaps.

Coffin frowned. "You're worried about people coming after you and you're a porn actor?" he said. "You think that's a good idea?"

"I'm doing gay stuff now," Cavalo said. "Two different worlds. Plus, I had some work done. I don't look the same."

"What kind of work?" Coffin said.

"Eyes, chin, nose, teeth, tattoo removal, the works," Cavalo said. "I even had my cock enlarged. Not that it needed it."

Coffin looked at Lola. "Not that it needed it," he said.

"What makes a guy get a penis enlargement?" Lola said, looking at the cover of the DVD Cavalo had given them. They were standing at the bottom of the carriage house stairs. "Insecurity? Is that it?"

"Vanity," Coffin said. "Ego. At least in Bobby's case."

"Still," Lola said, peering a bit more closely at the picture, "it *is* impressive. In a freakish kind of way. Bobby may not be the brightest bulb on the tree, but I can see why Kenji might have been interested."

"Interesting piercing," Coffin said.

"Wouldn't that hurt?" Lola said. "Like, a lot?"

"Colt Masters," Coffin said, flipping the box over, reading the back cover. "That's his porn name."

"It's got a nice ring to it," Lola said.

Coffin looked at her. "Ouch," he said.

Tony was leaning against his cruiser, eating something. Coffin waved him over.

"We have to go back inside for a minute or two," Coffin said. "If Mancini shows up, try to stall him."

"Will do," Tony said, taking a bite from a large, dripping sandwich. "How?"

"You'll think of something," Coffin said. "What are you eating?"

"Hoagie," Tony said, mouth full. He held the sandwich under Coffin's nose. "Want a bite?"

Coffin turned and walked toward the house. His left ear started buzzing again. His legs felt several inches too long. "What I want," he said, "is to get through the day without fainting or throwing up."

"I dated a performance artist a few times," Lola said.

The screening room was down a short flight of stairs from the kitchen, tucked in next to the storage/furnace room in Kenji Sole's basement. Coffin pushed the door open.

"She was developing this piece where she'd take off all her clothes, smear herself with shit—except it was really chocolate syrup—and recite the Pledge of Allegiance backwards. Then she'd invite members of the audience to come onstage and lick the chocolate syrup off."

"Genius," Coffin said.

Lola ducked her head, embarrassed. "It was supposed to be a statement about how society silences women by brainwashing them with jingoistic slogans. I forget how the chocolate syrup fit in."

There were no windows in the screening room; it felt airless and claustrophobic compared to the light and space of the rest of the house, and was barely big enough for its wet bar, L-shaped leather sofa, huge, wall-mounted flat-screen TV, and built-in floor-to-ceiling media shelving. Hundreds—maybe thousands—of DVDs had been stuffed into every available inch of shelf space.

"Wow," Lola said, pulling on a latex glove. "Cavalo wasn't kidding." She slid a DVD from one of the shelves. *"Moulin Splooge."*

Coffin looked over her shoulder. *"May the Foreskin Be with You,"* he said. "Look, here's a clever one—*Anal-ize This!"*

Lola curled her lip. "Ew," she said.

"There's some gay stuff here, too," Coffin said. *"Sailor Studs; Bad Boy Bikers."*

Lola squinted at Coffin. "Are you thinking what I'm thinking?"

"That maybe Ms. Sole had a more than purely academic interest in the subject matter?"

"You have to wonder when people say they're studying porn . . ."

"Why not Tolstoy? Or the lives of the razor clams?"

"It's kind of the Pete Townshend excuse," Lola said, "but what do I know?"

Coffin shrugged. "Exactly," he said. "We're just a couple of bourgeois ignoramuses. Not PhDs."

"Or psychiatrists," Lola said.

It was unnerving, Coffin thought, standing in that room, surrounded by all those DVDs with their stored memories of ritualized passion, or the banal stuff that passed for it in the porn industry, all those hundreds of men and women or men and men or women and women (or, or, or), variously coupled and conjoined, penetrating or being penetrated in all the standard ways—and others not so standard—scene after scene stored on plastic forever, the actors and actresses eternally young, eternally entwined. It was, Coffin thought, a strange electronic hell to end up in.

"Voyeurism," Coffin said. "On a grand scale."

Lola nodded. "It doesn't get any grander," she said.

"Unusual in a woman, isn't it?"

Lola thought for a second. "I guess so," she said. "I mean, most porn is made for guys, right? Gay or straight, still guys."

"What about romance novels?" Coffin said. "Bodice-rippers, or whatever they're called. Aren't they porn for women?"

"It's not the same," Lola said.

"Why is it different?" Coffin said. "Porn is porn, right?"

"Verbal versus visual," Lola said. "You guys are all eyes and no imagination."

Coffin sat on the sofa and rubbed his chin. He'd missed a spot shaving; the whiskers were spiky and thick. "So what's the scenario? Rape, murder, robbery?"

"Sure," Lola said. "Makes sense, right?"

"I don't know—it feels wrong." Coffin shook his head. "I don't see it as a rape thing."

"The nightgown," Lola said. "You don't wear a white lace baby-doll unless you're with someone. It's a nightie of consent."

"He could have forced her to wear it," Coffin said.

"I guess so," Lola said. "Seems like a bit of a stretch, though, you're right."

"So if it's not rape, then what?"

"Well," Lola said, frowning. "Maybe they're going to

have sex, get into a fight instead, then he kills her and robs the place."

"Maybe," said Coffin. "Maybe she has something he wants, he sleeps with her thinking maybe he can get it out of her, she won't give it up, he kills her and takes whatever it is."

Lola sat next to Coffin, her knee briefly touching his. "Maybe it's not the same person," she said. "Maybe person one has sex with her, kills her, and runs off. Person *two* knocks on the door, nobody answers, she's lying dead on the Persian rug, they step over the body and start looking for cash and jewelry."

"And computers," Coffin said. "So she's dead before they rob the place?"

Lola nodded. "Had to be before."

"Unless she came home, caught them in the act—"

"Took off all her clothes and put on a see-through nightie while threatening to call the cops—"

"Maybe she and the killer are having sex," Coffin said. "They have a fight—he trashes the place, she tries to stop him, and he stabs her."

"Maybe she trashes the place, strips, puts on the nightie and stabs herself. Five or six times. With an eight-inch chef's knife."

Coffin laughed, a short, sharp bark. They sat silently for another minute, looking at the floor-to-ceiling shelves full of porn.

"Curious about her film theory books?" Lola asked.

"Gack," Coffin said. "Not so much. Ever read any theory?"

"A little, in college. Everything's a text. You're a text, I'm a text, your car's a text. Beyond that I couldn't make heads nor tales of it."

"Nobody can," Coffin said. "That's the whole point."

* * *

Outside, Tony had wrapped most of the driveway in yellow crime scene tape, entirely closing off the entrance. Mancini and the two state police detectives were standing next to a big Lexus sedan as it idled in the street.

"Coffin!" Mancini waved Coffin over. "Tell your idiot cousin to clear this tape away, before I cut it down myself."

Coffin tapped his watch. "What kept you guys? Stop off for a clam roll in Eastham?" He looked at Tony, who had a long strip of crime scene tape stuck to his shoe. "Are you done?" he said.

"Not really," Tony said, "but I ran out of tape."

Coffin took a cigarette out of the pack in Tony's shirt pocket and stuck it into his mouth. "Maybe you should cut some of this down so Mr. Mancini and his friends can pull into the driveway."

"Thought you quit," Tony said, lighting Coffin's cigarette with a match.

Coffin blew smoke out of his nose. "I did," he said.

"Where's Chief Boyle?" Mancini asked, after he'd gone through the house. The two state police detectives were standing on the downstairs deck, waiting for the Crime Scene Services team to drive up from New Bedford in their shiny white van.

"He's an administrator," Coffin said. "He doesn't do actual crime."

"Lucky him," Mancini said.

He was wearing his Provincetown outfit, Coffin thought: perfectly pressed jeans, a black polo shirt buttoned all the way up, and sunglasses with blue oval lenses. His hair was gelled into a self-conscious rumple.

"Oh, come on," Coffin said. "You love a good, high-profile murder. Admit it. Nothing keeps your office in the public eye like a celebrity homicide."

The left side of Mancini's mouth turned upward a quarter of an inch. "No comment," he said. "What about you? How are the panic attacks? Any twinges in there?"

"One or two," Coffin said. "Thanks for asking."

"Well, I'm not just being nice," Mancini said.

"Ah," Coffin said.

Mancini looked at Coffin through his blue lenses. "What I'm trying to say is, are you up to assisting in this investigation? Officially?"

"Well," said Coffin. "This is unexpected. It's like the captain of the football team asking little old me to the prom."

Mancini shrugged. "Be a smart-ass, Coffin, if it makes you feel better. You don't like me, I don't like you, but you know the lay of the land up here, and that's useful to me. I owe it to the people of the Commonwealth of—"

"If I'm on the investigation officially," Coffin said, "you've covered your ass three hundred and sixty degrees. Case solved, you get credit for being smart enough to bring us in. Not solved, you blame the incompetent locals. That about right?"

Mancini lowered his voice. "I made a mistake last time, okay? What do you want from me—a written apology?"

"Last time," Coffin said, "we all made our share of mistakes. Except Sergeant Winters."

Lola was standing nearby, talking to one of Kenji Sole's neighbors—a very tall woman with thick legs and a big yellow hat.

Mancini pursed his lips. "Ah yes. The lovely and talented Sergeant Winters. Too bad she doesn't like boys."

"Too bad for who?" Coffin said.

"Come on, Coffin," Mancini said. "Don't tell me you wouldn't like a piece of that."

Lola's hair was dark blond, pulled back in a short ponytail that swung below the band of her uniform hat. She stood five feet ten inches tall and looked slimmer than her 155 pounds. Coffin liked her a great deal. It had been less than two years since she had saved his life.

"Don't worry," Coffin said. "I don't think you're gay."

Mancini grinned.

"If I'm in," Coffin said, "Lola's in, too."

"What," Mancini said, "afraid you'll end up in the drink again?"

"You never know," Coffin said.

"I'll talk to Boyle," Mancini said.

In the carriage house apartment, Bobby Cavalo stood by the window, watching the Crime Scene Services team unload equipment from their white van. He held a small black cell phone to his ear. The signal was terrible.

"I told you," he said. "It's gone. Whoever killed her must have taken it. All the DVDs, too."

A blast of static came from the cell phone. Cavalo could barely hear the voice on the other end.

"*It*. The computer," he said. "What else?"

There was another rush of static, a voice buried inside it.

"TV star?" Cavalo said. "What do you mean, did I find the TV star?"

"Not 'TV star,' you idiot," the voice said. "*DVR*. Did you find the fucking DVR?"

"DVR? You mean like a TiVo? I didn't see anything like that."

"You didn't fucking look, you fucking moron," the voice said through the static.

"There wasn't much time," Cavalo said. "I wasn't thinking. She was lying there dead, for God's sake, and the place was a mess. Maybe whoever killed her beat me to it."

"Well," the voice said, the connection suddenly clear, "if they did, they'd better lock their doors at night. That thing's worth a fortune."

"More than the computer?"

"You got pretty much everything that was on the computer, right? A half-dozen clips."

"Right. That's all I could find, anyway."

"A good DVR can store hundreds of hours of video," the voice said. "It's the freaking mother lode."

"You think he's on it?"

"If he was in her bedroom, he's on it."

"Maybe I can go back in," Cavalo said, "when all these cops pack up their shit and go home."

"Lotsa luck," said the voice. "They'll bring in a locksmith and rekey all the doors. They'll probably wire the place with an alarm system, too, if it doesn't already have one. You had your shot, unless you're planning to climb down the chimney like freaking Santa Claus."

"Fuck," Cavalo said. "I'd bet a million dollars it's still in there somewhere. It's like it's calling out to me. I can *feel* it."

Coffin sat in the new leather wing chair opposite Boyle's desk, watching the spot of glare on Boyle's scalp shift from side to side as the police chief shook his head.

"Absolutely not, Coffin," Boyle said. "Your goddamn panic attacks almost got you and Winters killed last time. No more homicide investigations for you."

"Fine with me," Coffin said. "What did you tell Mancini?"

Boyle steepled his fingers. "That he'll have to find his way around P'town without you, because you're not up to it."

"Fine," Coffin said. He started to get up.

"Wait a second, Coffin," Boyle said, holding up a hand. "Am I getting the impression that you *want* to participate in this investigation?"

"I hope not," Coffin said.

"You're trying to prove something, is that it? That you've still got the old mojo?"

"Nope."

"Well, I'm not going to put other officers at risk just so you can repair your ego." Boyle's phone buzzed. He punched the intercom button. "What is it, Arlene?"

"The attorney general," Arlene said through the phone's plastic speaker. "On line one."

"The attorney general?" Boyle said. "Of Massachusetts?"

"Yes, sir. Attorney General Poblano," Arlene said. "On line one."

Boyle pushed the blinking button. "Yes, sir," he said. "This is Chief Boyle. Yes, sir. That's right, sir."

A gull floated past Boyle's window, staring in at Coffin with one hard yellow eye.

"Both of them, yes, sir. No, sir—it's no inconvenience to me," Boyle said into the phone. "Absolutely. Happy to do it, sir. I'm sorry, what? Of course. Yes, he's right here." He held the phone out to Coffin. "It's the attorney general," Boyle said.

"Of Massachusetts?" Coffin asked, arching an eyebrow.

"Nobody likes a smart-ass, Coffin," Boyle said. "He wants to talk to you."

"Fine." Coffin stood up and took the receiver. "Coffin," he said.

"Detective Coffin? It's Art Poblano. I hope you don't mind that I've requested your help in this investigation."

As attorney general, Poblano was the chief law enforcement officer of the commonwealth. He was also a rising star in Massachusetts state politics; it was generally assumed that he would run for governor in the next election cycle or two.

"Happy to do what I can, sir," Coffin said. "On one condition."

"I've asked Chief Boyle if he can free up Sergeant Winters, too," Poblano said.

"You read my mind, sir."

"There's just one thing," Poblano said. "A favor I need to ask."

Coffin frowned a bit. "Shoot," he said.

Boyle glared at Coffin and tapped his watch crystal. Coffin turned away, letting the phone cord drape over his shoulder.

Poblano cleared his throat softly. "I need your discretion, Detective." He paused. "Kenji Sole and I were friends. It's possible that people in Provincetown may have seen us together. Now, our relationship was never intimate, but you know how people talk. Am I right, Detective?"

"Absolutely, sir," Coffin said.

"I feel a bit awkward asking this," Poblano said.

There was another pause; Coffin said nothing.

"Detective?"

"Yes?"

"I thought you'd hung up for a second."

"No, sir."

"I feel a bit awkward asking this, but I'd appreciate it very much if you'd let me know if my name comes up in the course of the investigation. Just a heads-up, is all I'm asking."

Coffin thought for a moment. "I don't see why not," he said. "We'll do what we can."

"That's all I ask."

"All right, then," Coffin said.

"If I can ever return the favor, Detective," Poblano said.

"You never know, sir," Coffin said.

"That's right," Poblano said. "You never know, do you?" Poblano paused, cleared his throat again. "Excellent work on that situation you all had out there a couple of years ago, by the way. Excellent work."

"Thank you, sir. Sergeant Winters deserves all the credit."

"Of course you'd say that. And how's your lovely wife?"

Coffin could hear Poblano leafing through what was probably his dossier. "Jamie, sir," he said. "We're not married."

"Excellent plan, Detective. I shouldn't have married mine, either." Poblano laughed at his own joke. "Don't forget now," he said, after a last moment of silence. "Keep me posted."

"Will do," Coffin said.

"What the hell was that all about?" Boyle said when Coffin had hung up.

"He wanted to know if I was sure I was up to the job," Coffin said.

"Well, are you?"

"We'll see," Coffin said.

"I'm not happy about this, Coffin," Boyle said, leaning forward in his chair and scowling. "Not one god-damn bit."

Coffin shrugged. "Me neither. What can I do?"

"One fuckup and you're done," said Boyle. "You faint, pass out, throw up, or so much as feel woozy and I'll yank you off this case so fast it'll make your head spin. Is that understood, Coffin?"

"I felt a little woozy this morning," Coffin said, "but it passed."

Boyle took a sip from the coffee mug on his desk, made a face, then took another sip. "I want daily progress reports. Understand? *Daily.*"

"Yes, sir, chief," said Coffin. "Since it's a matter of interest to Attorney General Poblano, I assume you'll be letting us drive one of the unmarked Crown Vics."

Boyle pursed his lips and nodded. The spot of glare on his forehead bobbed up and down. "Why not?" he said. "Maybe the freaking attorney general would like to come out here and take a crap on my desk while he's at it." Boyle dug in his desk drawer and tossed a set of keys at Coffin, who caught them in his cupped hands.

"Anything else you need, Coffin? A SWAT team, maybe? How about the K-9 unit?"

"We don't have a K-9 unit, sir," Coffin said. "Or a SWAT team."

"I expect a report from you in exactly eight hours, Coffin," Boyle said. "Now get the fuck out of my office."

Downstairs, in his basement office, Coffin doodled on a new legal pad.

"How are we supposed to coordinate with Mancini?" Lola said, propping her hip on Coffin's desk. "Boyle give you any direction?"

"Nope," Coffin said, drawing a cartoonish picture of a boat sinking in a calm sea. "It'll take Mancini a day or two to figure out what to do with us. Mostly we're just window dressing."

"To make it look like he's doing everything in his power—"

"To catch the ruthless killer of Kenji Sole." Coffin drew a survivor, swimming away from the wreck, and the dorsal fins of two sharks circling nearby. "I think we go back and talk to Cavalo again," he said.

"As a suspect?" Lola said, taking a sip from a can of Diet Coke.

Coffin thought for a moment. "No. I don't think so—but he is lying about something."

"How long he was in the house."

"Bingo."

"Which means he was doing something he shouldn't have been doing in there," Lola said.

"Right," Coffin said. "Otherwise, why lie?"

Lola scratched her head with the end of her pen. "The house is full of expensive stuff. Maybe he was looking for a souvenir."

"Some little keepsake," Coffin said.

"A nice Rolex," Lola said. "A diamond ring or two. To remember Kenji by."

"Such a sentimental boy." The fat sewer pipe that ran the width of Coffin's ceiling rumbled and swooshed; somebody had flushed a toilet upstairs. "There's a lot more going on with that guy than he's letting on," he said. "Either that or he's a pathological liar."

"Why not both?"

Coffin tapped Lola's soda can with his pen. "I don't know how you can drink that stuff. It tastes like formaldehyde."

"Soft drink of the pharaohs," Lola said. "It may kill you, but your body will be perfectly preserved for thousands of years." She stood up and picked a speck of lint from her uniform pants. "Think he'll give up the names of Kenji's other boyfriends?"

"In a heartbeat," Coffin said.

"Should we call Mancini or anything? Just to let him know we're going out to interview a witness?"

Coffin looked at her.

Lola smiled and punched Coffin in the shoulder. "Ha! Had you going for a second, right?"

Coffin rubbed his arm, which tingled. "Ow," he said.

The phone rang. It was a big putty-colored phone with a rotary dial. Coffin reached for the receiver and punched line one. "Coffin," he said.

"Mr. Coffin? It's Dr. Branstool from Valley View Nursing Home. I'm afraid I've got some bad news about your mother."

Coffin's heart flopped in his chest like a mackerel. He took a deep breath. "Is she dead?"

"No, sir—nothing like that. It's not a medical emergency at all."

"What, did she bite Mr. Hastings again?" Coffin said.

"No, there haven't been any more biting incidents, thank goodness." Dr. Branstool paused. Coffin heard him taking a deep breath. "I'm afraid, Mr. Coffin, that your mother is missing."

"Missing?"

"She wasn't in her room this morning when Natalie went to deliver her breakfast tray. We've just completed a thorough search of the facility, and she appears not to be on the premises."

"You lost my mother?"

"I'm terribly sorry, Mr. Coffin. Nothing like this has ever happened here at Valley View—certainly not since I've been director. I don't blame you at all for being upset."

"Good for her," Coffin said.

"I'm sorry?" said Dr. Branstool.

"I'll ask my colleagues to keep an eye out for her," Coffin said. "I doubt she's gone far." He pictured his mother climbing onto the Plymouth & Brockton bus to Hyannis, or thumbing a ride on the shoulder of Route 6.

"I certainly hope not, Mr. Coffin. She's quite a remarkable woman, your mother. Even in her condition."

Coffin held the phone at arm's length for a moment, then placed it back in the cradle.

"Problem?" Lola said.

"Mom's staged a jailbreak," Coffin said.

"Really? She busted out, huh?"

"Yep."

"Your buddy Kotowski still visit her over at Valley View?" Lola said as they climbed the basement stairs.

"You think maybe she had some help?" Coffin said.

Lola pushed open the big front door. "You never know, right?"

"Right," said Coffin, squinting in the sunlight. "You never know."

TWO

Coffin's friend Kotowski lived in a big, dilapidated house at the far west end of Commercial Street, only fifty yards or so from the long stone breakwater that divided the salt marsh from Provincetown Harbor. There were two hand-painted signs in Kotowski's scraggly front yard: one that read *$ELECTMEN FOR $ALE* and another that was a picture of a Jet Ski in a red circle with a diagonal line through it.

The sun was very bright. The incoming tide made low gurgling sounds between the breakwater's enormous stones. A couple of early tourists stood with their rented bikes in the middle of the traffic circle that marked the juncture of Commercial Street and Route 6, reading the bronze plaque that commemorated the Pilgrims' first New World landing in 1620.

"Kotowski?" Coffin called, knocking on the door. When there was no answer, he tried the latch (it was unlocked, as usual) and pushed the door open. Then he turned and held up one finger, giving Lola the "I'll just be a minute" sign before going in.

Kotowski was sitting in one of the ramshackle armchairs in his living room, wearing headphones, and wreathed in blue hashish smoke. He was long-boned and lanky, in his late fifties. He hadn't shaved in several days; his beard was grizzled and coarse. He held a long, small-bowled pipe in his right hand. A half-finished canvas sat on the easel: It was a painting of a man who looked a lot like Dick Cheney, sharp-toothed and demented, gnawing on the bloodied head of a man who very much resembled George W. Bush. Both men were immersed almost up to their necks in glowing green ice. Two other figures stood in the hellish background, their faces deep in shadow.

"Police!" Coffin yelled, knocking again.

Kotowski's eyes flicked open. His gaze was intense, sardonic. "I thought you said it was the police," he said.

"Funny," Coffin said. "I've got a question for you."

Kotowski took off the headphones. "Bach cello suites," he said. "Rostropovich. Transcendent stuff, Coffin. The humanity! The wheezing! You can almost see his ear hair! Smell the dandruff on his shoulders!"

"I was going to ask about my mother," Coffin said. "She's gone AWOL."

"Good for her."

"I was wondering if you had any idea where she might be."

Kotowski frowned. "She can't have gotten very far, I don't think. I doubt she has any money."

"She didn't say anything to you about wanting to run off?"

"Only every time I've talked to her in the past four years," Kotowski said.

"Nothing new in the past week or so?"

"No. Are you worried?"

"A little. She's pretty loopy."

Kotowski waved a dismissive hand and started to put the headphones back on. "It's P'town," he said. "She fits right in."

"Kotowski."

"Oh my *God*," Kotowski said. "What's next? The

bright light? The rubber hose? She made me promise not to tell."

"She has Alzheimer's," Coffin said. "She can't remember what day it is, most of the time."

"Okay, copper," Kotowski said, sighing theatrically. "You beat it out of me. She has a boyfriend."

"A *what*?"

"You heard me. Sam Taveres, retired fisherman. Widower. Very nice guy—still in possession of several of his faculties. About eighty, I think. Lives down the hall from your mother. You should visit more—maybe you'd know this stuff."

"She doesn't tell me anything," Coffin said. "Mr. Taveres have any family in town?"

"Beats me," Kotowski said. "You're the detective. Am I supposed to know everything?"

May was Coffin's favorite month in Provincetown. Winter and the damp chill of April were finally over; the beach rose and Scotch broom were in bloom. The good summer restaurants were opening, and the town was coming back to life: Guesthouse owners were painting trim and fixing roofs; a few pleasure boats puttered back and forth in the harbor. There were people around—unlike in the dark and lonely depths of winter when Coffin saw the same few faces on the street day after day—but the full onslaught of tourists had not yet arrived. They would not show up in any quantity until after Memorial Day, and even then not in earnest until the Fourth of July, when they'd appear in their bovine throngs, appetites raging, wallets fat with credit cards.

In late May, the drive from Town Hall to Mayflower Heights took five minutes. At the point where Bradford and Commercial streets merged, the houses on the harbor side of the road petered out—the bank above the beach being too narrow at that point for building—and the view of the water opened up gloriously: the small boats tugging at their anchor lines, the breakwater, MacMillan Pier and its mobile of gulls. The sun was just beginning to set, infusing the sky with pinks and lavenders; wisteria bloom and the salt tang of the rising tide scented the air. It was one of Coffin's favorite places in Provincetown. He wanted to park the big Crown Vic beside the road for a few minutes and sit companionably with Lola, watching the sky change color, breathing the perfumed air. He slowed a bit but didn't stop.

"Listen," Coffin said, standing at the bottom of Bobby Cavalo's front stairs. Faint music was coming from Cavalo's apartment.

Lola made a sour face. "What is that?" she said. "Justin Timberlake?"

"Who?" Coffin said, climbing the stairs.

"Justin Timberlake," Lola said. "He was in one of those boy bands."

"Boy bands?" Coffin said.

"Yeah, you know—Backstreet Boys, New Kids on the Block, 'N Sync? They were big in the nineties."

"I stopped listening to pop music when the Eagles broke up," Coffin said.

"The *Eagles*?" Lola said. "Really?"

"What do you want from me?" Coffin said. "I was in high school."

When they reached the landing, Coffin nodded at Lola. She pushed the door open, and they stepped silently into the living room.

Dance music blared from a boom box. Bobby Cavalo was kneeling on the futon sofa, energetically sodomizing the young woman crouched on her knees and elbows in front of him. She was blond and naked except for a pair of pink over-the-knee socks. Her hips were raised receptively, and her face was buried between the thighs of a second young woman, a brunette, who wore only a black lace camisole and lay propped on a pillow, half-facing the door. A slender young man, clothed, was filming them—a small silver video camera in his hand.

"Look," the brunette said, eyelids drooping, left hand still firmly in place on the back of the blonde's head. "Is the police." She had a heavy Eastern European accent.

Cavalo turned, eyes wide. "Fuck me," he said.

"Police?" the blonde said, looking blearily over her shoulder. Her hair was in pigtails.

"Bobby? Minka? Zelenka?" Coffin said. "Is this a bad time?"

When the girls had gotten dressed and the young man with the camera had agreed to give them a ride home, Bobby Cavalo sat on his futon-sofa, wearing a bathrobe and smoking a cigarette. A jade necklace and a man's Patek Philippe watch sat on the coffee table in front of him. "That's it," he said. "That's all I took. I swear."

Cavalo appeared to be in the process of packing for a trip. Clothes and shoes were strewn everywhere; an empty suitcase lay open on the bed.

Coffin picked up the watch. It was gold, with diamonds around the face. It felt heavy in his palm. "What is this, like, a twenty-thousand-dollar watch?"

"Fifty," said Cavalo. "Retail. Look, she was going to give me that watch."

"Sure she was," Coffin said. He put the watch back

on the table. "The necklace, too, right?" The necklace was made of twelve large jade beads, all intricately carved. Coffin held it up to the light. Each of the beads depicted, in tiny relief, a woman having sex with an animal: a tiger, a horse, a bear.

"I don't know, Bobby," Lola said. "We're talking felony theft. Even for a first offense, you're looking at pretty serious time. Of course, if you've got a record . . ."

"There's also the two girls," Coffin said. "They looked pretty young. Are you sure they're both eighteen?"

"Okay," said Cavalo. He held up his hands, palms out: *Stop, already.* "I shouldn't have taken them. It was a mistake, okay? I was in a total state of panic."

"Of course you were," Lola said. "Who wouldn't be?"

Cavalo frowned and tapped his cigarette ash into a coffee mug. "What do you want, really?" he said. "You're not here about the watch, are you?"

"We need the names," Coffin said. "Of Kenji's boy-friends."

"Fuck," Cavalo said. "I knew it." He stuck a hand out in the direction of the open suitcase. "Too goddamn slow. Story of my freaking *life*." His hands shook a bit as he lit another cigarette.

Lola took out her notebook. "You don't want to help us catch Kenji's killer?" she said. "How come?"

"Look," Cavalo said. "Remember when I told you people were looking for me? I wasn't fucking kidding. I can't be a witness in a murder trial, and I can't have a bunch of reporters snooping around. If I stick around here much longer I'm going to get killed, is what's going to happen. Plus, some of these boyfriends are going to be pissed if they find out I gave them up."

"Why's that?"

Cavalo took a deep drag and blew the smoke out

through his nose. "Kenji had kind of a thing for married guys—guys who were established, successful."

"I thought you said she was rich."

"She wasn't after their money. She just liked guys who were kind of older alpha types. She told me once she wasn't interested in fucking busboys." Cavalo picked up the jade necklace and stroked the carved beads with a manicured fingertip. "I think part of it was that they had something to lose if they got caught, you know? It gave her a charge, having that power over them."

"Names," Coffin said.

"I'll give you the names I know, but then I'm out of here."

Lola wrote fast as Cavalo rattled off a list of names: Stan Carswell, Ed Ramos, Tommy McCurry, Nick Stavros, a couple of others. When he was finished, she said, "You must have been close, the two of you."

"What," said Cavalo, "because she told me a lot of personal stuff?"

Lola tilted her head but said nothing.

"She was like that," Cavalo said. "She was a truth-teller. She always said exactly what she was thinking."

Coffin glanced at the list. "What about you? From what you've told us, I don't see how you were her type."

Cavalo smiled. "I guess for me she made an exception."

"There's something I'm having trouble with here, Bobby," Coffin said.

"What's that?"

"You say you're in a big hurry to get out of town. Your bag's half packed, even. But before you head out, you decide to shoot a little home video of yourself with Minka and Zelenka?"

Cavalo pursed his lips, nodding. "I know, it probably seems goofy," he said, "but it's business. One of the ways I get paid is by auditioning new girls. My friend Jordan tapes them, then we send the tapes to my producer in New York. He has connections in L.A. They like what they see, next week Zelenka and Minka might be workin' it out in SoCal, making some real money."

"Right," Coffin said. "While your producer friend holds on to their passports for them."

"It's a business," Cavalo said. "I didn't invent it. The girls make good money for not much work, and they don't have to scrub toilets and sleep on the floor of some fleabag motel. Know what they'd be doing back home in Bosnia, or wherever? Picking turnips, that's what. Or turning tricks on some street corner."

"Digging," Coffin said.

"What?"

"Turnips are a root crop. You don't pick them, you dig them."

Cavalo looked at Coffin, then at Lola. He seemed confused. "Are we talking about turnips now?"

"There's just one more thing," Coffin said.

"Oh, man," Cavalo said, shaking his head. "Here it comes."

"Don't leave town."

Cavalo threw up his hands. "I am *so* fucked. Do you guys know what you're doing to me?"

Coffin stood, walked over to the big front window, and gazed out at the harbor. The tide was out. A few small shore birds twittered back and forth in the puny surf, barely visible in the distance. "You're the principal witness in a homicide investigation, Bobby. If you take off, I'll have the state police bring you back. Then you can sit in jail for a few months until the investigation's concluded and the trial's over."

"You can't *do* that," Cavalo said, eyes flashing.

"Try me," Coffin said.

Lola closed her notebook. "Think of it as doing your civic duty, Bobby."

"Civic duty," Cavalo said, rubbing his temples. "Fuck *me*."

Outside in the Crown Vic, Lola flipped her notebook open. "Six boyfriends," she said."

"Interesting list," Coffin said. "Kind of an eclectic bunch."

"Bobby seems to have been minding Kenji's business pretty closely," Lola said. "I wonder why?"

"Maybe he sensed an opportunity," Coffin said. "Something he could use someday."

"He wasn't too happy when we told him not to leave town."

"No," Coffin said. "Not happy at all. What are the odds he skips before sundown?"

"Six married boyfriends, six jealous wives," Lola said. "I thought *my* life was complicated. I can't even date two people at the same time, let alone six."

"This is just the six we know about," Coffin said.

"Breeders," Lola said. She shook her head. "Fucking up marriage for the rest of us."

"Let's start at the top," Coffin said. "We'll hit Ed Ramos and Stan Carswell tonight, McCurry, Stavros, and the rest first thing tomorrow. If they all alibi out for the time of death, we'll have to take a look at the wives."

Lola turned the key in the Crown Vic's ignition. "Where to, then? Back to the office?"

"I've got to go home first," Coffin said. "Jamie's probably wondering what the hell's happened to me."

"How's she doing?" Lola said, taking a right onto

Route 6A. "I haven't seen her since she decided to do the whole fertility thing."

Coffin touched his mustache. It felt spiky and coarse, in need of trimming. "The Pregnyl's making her a little crazy, but otherwise she's doing fine. *I'm* getting a little worn out, though. I'm too old for this spawning deal."

Lola grinned as she steered onto Commercial Street at the Commercial/Bradford split. "Poor you," she said. "My heart bleeds."

"What," Coffin said, "do I hear a note of envy? What happened to you and what's-her-name?"

"Jen," Lola said. "She decided to get back together with her boyfriend."

"That sucks," Coffin said. "Sorry."

"I've got other prospects," Lola said. "Don't feel sorry for me." She patted Coffin's belly. "Maybe you should start going to the gym. Work on the old stamina. You know, a little conditioning."

Coffin looked out at the darkening water as it slid between houses on the harbor side of the street. The moon was rising, emerging from Cape Cod Bay like a huge, incandescent head. "Christ," Coffin said. "The gym. Now there's an inspiring thought. Nothing like lifting weights to the disco version of 'Don't Cry for Me, Argentina.'"

"A fate worse than death," Lola said.

"Right," Coffin said.

Even before Coffin stepped onto his screen porch, he smelled something burning. The front door stood open, and something was moving in the interior gloom. Some-*one*. Two someones, maybe, tangled together on the couch in an awkward, squirming embrace.

"Hello?" Coffin said, pulling open the screen door and stepping onto the porch. "Who's there?"

"Who the fuck are you?" said Coffin's mother, sitting up. She wore a cotton bathrobe, a long wool coat, and a pair of green Wellington boots. Her eyes were bright and hungry as a crow's, her long hair ratted, the color of galvanized steel.

"It's me, Ma," Coffin said, stepping into the living room. "It's Frankie. What are you doing here?"

"Moron," his mother said. "What does it look like I'm doing?"

She sat half astride a man who appeared also to be in his late seventies or early eighties. He wore a Greek fisherman's cap and had very bushy eyebrows. Coffin was grateful that both of them seemed to be fully dressed.

"Hi, Frankie," the man said. "Long time no see."

The low-ceilinged room was filling with smoke. Coffin strode into the kitchen and turned off the stove. Two eggs, burned to thin black wafers, smoldered in a cast-iron frying pan. The shells, he noticed, had been placed neatly into the cupboard, next to the juice glasses.

"Hi, Mr. Tavares," Coffin said, leaning his hip on the counter. "How's things at the nursing home?"

"Oh, you know," Mr. Tavares said. He had to struggle a bit to sit up. He took off his cap, ran a hand over his bald head, and put his cap back on. "Can't complain, I guess."

"Can't get it up is more like it," said Coffin's mother. She fixed Mr. Tavares with a flat, glittering stare. "But the rest of the old farts up there are drooling idiots, so what choice do I have?"

"What do you want from me?" Mr. Tavares said. "I'm eighty-three years old. I'm not a frickin' machine."

"They're looking for you up at Valley View, Ma. I imagine they're wondering about Mr. Tavares, too."

"That's their problem," his mother said, tossing her

hair. She had been beautiful once, but now, in the fifth year since being diagnosed with Alzheimer's, her face was gaunt and feral.

"I think I should probably take the two of you back, Ma," Coffin said. "Dr. Branstool called me at work. He sounded pretty worried."

Coffin's mother scowled. "Fuck Dr. Branstool and the horse he rode in on. Fuck 'em all. I'm not going back."

"Ma," Coffin said, "you can't stay here."

"The hell I can't. It's my house. I'll stay here if I want to."

Coffin rubbed his temples. His head was beginning to throb. "Ma. Give me a break, huh? We talked this over three years ago, and everybody agreed it would be best if you stayed at Valley View. Right?"

"I was daffy then," his mother said. "I'm better now. You like that mausoleum so much, you go live there. I'm gonna die in *my* house, when *I* say so."

"C'mon, Ma. You almost set the place on fire just now. It wouldn't be safe for you here. You know that."

"He's got a point, Sarah," said Mr. Tavares.

"Why don't you stay here and take care of me, then?" his mother said, standing up and straightening her robe. Her eyes were as bright and blank as glass beads. "That's what a *good* son would do, you ungrateful prick." She turned on Mr. Tavares and jabbed him in the chest with a knotty finger. "And you—when I want your opinion, I'll ask for it, noodle-dick."

"Sorry," Mr. Tavares said, eyebrows squirming. He looked miserable.

Coffin held up his hands, palms out. *Let's all calm down.* "I can't stay home and take care of you, Ma. I have to work. You know that. Somebody's got to pay the bills."

His mother sat down on the couch again. "They're trying to poison me up there," she said. "The dirty sons of bitches."

"Nobody's trying to poison you," Coffin said, sitting in his father's red easy chair. "You just don't like the food."

Coffin's mother smiled, foxy and malicious. "What's-his-face was worried, was he?"

"Very," Coffin said. "I think he's afraid I'm going to sue."

"Good. I hate that smug cocksucker."

"I don't like him much, either."

"Somebody called here a while ago," Coffin's mother said. "Some woman. Said something about being late. I hung up on her."

"That was Jamie, Ma. You remember Jamie, right?"

His mother pursed her lips. "She's that pale girl with the big tits. Looks like Vampira."

"No, Ma." Coffin didn't quite smile. "That was Julie. We got divorced years ago."

"Christ on a cracker," Coffin's mother said, shaking her head. "I'm losing my frickin' mind."

Coffin pulled his rumpled Ford Fiesta up to the curb behind Jamie's Volvo, put the shifter in park, and turned off the ignition key. The Fiesta quivered weakly, farted a small, pale cloud of oil smoke, and died.

Dropping his mother off at Valley View had been hard. Not that she hadn't gone docilely enough, finally: She had, escorted back to her room by Natalie, the day nurse. Still, there was a part of Coffin that felt guilty for committing his mother—again—to the care of strangers, Dr. Branstool and the nurses, those stout Cape Cod ladies who knew nothing about his *real* mother, the tough, funny woman she'd been before

Alzheimer's wormed its thorny tentacles into her brain. It was almost as bad as that first day, when he'd moved her into the nursing home with her suitcase and TV set and box of family photos. She'd wept and accused him of taking her there to die. Which was the truth, Coffin thought—if you wanted to be honest about it.

He climbed out of the car a bit awkwardly, unfolding his lanky frame. He barely fit behind the Fiesta's little steering wheel; driving it was like driving a carnival bumper car. Between the mortgage on his ex-wife's house, the alimony he still paid every month, his mother's upkeep at Valley View, and the soaring property taxes on her house, the Fiesta was the best car he could afford.

Coffin closed its sagging door. His postage stamp of a yard was studded with dandelions. A tangle of roses bloomed on the sagging trellis. Next door, Mrs. Rivera's wisteria wrestled her porch. The big, muscular vine was in full bloom, lavender testicles dangling. It smelled like a funeral, Coffin thought. He shook his head slightly, as if to clear it, and went inside.

"C'mon, big boy," Jamie said. "Give it to me!" She was bent over the bathroom counter, jeans and panties around her knees.

Coffin stood behind her, hypodermic needle poised the way the nurse had shown him—like a dart. "Sorry," he said. "I don't know why this is so hard for me."

Jamie turned and looked at Coffin over her shoulder. "I know, I know—it's not what you pictured when I asked you to poke me in the ass."

"Well, no," Coffin said, wincing as he stuck the needle into Jamie's backside. "Not exactly."

"Yow," Jamie said.

Coffin pressed the plunger with his thumb, then

pulled the needle out. "All done," he said. He dabbed a trickle of blood from her buttock with a square of toilet paper.

Jamie pulled up her jeans. "There's something very sad about this whole Kenji Sole business."

"Aside from the having been killed part?" Coffin said.

Jamie put her arm around Coffin's neck and kissed his cheek. "Her life seems kind of sad. All those boyfriends. All that porn. If you see other people as objects, aren't you missing something important?"

"She was in your advanced class, right?"

"Yep. A very dedicated little yogi—in great shape. Came to class four or five times a week. She told me once it was her best hedge against getting old."

Coffin pursed his lips. "Careful what you wish for," he said. "Let's have a drink."

In the living room, the stuffed goat's head stared down at Coffin with its clever yellow eyes. It had been repaired since Jamie shot it almost two years before, but its face was lopsided now, demented.

"Are you sure you should be drinking that martini, Detective?" Jamie said. "Aren't you on duty?"

"Duty, shmooty," Coffin said, taking a sip. The vodka was very cold, its medicinal bite very pleasant. He leaned back on his mother's uncomfortable Victorian sofa and stretched out his legs. "Do you really think Kenji was missing something? I was kind of under the impression she was having a good time."

"I guess it's just not really my idea of fun—too much drama. Can you imagine? Trying to keep up with all those men? For what?"

"I don't know," Coffin said. "Maybe the drama was

part of the kick. Maybe her ego demanded it—you know, being the center of attention."

"Then she must have been very insecure."

"How well did you know her?"

"Not, except to say hi, but she was kind of famous," Jamie said. "Or infamous, maybe." She lowered her voice conspiratorially. "There was whispering."

"What kind of whispering? Like gossip?"

"Definite gossip. All true, apparently. About her thing for other people's husbands." She lowered her voice again. "Shameless."

"Did she talk to you much?"

"Not a lot." Jamie kicked off her sandals and put her feet in Coffin's lap. They were elegant feet, Coffin thought—narrow, with high arches and long, almost prehensile toes. Jamie's toenails were painted sparkly red, like an electric guitar. "She wasn't one of the needy ones, and she didn't have a crush on me. She'd say thanks after class, but that was about it."

"Businesslike?" Coffin said.

"Superficially friendly," Jamie said, "but not ever going to invite the yoga instructor out for lunch or home for a cup of tea."

"Competitive with other women?"

"Well, duh," Jamie said, "but not toward me, that I was aware of." Jamie lowered her feet, leaned into Coffin's chest, and plucked one of the olives from his martini and ate it. "Yum," she said. "Somebody should sell olives soaked in vodka. They'd make millions."

"You may be onto something there," Coffin said, finishing his drink.

Jamie sniffed at his shirt and looked up at him. "Have you been smoking?"

"Only a little," he said.

"Frank. You promised. Nicotine's not good for your sperm."

"Sorry. It was a stressful morning."

"Frank?" Jamie said, nuzzling Coffin's neck.

"Mm?"

"I'm ovulating like crazy, you know."

"Really?"

"When did you say you had to go back to the office?"

"Soon."

"How soon?" Jamie tugged at Coffin's zipper. "Damn thing," she said. "Ah—here we go." She bent down and took his flaccid penis in her mouth.

"Jamie?" Coffin said.

"Hm?"

"Didn't we just do this, like, six hours ago? Shouldn't I have some time to recharge?"

There was a wet, popping sound. "Are you complaining?"

"No."

"Good. Because it sounded like you might be."

"No, no."

"Good. Now shut up and take your pants off."

"Jesus, Frank," Lola said, looking up. She sat at Coffin's beige metal desk, phone book open in front of her, foam cup of coffee at her elbow. "You look like something that just washed up on the beach. Everything okay?"

"Don't laugh," Coffin said. "Jamie's ovulating."

Lola laughed. "We're going to have to put you on a high-protein diet or something," she said. "That girl's about to wear you out."

"Ordering a pizza?" Coffin said, sitting in the hard visitor's chair opposite Lola.

"Just getting numbers and addresses of our boy-friends," Lola said. "Mancini called."

"And?"

"He got the prelim report from the ME's office."

"Wow. That was fast."

"Your friend Shelley Block sends her regards. You used to date her, right?

"Briefly," Coffin said. "She's a very nice woman, but I couldn't stop thinking about what she did for a living."

"You and your corpse phobia," Lola said.

Coffin leafed through the report. "Any surprises?"

"Nope." Lola glanced at her notes. "She was stabbed seven times in the chest and abdomen, once—the last one—in the heart. A couple of knife wounds on arms and hands indicate she tried to defend herself. Blood tests and toxicology report won't be back from the lab for a few days. Time of death around eleven o'clock last night."

"Sexual assault?"

"No physical indication of rape, but the ME did find semen in her vagina."

Coffin's eyebrows went up. "I thought you said there were no surprises."

"Sorry—it didn't surprise me. She *was* sexually active. To say the least."

Coffin frowned. "Can they tell how old the semen is? I mean, compared to the time of death?"

"Funny you should ask that," Lola said. She looked at her notes again. "Looks like the sexual activity happened shortly before she was killed. An hour or less."

"So if we can find out who she had sex with—"

"We might find the killer," Lola said, putting her notebook away. "Or not."

Coffin stood up. "Let's see if we can get Boyle to

authorize DNA testing for the boyfriends," he said. "In the meantime, let's go shake a few trees and see if anyone falls out."

Ed Ramos stood on his front steps, cringing a bit in the yellow glow of the porch light. He was a handsome man in his early forties, muscular and tanned, just under six feet tall. His hair was wavy and jet black. Coffin wondered if he dyed it.

"For Chrissakes, Frank—could you keep it down?" Ramos said. "The wife and kids are right inside."

Coffin rubbed his chin. It was bristly; he hadn't shaved in sixteen hours. He could feel his own hair getting grayer by the minute. "How many kids you got now, Ed?"

"Four by my first wife," Ramos said. "They're all grown and moved away, except for Nicky. And three with Sophie. They're eight, six, and two."

"Sophie doesn't know about Kenji Sole?"

"Jesus, Frank," Ramos said, glancing back at the house. The door was shut, but the front windows were open to the night air. "Keep it down, will you? Hell no, she doesn't know. I'd be divorced if she did."

"Why don't you come sit in the car with us?" Lola said. "Nobody'll hear us if we talk in there."

Ramos glanced over his shoulder again. "Bad idea," he said. "She's already getting suspicious. I can feel it." He shivered and looked at his watch. "Look, are we about done? Can we wrap this up?"

"Just a couple more questions," Coffin said. "How long had you been seeing Kenji?"

"I don't know," Ramos said. "A few months. Since January, I guess."

"Were you with her last night?"

"Last night?" Ramos looked scared, eyes suddenly

wide. "No. Not last night. I was here at home, watching TV with the kids." He glanced at his front windows. "Look, Frank—I'm sorry, but I gotta get back inside."

Coffin put a hand on Ramos's arm. "Hang on a minute, Ed. When was the last time you saw her?"

Ramos looked down. "Yesterday. Around lunchtime. She came down to the job site."

"Did you have sex with her?" Lola asked.

"Yeah," Ramos said, nodding slowly. "We drove out to Herring Cove and had a quickie in her car. Kinda threw my back out."

"Did you ejaculate inside her?" Coffin asked.

"Jesus, Frank," Ramos said. "That's getting pretty fucking personal, isn't it?" A large moth flew out of the darkness, circled the porch light twice, and bounced off of Ramos's forehead. It lay on the top step, throbbing its pale green wings. "Fuck," Ramos said, recoiling. "Look at that thing. It's the size of a fucking 747."

Lola picked the moth up gently by its thorax. "It's a luna moth," she said. "You almost never see them." It perched on her thumb for a moment, wings slowly pulsing. Then it flew at Ramos's face again.

"Jesus fucking Christ!" Ramos cried, waving his arms. "It's like a fucking vampire bat! Get it away from me!" The moth circled the light again and flew away.

"Ed," Coffin said. "They're going to find out. They're going to do DNA testing—the whole deal."

Ramos took a deep breath, let it out. "Yeah," he said, glancing back at the windows again and dropping his voice to a whisper. "I came inside her. She's bouncing up and down on my joint, yelling, 'Fill me up, baby!' What can you do?"

"Did you know you weren't the only guy she was having sex with?" Lola said.

Ramos made a wry little mouth. "Duh," he said. "Of course I knew. It's not like she tried to keep it a secret. Kenji was a very horny girl. Hell, that's why I liked her."

"How did you feel when you heard she was dead?" Coffin asked.

"How the fuck do you think I felt?" Ramos said. His eyes flashed in the yellow porch light. "Terrible. It's a terrible fucking thing. What kind of animal could do a thing like that?"

"Any idea who she was with last night?" Lola said.

"Nope. No idea. She didn't tell me much about her plans."

Coffin watched Ramos's face closely. "Any idea who might have wanted to kill her?"

"I got lots of ideas," Ramos said, lowering his voice even more. Coffin could barely hear him over the sound of the slight wind in the trees. "Could be, one of the wives found out. Could be, not all the guys she was humpin' were as laid-back about it as me."

Coffin looked at Lola.

"Are you thinking of anybody in particular?" Lola said.

"Wives—I don't know, except that mine was here all night last night. Claudia Stavros has got a hell of a temper on her, I can tell you that."

Lola looked at her list. "Claudia Stavros? Wife of Nick Stavros, I assume?"

"Bingo," said Ramos. "Selectwoman Stavros, to you."

"Yikes," Lola said. "What about jealous boyfriends?"

"I don't know anything for sure," Ramos said. "Just what Kenji told me, and the fact that he's been giving me dirty looks for about a month now."

"But . . ." Coffin said.

"But keep an eye on Stan Carswell," Ramos said. "Kenji was getting worried about him. I guess he fell in

love with her or something—he was getting all posses-
sive. Kenji said he was turning into a royal pain in
the ass."

A curtain moved in the front window, and Coffin
saw Ramos's wife, Sophie, looking out, half silhou-
etted against the inside light. "Eddie?" she said. "What's
going on out there? Is everything all right?"

"I'll be right in, hon," Ramos said. "Everything's
fine." He turned to Coffin and ran a hand over his thick,
black hair. "There's no way she's not going to find out
about this, is there?"

"Sorry, Ed," Coffin said. "She'll have to confirm that
you were both home last night. We don't have to talk to
her right now, but we will in the next day or so."

Ramos blew a slow stream of air out between his
pursed lips. "Well, I'm fucked, then. No way Sophie's
going to let this go."

"You're not going to be the only one, if it makes you
feel any better," Lola said.

"Actually, no," Ramos said, opening the screen door
and stepping inside. "It doesn't."

Stan Carswell's house was a faux Cape Cod McMansion,
built on the site of a teardown above Bradford Street. It
was three stories tall and shingled in cedar shakes that
shone silvery pale in the moonlight. A broad deck ran
the width of the top floor. When Coffin knocked, a shrill
fury of barking erupted inside, and two furry bodies
hurled themselves at the inside of the door.

"I hate little yappy dogs," Lola said. "They give me
the creeps."

Coffin smiled and knocked again. The little dogs
barked even more furiously. "My dad had a pug when I
was a kid," he said. "Named Oscar. Totally ferocious.
He'd hide behind a chair and jump out and bite you,

just for the hell of it. Horrible little dog, but Dad loved him. Even took him fishing sometimes."

A light went on inside. Coffin looked at his watch; it was almost eleven. "Maybe we woke him up," he said. The dogs barked madly.

"Shut the fuck up, you little monsters," said a man's muffled voice.

The dogs shrieked with bloodlust and hurled themselves at the door.

"Get back, for Christ's sakes," said the voice. The door swung open. A tall man in yellow pajamas and two tiny white dogs stood blinking in the beam of Lola's flashlight.

"Stan Carswell?" Coffin said.

The man squinted. His hair stuck out at odd angles, and he appeared to Coffin not to have shaved for several days. His pajamas had pictures of smiling monkeys on them.

The little dogs twinkled out onto the porch and sniffed Coffin's ankles.

"Yeah," Carswell said. "That's me. You'd be the cops, I guess. Come on in."

The inside of the house was almost completely empty. Soft track lighting glowed on pictureless walls. No rugs concealed the buttery-smooth hardwood flooring. There was no furniture in the cathedral-ceilinged living area except for two green plastic lawn chairs.

"Wife moved out last week," Carswell said, walking through the echoing room into the kitchen. The two small dogs trailed behind him. "Took the kids with her, and all the furniture, while I was at work. All she left was my clothes and Winkin and Blinkin here. Want a drink or anything? Coffee?"

Coffin looked at Lola, then shrugged. "Sure. Coffee sounds fine."

"What happened to Nod?" Lola said.

"Coyote got him," Carswell said, popping a white filter into the gleaming stainless steel coffeemaker. "Crunch, crunch. Nothing left but a few tufts of hair and a bad attitude."

Carswell scooped ground coffee into the filter. He rinsed the carafe in the sink, filled it with water, and poured the water into the machine. "There," he said, flipping the switch. "That ought to do it. I hope."

"New coffeemaker?" Lola said.

"Yeah. It's about all I've had time to replace. Or money. She cleaned out the bank accounts, too." He gestured toward the lawn chairs. "Have a seat."

"No thanks," Coffin said. "I'm fine."

"Me, too," said Lola. She leaned a hip against the kitchen island, equipment belt creaking. Coffin caught himself staring at the curve of her hip through her uniform pants and shook his head.

"Your wife found out about Kenji Sole?" Coffin said.

"Linda didn't find out," Carswell said, opening the enormous stainless steel fridge. "I told her." The fridge was empty, except for a carton of eggs, a twelve-pack of Heineken, and a container of half-and-half. Carswell retrieved the half-and-half and shut the door.

"Why tell her?" Lola said. "Did you want her to divorce you?"

"I wanted to be honest with her," Carswell said, shrugging. "I wanted her to know how I felt."

"Which was how?" Coffin said.

Carswell opened a cupboard and took out three mismatched mugs. He handed one to Coffin and one to Lola. Coffin's had the old New England Patriots logo on a white background: a man in breeches and a tricornered hat, hiking a football.

"I loved Kenji Sole," Carswell said. He looked at

Coffin, then Lola. "She was beautiful and exciting, and I fell in love. I couldn't just stay with Linda and pretend everything was okay."

"An honest man," Coffin said.

"After the fact," Carswell said, pouring a careful measure of half-and-half into his mug before filling it with coffee, "and we all know that doesn't count." He opened another cupboard, produced a tall, square bottle of Irish whiskey, and glugged a triple shot into his coffee mug. Then he walked into the living room and flopped down in one of the green plastic chairs.

"How did you feel about Kenji's other boyfriends?" Lola said.

"How do you think I felt?" Carswell said. His eyes widened, and he ran a hand over his hair, which stuck out even more erratically than it had before. He looked to Coffin as though he'd just stuck a fork into a short-circuiting toaster. "She was making me crazy. I wanted to marry her, but every time I brought it up she'd laugh."

One of the little dogs—Coffin wasn't sure if it was Winkin or Blinkin—jumped up into Carswell's lap.

"Get off me, you little freak," Carswell said, patting the dog on the head.

"What do you do for a living, Mr. Carswell?" Coffin said.

"I'm a psychiatrist," Carswell said. "I used to practice in Boston, but I got tired of my patients."

"How come?" Coffin said.

"I had a very wealthy clientele," Carswell said. "You wouldn't believe how boring rich people are. Everything's about me, me, me. After a while you just want to kill them."

Coffin and Lola exchanged looks.

"Figuratively, I mean," Carswell said.

"So you moved to P'town," Lola asked, "because you wanted more interesting patients?"

Carswell's face reddened. "It's a long story," he said.

"We've got time," Coffin said.

Carswell took a slurping sip of his Irish coffee. "A few years ago," he said, "Linda got involved with a woman. We had kind of an unconventional relationship for a while."

"What, like a ménage à trois?" Lola said.

Carswell nodded. "I was all for it at first. I thought what most straight guys would think—you know, *woo hoo*! But after a few weeks it was mostly a ménage à them, while I tried to sleep on the couch. It didn't work out."

"P'town just seemed like a good place to give it a shot?" Coffin said.

"Linda was worried about how the gossip might affect the kids if we stayed in Boston," Carswell said. "In P'town, all in all we were a pretty uninteresting alternative lifestyle."

"It doesn't really seem fair," Lola said. "Your wife got to have her affair, and you stuck around."

Carswell shrugged. "When I gave Linda the 'her or me' ultimatum, she picked me. She thought about it, mind you, but ultimately she wanted a life with me and the kids."

"But when the shoe was on the other foot?" Coffin said.

"I picked Kenji," Carswell said. "Am I a genius at relationships, or what?" The little dog licked Carswell's face, and Carswell pushed it off his lap.

"When was the last time you saw Kenji, Mr. Carswell?" Lola said.

"Jesus," Carswell said, eyes widening. "I'm a suspect."

"Nobody's a suspect yet," Lola said. "We still have a lot of people to talk to."

"I saw her a couple of days ago. She came by my office. I told her I wanted to break up with her."

"I thought you were in love," Coffin said.

"I was, but she was making me crazy. I couldn't take it anymore."

"So what did she say when you tried to break up with her?"

Carswell grimaced. "She talked me out of it."

"How?"

"How do you think?"

Lola tapped her notebook with her pen. "You mean she had sex with you? In your office?"

Carswell nodded and poked at Winkin glumly with his toe. "She liked to do things that were a little risky," he said. "For me, I mean. I think it was a control issue for her."

"Where were you last night, around eleven o'clock?" Coffin said.

"At the Captain Alden," Carswell said. "Getting shit-faced. It was drag karaoke night. I made a complete fool of myself."

"Did you perform?" Coffin said.

"To the best of my recollection, yes," Carswell said. "I sang 'Blue Suede Shoes' in a chartreuse wig, with a pair of fake boobs under my T-shirt."

"You keep that kind of gear around the house?" Coffin said.

"Sure," Carswell said. "Doesn't everyone?"

"He may not have a wife, kids, or any furniture," Coffin said, sitting in Lola's black Camaro, "but the man's got a great alibi."

"That's always something to be proud of," Lola said.

She slowed, then stopped in the middle of Bradford Street. "Check it out."

Two fat skunks were mating in the middle of the road. The male, hips pumping furiously, turned and looked over his shoulder, amber eyes blazing in the headlights' bright cone.

"Wow," Coffin said. "Pretty brazen. Must be mating season."

"Kind of late in the year for that," Lola said. "Maybe the cold spring slowed them down."

"Whatever you say, Professor."

The skunks, presumably satisfied, waddled off the blacktop and disappeared into the darkness.

"Where to?" Lola said, dropping the Camaro into gear. "Should we go talk to Tommy McCurry?"

"No," Coffin said, turning in his seat, hoping for a last glimpse of the skunks as Lola accelerated down Bradford. "It's too late. We'll get him first thing in the morning. Let's go to the Shack and have a drink."

"I'll drop you," Lola said, "but I'm not going in. That place gives me the willies."

"Me, too," Coffin said. "I have this recurring nightmare where I'm sitting at the bar and the parking lot cracks open and out pops Billy. He's all scorched, and when he opens his mouth, smoke rings come out."

"Jesus, really?" Lola said.

Coffin nodded. "I figure it's a metaphor. My subconscious thinks that Billy's leaving the place to me in his will was really his curse from the grave."

In fact, the Oyster Shack *was* a curse—a financial albatross of the first order. The property taxes were staggering, the building was slowly disintegrating, the liquor, beer, and food bills were all overdue, and Coffin was behind on payroll eight days and counting. He would have to sell the place—and soon—before it dragged him with it into bankruptcy, yet he found himself hesitating. He hated the thought of what it would inevitably become: luxury condos, maybe, or a mini strip mall crammed with T-shirt-and-taffy shops, or yet another upscale restaurant—small food on big plates—catering to the Mercedes SUV crowd.

Lola laughed. "You don't exactly seem like the business type."

"You're telling me. C'mon—drinks are on the house. The worst thing that can happen is you'll get a bad clam."

"That's what they all say." Lola flipped on the turn signal and swung the Camaro onto Shank Painter Road. "Anyway, I can't. I've got a date."

"A date?" Coffin said. "This time of night? Since when? With who?"

"Easy, Dad," Lola said.

"Sorry," Coffin said. "It just kind of took me by surprise."

Lola pulled into the Oyster Shack's potholed lot. "Me, too," she said. "It probably won't amount to anything. We're just meeting for a drink."

"You never know," Coffin said, unfolding himself from the passenger seat. "She could be the love of your life."

"She could," Lola said, "but I'm not holding my breath."

The Oyster Shack was quiet; the only customers were a discouraged-looking fisherman and an old woman whose false teeth sat on the bar next to her glass of Chivas Regal. Squid stood next to the beer taps, his back to the door, flipping channels on the crotchety Zenith that flickered behind the bar. Coffin's parrot, Captain Nickerson, climbed the bars of his cage.

"'Sup, Frank?" Squid said, without turning around.

He was tall and lanky, with sloped shoulders and enormous hands. His fingers were long, the fingertips oddly flattened, like suction cups.

"How'd you know it was me?" Coffin said.

"I can see your reflection in the TV screen," Squid said, pointing at the Zenith with one of his tentacle-y fingers. "It's all warped and freaky, but I can tell it's you." Squid turned, and touched his spatulate fingertips to his hair. It was dyed blue and gelled up into a faux-hawk.

"Join me in a drink?" Coffin said.

"Think we'll both fit?"

"Let's do the Talisker twenty-year-old," Coffin said. "A little water in mine. And let's have a dozen on the half-shell."

Squid poured the drinks, and Coffin sipped his meditatively: It tasted like peat smoke and old leather, a salty touch of seaweed on the tip of the tongue. On the Zenith, the Bruins were doing their best to lose to Atlanta. The ice appeared to have been painted a lurid green. The picture flickered and warped.

"Jesus Christ," said the fisherman. "When are you going to pop for a new TV? Why am I trying to watch a freakin' hockey game on this piece of shit?"

"Eat me!" said Captain Nickerson, bobbing his head.

"That TV is *not* a piece of shit," Coffin said. "It's vintage. It's part of our funky seaside ambience."

"Ha," said the fisherman, sipping his beer. "If I want funky seaside ambience, I'll go down to my boat and slide around in the fish slime."

Captain Nickerson bobbed his head. "Eat me! Eat me!"

"You tell 'em, Cap'n," Squid said. He shucked a dozen oysters in just under three minutes and set them in front of Coffin on their paper plate.

They'd been delivered that morning, Coffin knew,

fresh from Wellfleet. He squeezed a lemon wedge over the plate and could almost see the oysters cringing away from the juice's acid sting. Then he raised one of the gnarled shells to his lips, sucked the oyster into his mouth, and chewed it slowly.

"Happy, boss?" said Squid, pouring Coffin a beer.

"Very," Coffin said.

The door opened, and Kotowski walked in. He wore the same paint-spattered T-shirt, brown corduroys with holes in the knees, and green rubber flipflops he'd had on earlier in the day.

"You'd think a guy with all your money could at least try not to look like a bum," Coffin said, when Kotowski sat down on the stool next to his.

"It's my nature to look like a bum," Kotowski said. "Any word from your mother?" When Squid took his order, he asked for a Newcastle.

"Safe and sound," Coffin said. "You dress like a bum but suddenly you're drinking imported beer? What's the matter, Rolling Rock not good enough for you anymore?"

"They stopped making it in the glass-lined tanks of Old Latrobe," Kotowski said. "Before they sold the brand, every time I drank one I'd picture those funky-ass glass-lined tanks—you know, full of moss and drowned mice. It added a certain je ne sais quoi to the experience. Now they make it in some sterile factory in St. Louis. It's not the same."

"How's the work?"

"Terrible. I'm completely blocked. Haven't painted anything in days."

"Your mysterious collector isn't going to be happy about that. Or your gallery owner."

"That's the problem," Kotowski said. "It's like I've got this fucking collector guy, whoever he is, looking over my shoulder every time I pick up a paintbrush. It's making me homicidal."

"How much did the last one sell for? The Sarah Palin one."

"You mean *Moose Hunt*?"

Coffin nodded. *Moose Hunt* was a large painting of Sarah Palin dressed in dominatrix gear and brandishing a shotgun. She appeared to be about to shoot a man in a moose suit at very close range. Coffin had seen the painting several times, in various stages of completion. The moose suit was clownish, oversized and seedy-looking, complete with floppy antlers. The man inside it cringed in fear; he looked a great deal like John McCain.

"Not that much. One-thirty."

"Something tells me you'll snap out of your painter's block before too long."

Kotowski shrugged, sipped his beer. "Hey, I'll be the first to admit that I don't actually *deserve* to be making this kind of money. I think the guy's crazy, whoever he is."

"You've sold your soul," Coffin said.

Kotowski nodded. "Absolutely," he said. "I'm the socialist Taoist homosexual surrealist Thomas Kinkade. Next thing you know I'll be selling figurines."

"Thar she blows!" said Captain Nickerson.

They sat in silence for a few minutes. Outside, under the streetlight, a white plastic grocery bag blew across the parking lot, tumbling slowly like some primitive sea creature moving across the ocean floor.

"I hear you're investigating the Kenji Sole thing," Kotowski said, peeling the label off his beer.

"Lucky me," Coffin said.

"She was an interesting woman," Kotowski said. "Not altogether stupid. I actually kind of liked her."

Coffin sipped his beer. "I didn't know you knew her."

"I didn't *know* her, really," Kotowski said. "I probably had a total of three conversations with her. She liked art—went to a lot of gallery openings. Decent taste; knew the difference between a good painting and the dune-and-sunset crap in the tourist galleries. She came over to the house once to look at some work. This was about a year ago."

"She buy anything?"

Kotowski pursed his lips and shook his head. "No, but she put me in touch with my current dealer."

"No wonder you liked her."

They sat quietly for a few minutes, watching the Bruins glide over throbbing green ice.

"So," Kotowski said finally. "Any leads?"

Coffin grimaced. "Too many. I'm apparently the only straight guy in town that wasn't sleeping with her."

"I wasn't," Squid said.

"You're straight?" the old woman said. A lit cigarette was clamped in the set of dentures at her elbow. "Goddamn, I'm losin' my gaydar. I thought you was definitely a queer."

"Show us your tits!" said Captain Nickerson.

"You wouldn't have been her type, Squid," Coffin said.

"I wasn't boinkin' her, either," said the fisherman, "but Cap'n Rory was."

"Cap'n Rory?" Coffin said. "The guy that runs the sunset tours off MacMillan Pier?"

"Yup. She'd come down to his sloop there and off they'd go for a little sail. I seen him this mornin' when we come in—he was wicked nervous. It surprised me, how shook up he was."

"When was the last time you saw them together?" Coffin said.

"I don't know," the fisherman said. He took off his ballcap and scratched his head. He was bald on top, with a long ponytail in back. "We been out fishin' the last five days. Before that. Last week sometime. But they could have been together last night, for all I know. I'm tellin' you—Cap'n Rory was sweatin' fuckin' bullets when I seen him this morning. Like a freakin' hen on a hot plate, that guy."

The phone rang behind the bar. Squid answered it.

"Telephone," said Captain Nickerson.

"Hang on," Squid said into the phone. "He's right here." He held the receiver out to Coffin. "For you. Outer Cape Shellfish. They been tryin' to reach you all day."

"Shit." Coffin took the phone from Squid. "Coffin."

"Frankie? Johnny Guillemette here. I hate to be a pain in the ass, buddy, but we gotta get paid. You guys are, like, a month overdue."

"I'll have a check for you first thing tomorrow," Coffin said.

"Great," said Guillemette. "Hopefully things'll pick up for you once the season starts."

"Yeah," Coffin said. "Hopefully." He handed the phone back to Squid.

Kotowski raised an eyebrow. "Trouble, Lassie?"

"It's only impending bankruptcy," Coffin said. "No big deal."

"Oh, stop whining." Kotowski took a sip of beer. "Any idiot can run a bar. Your problem is you've got no idea how to market the place. That's why you don't have any customers."

"I hate customers," Coffin said.

"Of course you do. Customers suck," Kotowski said. "That's not the point."

Coffin ate his last oyster. "Next time some sleazeball

real estate developer offers me a pile of money for this dump, I'm taking it."

Kotowski sat up straight and scowled at Coffin. "Don't even kid about selling this place to developers," he said.

"I'm not kidding," Coffin said. "I'd sell it in a heartbeat."

"Billy's is a *landmark*," Kotowski said. "It's the last real thing in Provincetown. You're not allowed to sell it."

Coffin poked Kotowski in the bicep with his index finger. "You're rich now—why don't *you* buy it? Imagine the fun you could have, dealing with the beer distributors and the dry rot."

"Eat me!" said Captain Nickerson.

"What you need is a bar manager," Kotowski said. "I figure pretty much any dumb-ass off the street could do a better job than you."

"Hey, Squid," Coffin said. "How'd you like to be bar manager?"

"Of this place?" Squid said. "Uh, no thanks."

Coffin turned to the fisherman at the end of the bar. "How about you, Teddy? Want a job as bar manager?"

"Yeah, right," Teddy said. "That's like asking a guy if he wants to be captain of a sinking ship."

Coffin clapped Kotowski on the back. "Congratulations," he said. "You're just the dumb-ass for the job."

Captain Nickerson bobbed his head and swung frantically on his little swing. "Last call!" he shrieked.

"Hey, sweetheart," the old woman said, waving a ten-dollar bill at Squid. "You know how to make a Adios Motherfucker?"

"A what?" Squid said, sipping his scotch.

"Adios Motherfucker. It's a drink."

"If you can tell me what's in it, I can make it," Squid said.

"A shot each of vodka, rum, tequila, gin, and that blue stuff—what's it called . . ."

"Blue curaçao?"

"Yeah—curaçao. Plus some of that sour mix goo, and a squirt of 7-Up." She took the cigarette from between her dentures and sucked a long drag. "Chop chop, sweet cheeks. Tall glass, plenty of ice."

Squid frowned. "You really want that?"

"Damn straight," the old woman said, "and don't skimp on the booze."

Squid looked at Coffin, who shrugged.

"Okay, Pat," Squid said, "but don't blame me if you spend the night huggin' porcelain." He made the drink and set it in front of the old woman. It was bright blue, the color of Windex.

The old woman raised the glass in a mock toast and winked at Coffin. "Adios, motherfucker," she said.

Outside, the wind was picking up; the clouds raced overhead, backlit by the moon, glowing silver against the black night sky. Three gulls shrieked and fought over some bit of trash they'd pulled from the Dumpster. Coffin patted his pockets, then held up two fingers. "Got a smoke, buddy?"

Kotowski fished a half pack of Camel unfiltered regulars from his pocket and tapped one out. "Why not just ask me for a quarter?" he said.

"Can't smoke a quarter," Coffin said, cigarette dangling from his lip. "Got a light?"

"Need anything else?" Kotowski said. "A kick in the ass to get your lungs going?" He lit Coffin's cigarette with a battered Zippo, then lit one for himself. For a moment, the mingled smells of lighter fluid and smoke hung in the air between them.

"So," Kotowski said, puffing contentedly. "How's the

spawning coming along? Not that it's any of my business."

"You're right," Coffin said. "It's not."

Kotowski turned and regarded Coffin for a long moment. "That bad, eh?"

"Terrible," Coffin said. He shrugged. "I don't know—maybe terrible's too strong, but ever since the miscarriage the whole thing's had this edge of desperation. It's like we're trying to prove something now."

"That you're competent breeders, you mean."

"Something like that."

"I tried to warn you," Kotowski said, lifting a battered football helmet from the seat of his motorcycle and strapping it onto his head. "It's a total scam, all this fertility business. They rope you in. They make people think it's their right to reproduce—that they're entitled to it, and that nature's just being an asshole by getting in the way. Try these pills! That didn't work? How about a few shots? Once you start down the slippery slope there's no escape. Next thing you know you'll be whacking off into a cup in some clinic bathroom, staring at old copies of *Penthouse,* for God's sake—and paying thousands of dollars for the privilege. I can't think of anything more pathetic."

Coffin shrugged. "Been there, done that," he said. "When they did my sperm count. They actually had quite a variety of magazines. *Playboy. Penthouse. Field and Stream.*"

"*Field and Stream*? That's just sick."

Coffin laughed.

"How long has it been now?" Kotowski said. "A year?"

"Almost two. I still dream about it—all that blood." Coffin shivered and took another drag of the cigarette.

"You should really be seeing a shrink, you know,"

Kotowski said, climbing onto the dented Honda. "You're completely crazy."

"This is news to you?" Coffin said.

Kotowski blew out his lips like a horse. "Don't be ridiculous. Your mental illness is what makes you interesting. To the extent that you're interesting at all." On the third kick-start, the motorcycle backfired like a small cannon, then roared to life. Kotowski cranked the gas and popped the clutch, burning rubber as he pulled out onto Shank Painter Road.

"I don't usually do this on the first date," Lola said. She took a long drink of water from the bottle on the nightstand. A young woman lay next to her. They were both naked. All the lights were out. A tall pillar candle burned on the dresser; it smelled like vanilla.

"Don't usually do what?" the young woman said, brushing a strand of blond hair from Lola's eyes. Her name was Kate Hanlon. She was tall and slender, dark-eyed, very pretty. "Cook a fabulous late supper? Open an outrageously expensive bottle of wine? Seduce a younger woman?"

"All of the above," Lola said. Then, after a pause, "You're not *that* much younger."

Kate traced a fingertip over the scar on Lola's belly. "This is really something," she said.

"It's ugly, I guess," Lola said, "but I feel like I earned it."

"What happened? An accident?"

"Job-related," Lola said. "A couple of years ago. Guy with a knife."

"Wow. That's so crazy. You weren't wearing one of those protective vests, I guess."

"No," Lola said. "I should, but they're kind of bulky and hot."

Kate sat up, eyes bright in the candlelight. "Okay,

look," she said. "If we're going to be in a relationship, that's got to be a rule. You have to wear one of those vests."

Lola smiled and kissed her hand. "Are we in a relationship?"

"After what you just did to me?" Kate said. "We'd better be."

Just over a mile away, Coffin and Jamie lay awake in their bed, listening to the slow rush of the wind through the neighbor's cedar trees.

"Tired, Frank?" Jamie said, propped up on one elbow.

"Very," Coffin said. He reached across Jamie's hip, took a cigarette from the pack on the nightstand, and lit it with a plastic lighter. The taxidermied owl on the wardrobe stared at him with what looked like startled outrage, ear tufts awry, amber eyes glowing in the light of the votive candle on the windowsill.

"Bad day," Jamie said, patting his arm.

"Terrible day. I thought I'd probably retire before I had to investigate another homicide. I sure as hell didn't think we'd have another one so soon. I mean, what are the odds?"

Jamie put her hand on Coffin's bare chest. "I wish you didn't have to deal with this," she said. "You forget, sometimes, living out here—how awful people can be."

"I've been thinking about Stan Carswell and Ed Ramos," Coffin said. "Boy, have they fucked up their lives. One day you're a married guy with a couple of cute kids, reasonably content, and the next day along comes Kenji Sole."

"She must have been like something out of a Greek myth," Jamie said. "Irresistible. Men all over town jumping out of their wrinkle-free Dockers, ditching their families and groveling at her feet. For what? A little bit of fucking?"

"She made them feel desired," Coffin said. "Here they were, these basically ordinary schlubs with their wives and kids and mortgages, pretty much resigned to a houseful of plastic toys and kids yelling and utilitarian sex with the wife three times a month. Kenji Sole was the possibility of something more exciting. Not to mention the fucking."

"A tad too much empathy there, mister," Jamie said, tweaking Coffin's nipple.

"Ow! No fair. You asked."

"Well," Jamie said, pulling the sheet up to her breasts and turning her back to Coffin, "you didn't have to get all wistful about it."

"What," Coffin said, nuzzling the back of her neck, "are you mad at me?"

Jamie sighed and rolled her hips against his groin. "Yes," she said, "but that doesn't mean you're off the hook, pal."

"Frank!" Jamie was in the bathroom.

Coffin could barely hear her. The bathroom seemed very far away, down a long, narrow corridor. The door was open a crack, and a wedge of yellow light fell out. Otherwise the house was dark.

"Frank, oh my God—!"

Coffin couldn't move. His arms and legs felt as though they were tied to the bed with big rubber bands. He tried to sit up but fell back again.

"Frank! Oh, God, it happened again."

Then Coffin was in the slanted hallway outside the bathroom door. Jamie stood at the sink, wiping at the blood with a white towel. Blood on her bare legs. Blood in the toilet and on the floor. The towel dark with blood . . .

"Frank," Jamie said, looking up at him. "Frank, it's okay."

Coffin opened his eyes. He was in bed. Jamie was sitting up beside him.

"It's okay, Frank," she said.

Coffin drank water from the plastic bottle beside the bed, wiped a hand over his mouth. "Jesus Christ."

"Bad dream?"

"How could you tell?"

"You were yelling," Jamie said, stroking Coffin's hair. "Sort of."

"What did I say?"

"I don't know. Not really words, but you sounded upset so I woke you."

"Sorry," Coffin said. "Me and my freaky subconscious."

Jamie yawned and nestled her shoulder into Coffin's armpit. "Can you tell me about it? Might make you feel better."

The stuffed owl glared from the top of the wardrobe. Coffin shook his head. "Nope," he said, lightly rubbing Jamie's back. "It's gone now. I can't remember a thing. Let's go back to sleep."

"Okay," said Jamie, eyes flickering shut. She patted Coffin's chest. "Everything's okay . . ."

THREE

Coffin woke up at 6:57 A.M., three minutes before the alarm was set to go off. He was alone; Jamie had evidently gotten up early. He hoped briefly that she was downstairs, drinking coffee and reading the paper—but the house felt empty; the only sound was the slow drizzle outside. Coffin sat up and looked out the window. His neighborhood of gray-shingled houses was wreathed in mist. The small rain dripped from the telephone wires and puddled in the street. Coffin lit a cigarette, pulled on a pair of sweatpants, and went downstairs.

There was a note from Jamie on the kitchen counter.

Mister Wistful,
Sorry I couldn't stick around till you dragged your ass out of bed. I've got an early class and there's nothing in your fridge except pickles and beer. If you're not too tired tonight, let's have dinner and maybe some of that utilitarian sex you were talking about. Does it involve actual utilities, or is that too much to hope for?
xxx J

When the coffee was ready, Coffin poured a cup and stirred in sugar and half-and-half. He sat at the kitchen table with a legal pad and a pen, lit another cigarette, and wrote:

1. *Cap'n Rory—why so nervous?*
2. *Tommy McCurry*
3. *Nick Stavros*
4. *Talk to Mrs. Ramos*
5. *Check Carswell's alibi—anybody see him?*

Then what?
Coffin tapped the legal pad with his pen. He picked up the phone, dialed Lola's number, and got her voice mail. He hung up and called her cell.

"Hi, Frank," she said, on the fourth ring. She was breathing hard. Coffin could hear music in the background, and a whirring sound.

"Where are you?"

"At the gym," Lola said. "On the treadmill. What's up?"

"If you were robbing someone's house, which would you take—the computer or the fifty-thousand-dollar watch?"

There was a blast of static, then silence. Then Lola said, "Frank? You still there? A seagull must have landed on the cell tower."

"Kenji's computer. The one the killer took. What do you think was on it?"

"Something embarrassing," Lola said. Then, after a static-filled pause, "Something incriminating."

"Like what? For who?"

"She was into porn and married men. You tell me."

Coffin's phone blooped. "Hang on," he said. "I've got another call." Coffin hated call waiting; it seemed like a symptom of some great American rudeness, further proof that Western civilization was in precipitous decline. He pushed the TALK button.

"Coffin," he said.

"We've got a situation here, Coffin." It was Chief Boyle. "And its name is J. Hedrick Sole."

"Kenji's father," Coffin said.

"I *know* that, Coffin. He just spent the last ten minutes threatening to sue me, you, and everyone else he could think of. He's demanding to know who killed his daughter."

"Tell him we've got it narrowed down to ten or fifteen people," Coffin said. "Maybe."

"Very funny, Coffin. He wants to talk to you. He's sitting in my outer office with some crazy woman and a monkey. A fucking *monkey*, Coffin. Get your ass down here, pronto."

Coffin hit the TALK button again, but Lola was gone—nothing on the line but a low, dismal whooshing sound. The stuffed goat's head leered from the living room wall.

"God," Coffin said, "I love this job."

After she'd run three miles on the treadmill, Lola checked her pulse, wiped her face with a towel, and took a long drink from her plastic water bottle. She took her time stretching, then working her way through the circuit of weight machines. She did a light free-weight workout: dumbbell curls—less weight than usual because the bone chip in her elbow was giving her trouble; three sets of butterflies; three sets of light bench presses—only 190 pounds, since she had no spotter. Then a long, hot shower in the busy locker room.

For Lola, public showers had always been a kind of test. In high school, when they'd all showered after

gym or basketball or soccer practice, Lola had found
herself looking at the other girls' bodies with what she
guessed was more than the usual curiosity. It was normal, she'd been told, to register how those bodies were
shaped and compare them to her own. Normal. It was
not normal, though—and she'd been told this also—to
catch oneself glancing at their erect nipples, admiring
the way the water coursed over the curves of their but-
tocks; *not* normal to find them beautiful, to want to
touch them and have to make herself look away. Yet
she did these things, and ached for those girls, and
knew that whatever she was, she wasn't quite what
she was supposed to be, wasn't quite *normal*—not by
the narrow standards of her Wisconsin high school, at
least.

Not that she hadn't been attracted to boys, too,
sometimes—although not much lately, and maybe she'd
never really been attracted to them as much as she felt
she *should* be attracted to them. Still, mostly it was
girls that filled her dreams, girls she wanted to kiss,
girls she fell in love with, desired, longed for alone in
her narrow bed.

Now, Lola knew, she could have all the girls she
wanted. The trouble lay in finding someone real, someone who wasn't looking for a mother or big sister or,
worse, a safe, substitute father, or something even
weirder, even less about her, Lola, the person—*I've
been bad, Officer Lola; are you going to arrest me?*
Maybe that was Kate: There was promise there, certainly. She touched her scar and let the hot water stream
over her shoulders and back. She felt the gazes of the
other women in the locker room—one, a pretty blonde
with pierced nipples, naked under the next shower head,
meeting her eyes for a moment, then again. *Good,* Lola
thought, gazing back. *Let her look.*

* * *

J. Hedrick Sole was, Coffin thought, a scary old fucker. He was tall—at least six feet four inches—and very thin. He had long white hair and pale gray eyes that bulged as though they were about to squirt napalm. His suit was charcoal gray and very well cut, a perfect quarter inch of white shirt cuff extending beyond the sleeves. He wore a tie made of raw indigo silk and Italian shoes the color of saddle leather, which, Coffin guessed, probably cost a thousand dollars. The effect was impressive, until Coffin noticed that J. Hedrick Sole's fly was open.

Boyle sat at his desk, scowling. "Detective Coffin," he said, "this is Mr. Sole."

The old man levered up from his chair and stuck out a bony paw. A chunky gold Rolex hung loosely on his wrist. "Jerry Sole," he said, gripping Coffin's hand with surprising strength. "Great pleasure meeting you. Hope we didn't get you out of bed."

"I was up," Coffin said. "Where's the monkey?"

Sole grinned. His teeth were yellow and sharp—not dentures, Coffin thought. "My companion—Priestess Maiya—has gone out in search of a cafe latte. She's taken Gracie with her." Sole's voice was low and modulated, like an undertaker's.

"Gracie is the monkey," Boyle said.

Sole tilted his head. "I've been reading about you, Detective. Excellent work on those serial murders a couple of years ago. Very impressive."

"If you say so," Coffin said. Sole's way of speaking reminded him of a bad television actor; the inflections seemed arbitrary, purely for effect.

"Taciturn," Sole said, still gripping Coffin's hand. "Modest. I like that. Good old Yankee reserve. People talk too much these days. Talk, talk, talk." He chuckled, but then his face grew serious. "Tell me, Detective. What progress have you made in investigating my daughter's murder?"

"None whatsoever," Coffin said.

Sole's bushy eyebrows shot up. He released Coffin's hand as though it had given him a shock.

"Which is about what you'd expect," Boyle said. "Considering we've had the case for just over twenty-four hours."

"Surely you have *suspects*," said Sole. "Some sort of unifying *theory*."

"Not yet," Coffin said. "Nothing as defined as that. We've interviewed a few people, picked up a little gossip. The forensic specialists might be able to give us more information, but that'll take time. You're an attorney, right?"

"Indeed. I specialize in corporate law, with a bit of estate work on the side. Though these days I'm mostly retired."

"Then maybe you haven't had much experience with the way a homicide investigation typically works."

"Only in a very limited way."

Boyle raised a warning hand. "Coffin—"

"Around thirty-six percent of homicides nationally go unsolved," Coffin said. "Of the ones that are solved, about a quarter turn out to have been committed by strangers. The rest are committed by family, friends, and acquaintances."

J. Hedrick Sole nodded his craggy head. "I see where you're going," he said. "Probability."

"Exactly," Coffin said. "Unless the killer feels immediate remorse, calls 911, and waits quietly for the police to arrive—which happens more often than you'd think—we usually start by interviewing the victim's family and friends, neighbors, coworkers. We try to establish a timeline of the victim's movements before the murder. At the same time, we look for inconsistencies or contradictions in their statements, which may lead to things like search warrants and further forensic investigation."

"Looking for bloodstained clothing in the suspect's hamper, that sort of thing," said J. Hedrick Sole. "Chemical swabs and ultraviolet lights."

"Right. Anything that might link the suspect to the crime. Occasionally it works the other way around, and we find some bit of physical evidence that ends up driving the investigation, instead of just reinforcing what we already suspect. When I was a homicide detective in Baltimore, we once found a glass eye under a victim's sofa."

"Not the victim's, I take it."

"Exactly," said Coffin. "Turned out it belonged to the guy down the hall."

"He was the killer?"

"Yes."

"Either he was very stupid or you were very lucky."

Coffin nodded. "We were lucky he was so stupid."

"I see." Sole sat down, slowly. "I take it you found no glass eyes in my daughter's house."

"No, sir," Coffin said. "It's possible the forensic specialists may have found something interesting—we'll get their report in the next few days—but I wouldn't hold my breath."

"So, assuming Kenji's murder is not one of the thirty-six percent that go unsolved, how long is the investigation likely to take?"

"Several days if we're very lucky. Several weeks if we're not."

"Pray for luck, then, Detective," Sole said. "Several weeks is unacceptable. I shall do all in my power to see that your investigation moves forward in a timely manner." His eyes bulged ominously.

Thyroid problems, Coffin thought. *Either that or he's doing speed.*

"I explained to Mr. Sole that the Cape and Islands DA's office is leading the investigation, along with the state police," Boyle said, "and that you're only a consultant on the case."

"And I explained to Chief Boyle that I've met Mr. Mancini and found him a preening imbecile." Sole shook his head. "If this case is to be solved, I doubt very much it will be solved by Vincent Mancini."

"Since we're in the process of interviewing family and friends," Coffin said, "I wonder if you'd mind coming down to my office. I have a few questions I'd like to ask you about your daughter."

"By all means, Detective. Anything I can do to help."

The office door flew open. A young woman in what appeared to be a black wedding dress sailed into Boyle's office. She held a tall paperboard coffee cup in one hand. A green monkey sat on her shoulder, nibbling a biscotto. She extended her free hand to Coffin, palm down, as though she expected him to kiss it. It was encased in a black lace glove that ended just below her armpit. "Priestess Maiya," she said. "You must be Inspector Coffin."

"He's a detective, dear," J. Hedrick Sole said. "Not an inspector."

"Whatever," said Priestess Maiya. "Your fly's open."

The monkey stared at Coffin. Its eyes bulged. J. Hedrick Sole's eyes bulged. Outside, the rain fell harder.

Downstairs in Coffin's basement office, a small drop of fluid dangled from the overhead sewer pipe for a moment, then plunked softly onto the desk.

"Good God," said Priestess Maiya, looking up at the sewer pipe, then down at Coffin's desktop. "What was that?" She sat in Coffin's orange plastic guest chair while J. Hedrick Sole waited in the hallway.

"Condensation," Coffin said. "I think."

"You hope," said Priestess Maiya. Gracie the monkey perched on her shoulder, regarding Coffin with wide, astonished eyes.

Coffin opened his desk drawer and took out a felt-tipped pen and a legal pad. "Can I ask what your real name is, just for our records?"

"My legal name is Priestess Maiya. I changed it four years ago."

"Changed it from what?" Coffin said.

"McGurk. Ruth McGurk."

He looked up from his legal pad.

"M-C-G-U-R-K," said Priestess Maiya.

"So the last time you saw Kenji was around a month ago?"

"Yes, early April. A Saturday."

Coffin opened his desk calendar. "The first Saturday in April was the fifth. The next Saturday was the twelfth."

"I was in Amsterdam on the twelfth, I'm pretty sure, so it must have been the fifth. We had lunch at this noodle shop in Chinatown. Vietnamese. Quite good. I had the tripe."

"Tripe?"

"Yes, you know—cow intestine."

"Do you remember the name of the noodle shop?"

"Phó Bo. Little hole-in-the-wall with a dirty floor, just across from New England Medical Center."

"Whose decision was it to meet there?"

"Mine," said Priestess Maiya. "I've been there several times. It has a very special energy—a specific kind of chi. Do you know about chi, Detective?"

Coffin scratched his ear with his pencil eraser. "Life force, isn't it?"

Priestess Maiya smiled and clapped her hands together. "Very good, Detective."

"What did you talk about over lunch, the three of you?"

She leaned forward conspiratorially and put her elbows on Coffin's desk. Her eyes were almond-shaped and very dark. "Kenji was not a *happy* person," she said, "and she didn't want the people in her life to be happy, either. She was driving her poor father *crazy* with all this business about the will." The monkey hopped from her shoulder to the desktop, then skittered onto the pile of papers in Coffin's in-box and bared its little fangs.

"Whose will?" said Coffin.

"Jerry's will, of course," said Priestess Maiya, leaning back again and regarding Coffin through narrowed eyes. "But you already knew that. What else do you know that you're pretending not to know, Detective?"

"I've only heard bits and pieces. It would help if we had the whole story."

Priestess Maiya took a silver cigarette case and a long cigarette holder from her purse, screwed a cigarette into the holder, and lit it with a small gold lighter. "I love smoking," she said, exhaling a thick blue stream, "but I hate having smoked."

"About the will," said Coffin. He pushed the glass ashtray across his desk.

"Well, Kenji was very upset that Jerry had changed it, you see. She was the principal heir in the previous will— would've gotten the lion's share of his estate, after the various charities and things took their little bites."

"Not anymore," Coffin said.

"No," said Priestess Maiya. "Jerry's a very generous man, and he believes in my work, of course."

"Of course," said Coffin.

"Not that it matters the least little bit to Priestess Maiya." She took a long drag from her cigarette and exhaled through her nose. "I've always been quite good at raising money to support my work. It's what Jerry wants, though."

"How much money are we talking about, exactly?"

Priestess Maiya waved a black-gloved hand. "Oh, God. I don't even know, really. Millions, I suppose."

"Ten million?" Coffin asked. "Twenty?"

"Something like that," said Priestess Maiya, removing the cigarette from its holder and stubbing it out in the ashtray.

Coffin tapped a pencil on his notepad. "Kenji had her own money, right? From her grandfather?"

"Exactly. Great sacks of it. So of course it wasn't really about the *money*, Detective."

"No?" Coffin said, not liking the way the monkey was squatting in his in-box.

"Oh, now, don't be a dull boy, Detective. It was a *Daddy* thing, of course."

"A Daddy-has-a-girlfriend thing?"

"Precisely. Daddy's getting *laid*. *Bad* Daddy. Classic Electra complex."

"So, back to the noodle shop," Coffin said. "Phó Bo. You said hello, you sat down, you ordered cow intestine."

"Then Kenji launched into this tirade, Detective—I'm not exaggerating—this absolute *tirade* about how she was going to put a stop to it. That's what she said, 'put a stop to it.'"

"Did she say how she planned to go about it?"

Priestess Maiya rubbed her temples. "God. It was awful. She said she was going to take Jerry to court and have him declared incompetent unless he cut me out of the will."

"So what did Jerry say?"

"Well, Jerry's *entirely* competent, and a very proud man. He told her she was welcome to try, but if she did he'd countersue, and of course cut her out of the will entirely. Then it got ugly."

"Ugly how?" said Coffin.

Priestess Maiya batted her long eyelashes. "She accused Priestess Maiya of all *sorts* of terrible things. You'd think I had her poor father under some sort of *spell*." Her face turned serious, her mouth flattening into a tight line. "She made threats, but I didn't take them seriously."

"Threats other than the lawsuit and the competence thing?"

"Physical threats—against me. She threatened to have my legs broken and, in her words, my tits cut off. What sort of person would say a thing like that, Detective?"

The monkey made a loud chittering sound and scrambled up Priestess Maiya's arm. Two small, glistening turds lay in Coffin's in-box.

"Son of a bitch," said Coffin.

Priestess Maiya tickled the monkey under its chin. "Gracie," she said. "What a naughty thing to do."

The door swung open, and Lola stuck her head in. "Mind if I sit in?" she said.

Coffin forced himself to stop staring at the monkey turds. "Priestess Maiya, this is my partner, Sergeant Winters."

Priestess Maiya smiled and held out a gloved hand. "Charmed," she said. "Have you ever done any sort of performance work, Sergeant Winters?"

"Me?" Lola said. "I'm tone-deaf."

"I can't believe that monkey crapped in my in-box," Coffin said.

"Hi, monkey," Lola said, stroking Gracie's round head with her finger. The monkey closed its enormous eyes and sighed.

"So," Coffin said after he'd dumped the two slender monkey turds into the trash can. "How did the conversation end—after Kenji threatened you?"

"I said I was going to perform a purification ritual for Kenji, to try to cleanse her of all the rage she was feeling. She told me to go screw myself. So Priestess Maiya got up and walked out. Jerry came, too."

"That's the last contact you had with Kenji before she died? No other conversations or meetings?"

"Nothing after that, no. Not directly."

"Indirectly?"

"A letter or two from her lawyers, that was all. Routine inquiries. Jerry passed them on to his staff and that was the end of it. There was really nothing they could do, and they knew it."

"When was the last time you were in Provincetown, Priestess Maiya?"

"Oh, months ago. Last summer—we came out for a visit, Jerry and I."

"Not since then?"

"No."

"And if you don't mind my asking—"

"Don't be shy, Detective."

"Where were you on Friday night, between eight and midnight, say?"

"Jerry and I stayed in that night. He wasn't feeling all that well, and I decided to stay home with him."

"Nothing serious, I hope."

"Just a bug. Some twenty-four-hour virus, apparently."

Coffin tapped his pencil on the edge of the desk, then turned to Lola. "Anything you'd like to ask the priestess?"

Lola pursed her lips. "What are you a priestess *of*, exactly?"

"My vagina is the door to a great and holy temple, Sergeant Winters. So is yours."

"Okeydokey," said Lola, eyebrows raised.

The monkey bared its little fangs at Coffin. He bared his back.

"Gee," said Lola after they'd interviewed J. Hedrick Sole and the old man and his girlfriend had driven away in his chauffeured Bentley. "Think they worked on their stories?" She flipped through Coffin's notes, comparing them to her own. "They're almost word for word in places. *Put a stop to it. Cut her tits off. Routine inquiries.*"

Coffin pulled on his leather jacket. "Goes without saying. He's a lawyer." He paused. "What do you think— is she a suspect?"

"Well, there's motive, maybe—Kenji can't have Daddy declared incompetent if she's dead—but I'd want to see those letters from Kenji's lawyers. They both called them 'routine inquiries.'"

"Every time I've gotten a letter from a lawyer," Coffin said, as they climbed the stairs to the ground floor, "it's either been a bill, a threat, or bad news. Never a routine inquiry."

"Cavalo said Kenji hired a private detective to dig up the dirt on Priestess Maiya. I wonder what they came up with."

"Me, too," Coffin said. "I'll bet the PI worked for her lawyers." He pushed the big front door open. The drizzle had stopped. A small troop of starlings picked their way across the lawn, near the base of the World War I monument. The grass seemed very green in the muted light. "Torkel, Baldritch, Nash, wasn't it?"

Lola pulled her notebook from her purse, flipped it open. "That's what J. Hedrick said, yes. You've heard of them, I take it?"

"Very prominent Boston firm. Highly regarded, nasty in a clinch. Known for high-profile lawsuits and generally dragging their opponents through the mud."

"Sole and Priestess Maiya would have to know we'd follow up. Why would they lie about the letters being 'routine inquiries'?"

"Maybe he figures we're too busy, too dumb, or too incompetent," Coffin said. "Maybe what sounds like a threatening letter to me *is* routine to a professional litigator like Sole."

"Maybe," Lola said, as they climbed into the big, unmarked Crown Vic, "but I'd still like to see those letters."

"I'm more interested in the PI's report," Coffin said. "A trip to Boston may be in order."

Lola poked him in the ribs with the car keys. "Hoping for pictures, Frank?"

"I know my rights," Coffin said. "I'm not saying anything. Hey, I almost forgot—how was your date?"

Lola turned the key, and the Crown Vic's big V8 rumbled to life. "Good," Lola said.

"Good? That's it? *Good?*"

"*Okay*, Mr. Nosy," Lola said. "Better than good. Very good."

"*Very* good," Coffin said. "Now we're getting somewhere. How about hot? Would you say it was a *hot* date?"

"Sure," Lola said. "Hot. A hot date. There—happy now?"

"I can't believe you're holding out like this," Coffin said. "I tell you everything, but I have to pry and pry and all I get is 'good'?"

Lola rolled her eyes. "Oh. My. God. You want the play-by-play, is that it? You're a total voyeur, did you know that? You and Kenji Sole."

"What can I say? I live vicariously through you."

"We had dinner at my place, a nice bottle of pinot noir. Very low-key."

"A minute ago it was a hot date, now it's low-key."

"Jesus. You're relentless. You want to know if we had sex, right? That's what this is about."

"That's coming from you. I didn't say that."

"Okay, fine. We had sex. For *hours*. Hot. Lesbian. *Sex*. Satisfied?"

Coffin rolled down the window, lit a cigarette. "Oh yeah," he said.

Lola laughed. "J. Hedrick and Priestess Maiya didn't really drive all the way out here to tell us to work harder, did they?"

"No," Coffin said. "It was a preemptive strike. They wanted to get their statements on the record. That way they don't look like they're hiding anything."

"But if they're that worried about looking like they're hiding something, they must be hiding something."

Coffin shook his head. "Their whole response is so *premeditated*," he said. "Where's the grief? His daughter was murdered less than twenty-four hours ago, for God's sake."

Lola shrugged. "He's grieving on the inside, maybe?"

"Maybe," Coffin said.

Lola's sleek black cell phone was on the console.

Coffin flipped it open and checked for a signal. "Two bars," he said. "I guess the wind's blowing in the right direction." He dialed 411. "Boston, Massachusetts," he said, after a long moment. "Torkel, Baldritch, Nash. T-O-R-K-E-L. It's a business."

FOUR

MacMillan Pier stretched 1,270 feet into Provincetown Harbor and was sixty feet across at its widest point. The concrete deck was supported by hundreds of wooden pilings, each the thickness of a large man's torso, and with the tide halfway out stood about eight feet above the dark, choppy surface of the water. Still, to Coffin the pier seemed insubstantial; he could almost feel it swaying in the breeze.

"I hate this fucking guy already," Coffin said, looking down at Cap'n Rory's sailboat, the *P'town Princess.* "Let's just arrest him and call it a day."

Lola tucked a strand of hair back under her uniform hat. "Who is he, again?"

"Cap'n Rory," Coffin said. "He was seeing Kenji Sole, but he wasn't on Cavalo's list. I heard he was acting weird the morning after she was killed."

"So, you want to arrest him for acting weird, or because he lives on a boat?"

"The second thing," Coffin said. "I mean, what kind of an asshole lives on a fucking boat?"

As bad as the pier was, the rickety aluminum gangway down to the deck of Cap'n Rory's boat was infinitely worse. Coffin's stomach lurched; he gripped the gangway's flimsy rope rail with both hands.

"You okay, Frank?" Lola said, descending a few feet ahead of Coffin.

"Fine," Coffin said, trying not to look down. "Just perfect. Do you have to bounce like that?"

"Jeez. Sorry."

"Stop laughing. It's not funny."

"It's really hard to stop laughing when somebody tells you to stop laughing," Lola said.

"Fine," Coffin said, "but it'll be your fault if I barf."

Cap'n Rory didn't look like much, Coffin thought. He was fiftyish, short, balding, and bandy-legged. He wore swimming trunks and a Hawaiian shirt even though the day was still windy and raw. The trunks were orange and stained on the right leg with something that looked like lime Popsicle.

"The last time I saw Kenji was over a month ago," Cap'n Rory said. He sat in a deck chair on board the *P'town Princess*, smoking a long, fat cigar. "She dumped me. Said she needed to cull the herd." His voice was gravelly. The sound of it made Coffin reflexively clear his throat.

"Cull the herd?"

"Yeah, you know—reduce the inventory. She had too many boyfriends. She could only keep track of so many at a time. She'd add a couple of new ones and lose one or two that she wasn't really into anymore. It was like a collection she was always tweaking, know what I mean?"

"How did that make you feel?" Lola said. "Getting dumped like that."

Cap'n Rory shrugged. "No big deal," he said. "Kenji was a hot broad and all, but I get more pussy than I know what to do with. No offense, Officer."

"You *do*?" Coffin said.

"It's the boat," Cap'n Rory said. "Seventy-three feet of chick magnet. Young, old, skinny, fat—they can't resist it."

"Really?" Coffin said, squirming in his deck chair.

"I shit you not, my friend," Cap'n Rory said. "It's the romance of the frickin' sea. No joke."

The *P'town Princess* bobbed gently against her tether. Coffin closed his eyes. He could feel a sheen of sweat, slick on his forehead.

"So you were aware that Kenji had other boyfriends," Lola said.

Cap'n Rory nodded, eyebrows raised. "Oh, fuck yeah. If you were human and had a dick, you had a shot with Kenji. But mostly she liked rich, handsome guys. Go figure."

Coffin tilted his head. "So you're saying that when Kenji ditched you for, like, six other guys, that didn't piss you off even a little?"

Cap'n Rory puffed at his cigar, then held it out at arm's length. "See that?"

"Dr. Freud would be envious," Coffin said.

"Cuban," Cap'n Rory said. "It's an El Presidente— same exact cigar Castro used to smoke. Maybe the best cigar on the planet. Kenji gave me a box of 'em the night she dumped me. Then she fucked my brains out. How pissed off could you be?" He shrugged again. "Kenji may have been a bitch, but she was a classy bitch."

"Did Kenji ever ask if she could videotape the two of you together?" Lola asked.

Coffin looked at her, head tilted. She shrugged very slightly.

Cap'n Rory's face reddened a bit beneath its tan. He chewed his cigar for a moment, then shook his head.

"Nope," he said. "I don't think so, but nothing she wanted to do would've surprised me. She was a kinky girl."

"In what way?" Coffin said.

"It was all about control," Cap'n Rory said. "Kenji got off on being in charge."

"So, what," Coffin said, "whips and chains? That kind of thing?"

"It was never like the whole dungeon scenario," Cap'n Rory said. "More like silk scarves and a Ping-Pong paddle; light S&M, I guess you'd call it. Beyond that I drew the line. That's partly why she dumped me."

"Drew the line how?" Lola said.

"The strap-on," Cap'n Rory said. He took the cigar out of his mouth, eyed it, shrugged, and puffed it back to life. "She had a big black one, about a frickin' foot long. When I saw that thing coming at me, I started yelling 'avocado' like crazy."

"Avocado?" Coffin said.

"Yeah," Cap'n Rory said. "That was our safe word. If you said 'avocado,' it meant she was supposed to stop."

A seagull landed on top of the *P'town Princess*'s mast, shrieked, and flew away. Coffin looked at Lola. Her eyebrows were up, and her mouth was pressed tight. She was trying not to laugh, Coffin realized.

"So what are you nervous about, Cap'n Rory?" he said, wincing as the breeze freshened, stirring the harbor into a barely perceptible chop.

"Me? Nervous? Who says?"

"The word," Coffin said. "The word is, you were acting extremely nervous yesterday morning."

"You know. The morning after Kenji was killed," Lola said.

"Extremely," Coffin said, "nervous. How come?"

Cap'n Rory's face darkened. He looked down at the

deck. The cigar drooped in his hand. "Aw, fuck," he said. "Am I gonna have to get a lawyer?"

"Depends," Lola said. "Did you kill her?"

"Hell no, I didn't kill her," Cap'n Rory said, waving his fat cigar. "I wouldn't kill anybody. I told you—I *liked* her."

"Then why would you need a lawyer?"

"I don't have to talk," Cap'n Rory said. "I know my rights."

"We're not here to bust you for smuggling," Coffin said, "if that's what you're worried about. This is about the murder."

"You won't tell anybody? You give me your word?"

"Sure," Coffin said. "We give you our word. Just tell us the truth."

"It's got nothing to do with smuggling," Cap'n Rory said. "It's Linda. She's pregnant. She says it's mine, and she wants child support."

"Linda?" Coffin said, scratching his head.

"Linda Carswell," Cap'n Rory said. "You know—Stan's wife."

"You're sleeping with Stan Carswell's wife?" Coffin said, incredulous.

Cap'n Rory winked. "Why not? The girl could suck a golf ball through a twenty-foot garden hose."

"I thought she left town," Lola said.

"Yeah—all the way to Wellfleet. Nice little sail."

"So that's it?" Coffin said. "You were upset because you're going to have to pay child support to Linda Carswell?"

"Don't laugh," Cap'n Rory said. "I'm seriously screwed. Every nickel I make goes right back into the boat."

"And we can't tell anybody because—"

"Because if word gets out, she gets diddly in the divorce settlement with Stan. She'll fucking kill me."

Coffin and Lola exchanged looks.

"Speaking metaphorically, of course," Cap'n Rory said, scratching his chin with a dirty thumbnail.

Coffin persisted. "If she has another kid, won't Stan be able to figure out it's not his?"

Cap'n Rory sucked at his cigar, but it had gone out. He fished a silver lighter from his shirt pocket and flipped it open. "Maybe, maybe not," he said, torching the end of the cigar into a symmetrical red coal. "Stan's not exactly the sharpest tool in the shed. Hey—want to hear a joke? It's a good one."

"Sure," said Coffin. "Why not?"

"Okay," Cap'n Rory said, holding up his thumbs. "What's got two thumbs and really likes a blow job?"

"I give up," Coffin said.

Cap'n Rory grinned and turned his thumbs inward, so they pointed at his chest. "This guy," he said.

"Holy crap," Lola said when they were safely back in the Crown Vic. "I had no idea you breeders carried on this way. This town is a snakepit."

"Things have got to be fucked up when my life is suddenly a model of normalcy," Coffin said.

Lola laughed. She had a rich, easy laugh that made Coffin feel good. "You *are* pretty normal," she said. "For a straight guy."

Lola drove the length of Commercial Street, past the Coast Guard station and its lonely volleyball net, past Stanley Kunitz's house, standing empty now that the former poet laureate was dead, past the Red Inn and a few clusters of older cottages, all recently condo-ized. The water glittered in the tight spaces between the houses on the harbor side of the street. They passed Kotowski's hulking, ramshackle house and the stone breakwater, a low, porous dike dividing the salt marsh from the harbor, built in 1911 to protect the waterfront from a massive storm surge in the event of a gale or hurricane.

At the end of Commercial, Lola turned right onto the eastern terminus of Route 6. The salt marsh percolated silently on their left. A broad plain of mud and cordgrass, the salt marsh was fully submerged at high tide, exposed and ripe-smelling when the tide was out. Home to many species of birds and shellfish, it had always seemed alive to Coffin, breathing seawater in and out like a big, spartina-haired lung.

Up the hill, to the right, the Moors condo complex stood abandoned, some of the buildings skeletal and rickety, still for sale two years after the project had been abruptly halted. During the day the half-built condos seemed pedestrian enough, but at night they were ghostly, translucent, the moon and stars shining through their sagging frames.

"So what was that about Kenji videotaping Cap'n Rory?" Coffin said. "Trying out a hunch?"

Lola grinned and ducked her head. "Yeah," she said. "You win some, you lose some."

Coffin waved a hand. "You might be onto something," he said. "I mean, there's got to be some kind of psychological connection, right?"

"Between the boyfriends and the porn?" Lola said. "Definitely. I'm not sure I really get it yet, but it's got to be there."

"If your two big passions in life are boyfriends and porn, why not try to combine them somehow?"

"You could watch porn with the boyfriends—"

"Peanut butter on my chocolate—"

"Or you could figure out a way to put the boyfriends *into* the porn."

"Great theory," Coffin said, after a short silence. "I like it."

"Too bad it's completely made up," Lola said.

"Well," Coffin said, "there's that."

After a mile or so, Lola turned left onto the Province Lands Road and drove past the entrance to Herring Cove beach and then for several miles between the dunes, Cape Cod Bay visible here and there on the left, a blank stretch of scrub pines and sand on the right, crimson beach rose in bloom, dune grass turning from its winter silver to a bright acid green.

The Province Lands Visitor Center was a two-story octagonal building that sat on a high dune, a hundred feet or so above sea level, with a dramatic view of the Atlantic Ocean and the long curve of camel-colored sand sweeping off to Pilgrim Heights, Marconi Station, and Nauset Beach. In fact, Coffin thought, the visitor center bore a passing resemblance to the Smokey Bear hat that sat on Tommy McCurry's desk. Tommy McCurry was a National Park Service ranger; he directed the visitor center.

"Let's take a walk," McCurry said, putting the Smokey Bear hat on his head. "I can't talk about this here."

"Sure," Coffin said. "Let's take a walk."

They passed through the big main room with its lively photo exhibit on dune and marine life and stood outside on the deck. A layer of thick, low cloud hung over the ocean, and the breeze was damp and cold. It was just after ten o'clock. There were no visitors.

"You guys could have called ahead," McCurry said, lighting a cigarette. He was tall and thick through the chest, like someone who lifted weights. He did not appear to be cold in his ranger uniform: gray short-sleeved shirt, green knit pants. He wore a thick gold wedding band on the appropriate finger.

"We like to just pop in on people," Coffin said, lighting a cigarette of his own. Something about the slow-heaving ocean made him want to smoke. "The conversation's more spontaneous that way."

Lola took out her notebook, flipped it open. "Where were you night before last, between 9:00 P.M. and 1:00 A.M.?"

"Home with the wife and kids," McCurry said. "All five of them."

"Five?" Coffin said.

McCurry laughed. "We had the first three bang, bang, bang, then figured we were done, but we had a 'woops' a couple of years ago that turned out to be twins."

"When was the last time you saw Kenji?" Lola said.

"Thursday night," McCurry said. "The night before she was killed. We had a regular thing on Thursday nights."

"Why was that?" Coffin said. "Wife working the late shift?"

"She liked to go out with the girls and play bingo at the VFW hall. She thought I was out with my buddies at the Old Colony. We had a regular sitter."

Lola frowned. "She never checked up on you?"

"I don't know—I was never there. She never said anything, if she did."

"So you were at Kenji's house Thursday night," Coffin said, "or someplace else?"

"Kenji's place. Unless it was some spontaneous lunchtime thing, we almost always got together there."

"Nice view up there on Mayflower Heights," Coffin said.

McCurry laughed. "Like we were looking out the freakin' window."

"Was that her choice or yours?" Lola asked.

McCurry's face darkened; then he shrugged. "It was mutual, I guess. It's pretty private up there, most of the time."

"Most of the time?"

"The last time I was with her, we got interrupted. We're right in the middle—you know—and somebody walks into the house, starts calling Kenji's name."

"She didn't lock the door," Lola said.

"Nobody locks their door in P'town," McCurry said. "Do they?"

"Who walked in?" Coffin said.

"Stan Carswell." McCurry's mouth tightened. "He was drunk and kind of weepy. He kept saying he wanted Kenji to marry him. Said he was in love with her."

"A bit of an awkward moment," Coffin said.

"Considering Kenji and I were both naked and smeared with massage oil, yeah, kind of," McCurry said.

"So," Lola said, "what happened?"

"We were up in Kenji's bedroom, going at it. Stan comes in downstairs and starts yelling for her. Says he knows she's home. So she puts on a little nightie and goes downstairs to talk to him."

"Did he know you were there?"

McCurry's mouth bent into a half smile. "He must have. Not me specifically, but someone."

"Because?"

"First, because it's Kenji. She didn't spend a lot of evenings sitting home alone, you know? Second, you go to see your girlfriend and she comes out of her bedroom covered in oil and wearing nothing but a see-through negligee, what would *you* think?"

"Did you see Carswell? Talk to him?"

"I stayed put in the bedroom till Kenji got him out of there. Didn't want Carswell ratting me out to my wife, you know?"

"You're sure it was him?"

"Sounded like him. Kenji said it was him." McCurry shrugged. "I'm guessing it was him."

"What about you?" Lola said. "Did you ever get jealous?"

"Of Kenji?" McCurry took a deep drag from his cigarette and exhaled a stream of smoke. "Nah. She was great in some ways—"

"Like in the sack, you mean," Coffin said.

McCurry stared at him for a second. "That, too," he said. "She was great in some ways, but she was also a pretty freaky girl. Not somebody you'd want to have a serious thing with."

"So you had an unserious thing," Lola said.

"A freaky, unserious thing," Coffin said. "While the mrs. played bingo."

McCurry watched a Porsche convertible pull into the parking lot. It was yellow. Two slender men got out and walked down the dune path to the beach, holding hands.

"Look," McCurry said. He put his hands in his pockets and shrugged his shoulders. "I know—I'm an asshole. Kenji kind of had that effect on people. Sooner or later she brought out your inner jerk."

"You were okay with that?" Lola said. "The way she brought out your inner jerk?"

"No," McCurry said. "I wasn't proud of it, if that's what you mean."

"Then why not break up with her?"

McCurry looked down for a moment, and Coffin knew he was trying to decide whether to lie or tell some part of the truth.

"You didn't break up with Kenji," McCurry said, meeting Coffin's eyes. "She kept you until she was done with you. That's how it worked."

"Or what?" Coffin said. "She'd tell your wife?"

"Your wife, your boss, whoever. She'd ruin you. I think that's why she liked married guys. Once she pulled you in, she could control you."

"She said that?"

"Not in so many words, no," McCurry said, "but it was strongly implied."

Coffin smoothed his mustache. One long, wild mustache hair keep curling into his nostril. It made him want to sneeze. "Did Kenji ever film the two of you having sex together?" he said, when the urge to sneeze had passed.

McCurry's eyes widened slightly. "No," he said. He thought for a second. "Not that I was aware of."

"Not that you were aware of? What does that mean?"

"It means I was never aware of being filmed by Kenji," he said. "Why is that hard to follow?"

"What about the other boyfriends? Did she film them?"

McCurry shook his head. "Not that I was—"

"Aware of," Coffin finished. "Got it. But you're not going to say it didn't happen. How come?"

Coffin watched McCurry trying to formulate his answer. He'd seen witnesses do it a thousand times: try to guess what the cops knew, try to figure out how much to tell them.

McCurry took a deep breath, let it out. "Because it occurred to me that she might. More than once. I'm not sure why. I thought I was probably just being paranoid—but it's the kind of thing she might have done."

"The control thing," Coffin said.

"Right. It's one thing to rat you out to your wife or your boss. It's another thing entirely to show them the video. You know?"

"Hey, look," Lola said. She was gazing out at the ocean, shading her eyes with one hand. "Whales."

Coffin looked. Two dark, enormous creatures were rolling together in the swell a couple of hundred yards offshore, half obscured by the roiling sea. Now and then a long flipper emerged from the water, or the broad, bladelike flukes at the end of a tail. A plume of steam huffed from a blowhole; then Coffin heard a sharp gasp—a whale, taking a huge breath.

"Humpbacks," McCurry said. "They've been out here all week, putting on a show. Yesterday they were breaching like crazy."

"I think they like each other," Coffin said. "Are they mating?"

"Nah." McCurry waved a hand. "They do that down in the tropics. They're eating. The sand-eel hatch was a month ago—there's gazillions of 'em out there. Perfect whale food."

"I don't know," Lola said. "Whatever they're doing, it looks friendlier than just eating."

Coffin squinted. The whales seemed to be rubbing against each other, flapping at the water gently with their enormous pectoral fins.

"Hold on a sec," McCurry said. He went inside and came back with a big pair of binoculars. "Huh," he said, after raising the binoculars to his eyes and gazing at the whales for a long minute. "Actually, there's never been a documented observation of humpback whales mating, and it would be really weird for a female to still be in estrus, this late in the year—but it sure looks like *something's* going on out there."

"That was interesting," Coffin said, on the short ride back into town center from Race Point. He was looking out the window at the sprawl of new, mostly unsold houses cluttering the beech woods south of Route 6.

"Which part?" Lola said. "The whales fucking, the thing about Stan Carswell showing up at Kenji's house drunk and weepy, or the part where McCurry lied about being filmed by Kenji?"

"All of the above. I think we need to have another talk with Carswell. We also need to take a second look at Kenji's house. Something funky was going on there. McCurry made breaking up with Kenji Sole sound like trying to get out of the Mafia."

Lola stopped at the light on Route 6. "Now?" she said.

"Let's grab a bite first," Coffin said. "I'm starved."

"Do you buy McCurry's thing about the way Kenji seemed to bring out the worst in people? Or do you think he was just rationalizing his own bad behavior?"

"She seems to have brought out the worst in whoever killed her."

"Yeah—but the other guys, too. They just seem like ordinary *guys,* you know? Maybe not geniuses, and not exactly Mother Teresa, any of them, but not totally terrible people, either. I mean, you sort of have to feel bad for Stan Carswell and Ed Ramos. Even McCurry, in a way."

"They made a choice," Coffin said. "They *wanted* to fuck up their lives—Kenji was just the excuse."

"Thanks, Dr. Phil," Lola said, giving Coffin a sideways glance as they crossed Route 6. "What about the power of *love*, baby? Haven't you ever known anybody like that—that could make you do stuff against your better judgment?"

Coffin laughed, rolled down the window, and lit a cigarette. "Well," he said, "there's my uncle Rudy, but that's not quite the same thing. I guess you could say my ex-wife brought out the worst in me for a while, although it was bubbling pretty close to the surface toward the end of our marriage."

Lola waved at the cigarette smoke swirling inside the Crown Vic. "That's all I'm saying. Some people just know how to push your buttons. They like a little conflict—a little drama."

"Plus, if they can implicate you, that gives them power," Coffin said. "Once you've compromised your marriage, there's always the implied threat that they'll expose you."

Lola nodded. "Unless you do what they want. It's a pretty fucked-up dynamic."

"Been there, done that?"

Lola narrowed her eyes and glanced at Coffin. "Kind of," she said.

"Oh, come on," Coffin said. "Don't go all strong and silent on me. Let's share."

Lola snorted. "I live for your amusement."

"Okay, fine. I'll tell the story and you stop me if I get too far off track." He rubbed his chin. "Where do we start? It was in college—"

"Law school."

"Okay, now we're getting somewhere. You were in law school, and you had a steady thing going with a nice girl named Becky—"

"Becky?"

"Okay, not Becky. So, not Becky is all about cuddling in front of the fireplace and tea and nice little cookies—"

"Annie. Her name was Annie."

"But something was missing," Coffin said. "The erotic spark. She was *too* nice. *Too* sweet—like she was afraid of herself, almost."

Lola stopped at the light on Bradford and clicked on the turn signal. "This is creeping me out a little," she said.

"Not really what you'd want in the old sackeroo," Coffin said.

"The old sackeroo?" Lola said, turning into the parking lot across from Town Hall. "Did we just leap back in time to, like, 1948?"

"You know what I mean," Coffin said. "I'm right, right?"

"We'll see," Lola said. "Keep going."

Coffin cleared his throat. "So this girl walks up to you one day after class and asks you out. Just like that. She's not as pretty as Annie, but she's *hot* in this way you can't quite put your finger on."

"She's *stacked*," Lola said, elbowing Coffin in the ribs.

He shot her a look. "Look, if you're going to sit there and make adolescent jokes—"

"Sorry," Lola said.

"She's a Brooklyn hipster chick," Coffin said. "She's got a couple of ironic tattoos and a spiky hairdo and a clit ring."

"Northampton," Lola said. "She's from Northampton."

"She's totally out, too," Coffin said. "Which is sexy all by itself."

"That part's actually true," Lola said. "She wasn't afraid to take a chance that she might be wrong about me. I mean, do I *look* like a lesbian?"

"No fair," Coffin said, pushing the door open and climbing out. "Trick question. Let's walk over to the Portuguese Bakery and get some doughnuts."

Lola grinned, climbed out of the Crown Vic, and put her hat on. "So you're saying I do. You think I look like a lesbian."

"Now you're harassing me," Coffin said.

"Go on with the story," Lola said. "It was just getting good."

"Okay, fine. So you go out for a coffee—you know, no big deal—and the next thing you know you're at her place, having sex on the couch."

"Hot *lesbian* sex," Lola said, as they crossed Commercial Street.

"Fucking," Coffin said. "In the best possible sense of the word. *Abandon*. Nothing off-limits. No earnest discussions about the gender politics of the dildo. That was Becky." Inside, the bakery smelled like grease and sugar and coffee.

"Annie," Lola said.

"But this is what's-her-name," Coffin said. "Agnes."

"Jen," Lola said. "Having fun?"

"I told you—I live through you vicariously," Coffin said. He pointed at a platter full of flat, sugary, fried-dough confections inside the glass counter. "*Duas malasadas, por favor*," he said to the man behind the counter. "How are you, Ernie?"

The counterman shrugged. He was a little older than Coffin, with a thick black mustache that might have been dyed. He wore a white apron, white pants, and a white paper hat. "I could moan an' groan," he said, "but who the hell would listen? How's your ma, Frankie?"

"Not bad, considering," Coffin said. "Some good days, some not so good."

"Same for everybody, ha?" Ernie said, reaching into the display case with a slip of wax paper. "Some days good, some days not so good." He picked out six of the Portuguese doughnuts and pushed them into a white paper bag. "A couple for your cousin Tony, too. He's lookin' a little skinny lately. What can I get for the young lady?"

Lola peered into the big glass counter full of cook-

ies and pastries and cakes. "Uh, just coffee," she said.
"Thanks."

"Coffee for me, too," Coffin said.

The counterman poured coffee into foam cups. Coffin sipped his—it was bitter and scorched, as though it had been sitting on the hot plate a long time.

"On the house, Frankie," Ernie said. "Give your old ma my best regards."

Coffin sat at his desk eating a malasada and sipping bitter coffee, which he'd doctored heavily with cream and sugar. The block walls were painted Di-Gel green and glowed sickly in the buzzing fluorescent light.

"There was more to it than just the sex thing, though," he said, tipping back in the orange plastic guest chair, propping his shoulders against the file cabinet. "Agnes was smart and funny and kind of *mean* about people, in a way that drew you in. She saw right through you; it was like she could read your weaknesses and all your dark, ulterior motives before you even opened your mouth. She had you pegged within twenty minutes— and she knew how to use all of it against you."

"Do you think of me as having dark, ulterior motives?" Lola said, twirling her uniform hat on her index finger.

"That's neither here nor there," Coffin said, pushing the last bite of greasy, sugary doughnut into his mouth. "How did the Lola-Agnes-Becky love triangle resolve itself? Was there a huge, ugly scene?"

"You tell me."

"Okay," Coffin said, sipping the scalded coffee. "Let's see." He ran a hand through his hair, feeling for the dime-sized bald spot on the crown of his head with a fingertip. "You fessed up after a few weeks. It sucked. Becky took it hard."

Lola raised her eyebrows, nodded. "There was weeping."

"*Copious* weeping," Coffin said. "Like you'd chopped up her cat with a chain saw or something. You were the worst person on the planet."

"I never liked that cat," Lola said. "She was a neurotic little barfer."

Coffin scribbled something on a slip of paper. "And the cat's name was?" he said, folding the paper in half.

"Emily," Lola said. "After Emily Dickinson, of course."

"Ha," Coffin said. He stood up, unfolded the scrap of paper and handed it to Lola. The word "Emily" was scrawled across it.

"Okay," Lola said. "You're definitely creeping me out. Are you done yet?"

Coffin sat back down in the squeaky office chair, put his feet up on the desk. "So you try to make a go of it with Agnes. The first few weeks are kind of great—intense and guilt-soaked, but the sex is better than ever. You move in together. Then, out of the blue, she decides she wants to date other people. She kind of misses men, she says. Someday she might want to have a baby, she says."

"Seriously," Lola said. "Let's stop."

Coffin stopped. "Sorry," he said. Neither of them said anything for a few seconds. Then he said, "Seriously. I didn't mean to cross a line there."

"It's not that," Lola said.

"Good."

"It's just hard to talk about. Things with Jen got really codependent and freaky for a while. I tried to move out once, and she literally lay down in the driveway behind my car as I was about to back out. I kind of started to hate her."

"But you were locked in."

"Right—when you ditch somebody for a new relationship, your impulse is to make the new thing work, no matter what. Otherwise you look like a fool."

"Been there," Coffin said. "Done that."

Lola twirled her uniform hat meditatively. "So Jen and I are up in New Hampshire at her aunt's lake house, out in the middle of nowhere. It's this amazing, serene place, mist rising off the lake in the moonlight, loons calling—totally beautiful, nobody around. With anybody else on the planet, I'd be having a great time."

"Sarah Palin?" Coffin said, pulling a stapled report from his in-box and leafing through it.

"Ew," Lola said. "Thanks for *that* thought, Frank."

"Sorry."

"But I'm not having a great time with Jen. She's in full-on freaky mode—one minute she wants to go skinny-dipping and have sex on the dock, next minute she's picking a huge fight with me about how to stack the firewood."

"The firewood?" Coffin said, looking up.

"Right, and every other damn thing. What to have for lunch, the most environmentally sound dishwashing method, you name it."

"Not fun."

"No, and I'm stuck there. We only brought one vehicle, and I can't just ditch her."

"Ack," Coffin said.

Lola leaned forward and put her elbows on the desk. "I wanted to kill her."

Coffin waved a hand. "If you've never wanted to kill someone, there's probably something wrong with you."

"No. Seriously. The thought of cracking her over the head with a canoe paddle or drowning her skinny ass in the lake was *pleasurable*. Homicidal ideation, Frank.

I actually had to consciously stop myself from thinking about it."

"So, how close was it?"

"Close. A couple of times."

Coffin grinned. "Kind of hard to go back to walks in the rain and candlelit hot tubs after a moment like that."

"Yeah, that trip was pretty much the end of the romance—what was left of it."

Coffin leaned back and laced his fingers on top of his head.

"What?" Lola said. "Stop looking at me like that."

"Did you ever tell her?" Coffin said.

"That she almost ended up at the bottom of Lake Winnipesaukee, you mean?"

He nodded.

"No. Are you kidding me? I'd have never heard the end of it. Then I *would* have had to kill her."

Coffin held up the report. "Final autopsy on Kenji Sole."

"Holy shit—you just let me keep talking?"

"Three deep stab wounds to the chest including the one that killed her, two to the abdomen," Coffin read. "One shallower wound to the back, apparently struck a rib. Three defensive wounds: two on the left forearm, one on the right. So she was stabbed nine times altogether. All wounds appear to have been caused by the same knife."

"The one sticking out of her chest," Lola said, looking over Coffin's shoulder.

"Bingo. The depth of the wounds indicates the killer was angry—"

"Duh."

"And reasonably strong. Also, entry angles of some wounds indicate the perpetrator may have been taller than the victim, or standing above the victim."

"She was what, five foot six?"

Coffin flipped back to the first page. "And a half," he said.

"So an angry killer, taller than the victim, reasonably strong. What does that tell us?"

"Nothing we didn't already know," Coffin said.

"No mutilation," Lola said. "No wounds to the genitals. No sign that she was tortured."

Coffin turned a page. "No cuts to the throat. No sign that she was bound."

"None of the hallmarks of a sexual psychotic killer, in other words. Or of an execution." Lola tapped the report with a fingertip. "The last wound was the one that killed her—punctured the left ventricle. Death almost instantaneous."

"An important detail," Coffin said. "The killer was enraged enough to kill but not crazy enough to keep going after Kenji stopped struggling."

"The wound in the back is interesting," Lola said. "Was she stabbed in the back first? Or did she turn and try to escape?"

"If the first wound is to the back, then maybe the killer was concealed and jumped out," Coffin said. "A sneak attack."

"Hiding in the kitchen, maybe," Lola said.

"Makes sense. Then is it a jealousy thing? The killer's in the kitchen, Kenji's in the living room with a boyfriend—"

"On top, apparently."

"Or behind," Coffin said.

"Right," Lola said, cheeks turning a faint pink. "Almost forgot."

"The killer grabs a knife, runs into the living room, stabs her in the back—"

"But the blow hits a rib, doesn't do much damage."

"Hurts like a sonofabitch, though. Definitely gets her attention. Kenji jumps up, and the killer keeps stabbing her as she's trying to back away."

"One question," Lola said.

Coffin held up a finger. "What's the boyfriend doing while Jealous Person is stabbing the woman he's been having sex with until, like, a second ago?"

"Right. Does he run away? Stand there and watch it happen?"

"What, naked? And wait for the killer to turn on him?"

"So he runs away—but doesn't call the police. Why not?"

"He's married. Wants to stay that way."

"Or wants to protect the killer," Lola said.

Coffin rubbed his chin. Neither of them said anything for a long moment.

"So, let's say the wound to the back isn't from the first blow," Coffin said finally. "Then what?"

"Depends," Lola said. "On what CSS comes up with. If there's no blood in the kitchen—"

"Then it's a lot less clear," Coffin said. "If there *is* blood in the kitchen, some spatter, at least, it could be that the argument starts there. They've just had sex, say—"

"He's ejaculated inside her."

"Or someone else did, an hour or two prior."

Lola sat down in the orange plastic desk chair across from Coffin's desk. "I'm getting a headache," she said, rubbing her face with both hands. "Too many ors."

"They've just had sex, they're fighting about something, he or she grabs a knife and stabs Kenji in the belly—or she blocks the blow with her arm. Kenji runs to the living room, starting to bleed like hell. More stabbing, not much struggle, the end. Killer tosses the place and leaves."

"Shit," Lola said. "I forgot about the tossing part, almost."

"Or," Coffin said, "they're in the living room postsex. They're having a fight. He's in a rage, he's looking around for a weapon—"

"He says, 'Hold on a sec—stay right there, I'll be back in two shakes with a big-ass knife.'"

"Trots out to the kitchen, grabs big-ass knife, trots back into the living room—"

"Still in a murderous rage, stabs her in the chest, et cetera."

"Doesn't make sense that way, really," Coffin said. "You'd use whatever weapon was at hand, probably, if you were that angry. The fireplace poker, or a statuette or something. Or your bare hands. You wouldn't run to the kitchen, grab a knife, and come back. Too much time to think things over. Maybe."

"Maybe," Lola said. "What about the tossing part, though? If it's a jealousy thing, or they're having a lovers' quarrel, it doesn't make any sense either. You have a fight or catch her with another man—"

"Or your husband. Or—"

"Or *whoever*," Lola said. "Then, as an afterthought, you decide there's a computer and who knows what else you really, really need to look for?"

"Now *I'm* getting a headache," Coffin said. A drop of condensation fell from the sewer pipe and splattered on the autopsy report. He wiped it off with his sleeve.

Lola shook her head. "This whole thing really bugs me," she said. "As a woman, I mean."

Coffin slid the autopsy report into a manila folder, then put the folder into his desk drawer. "It's hard not to judge her," he said.

"You want to say that a woman should be able to have as many partners as she wants," Lola said, picking a

speck of lint from her uniform. "Whenever and wherever she wants, without having to worry about getting
killed." She looked up at Coffin. Her eyes were very
blue. "It ought to work that way."

Coffin nodded. "It ought to," he said, "but ought to's
got nothing to do with it." He picked up the phone and
dialed a number.

"Who are we calling?" Lola said.

"Nick Stavros. His office." He held up a finger. "Hi,
Marcy, this is Frank Coffin. Is he in? Out of town till
when? Have him call me, yeah. It's important. Thanks."
He put the receiver back in its cradle.

"You know Stavros's office number? Just off the top
of your head?"

"I've known Stavros since I was a kid," Coffin said.
"Hell, we're lodge brothers."

"*Lodge* brothers? You're in a *lodge*?"

Coffin nodded. "Masons."

"You're a *Mason*? Jesus, Frank. You're a man of
mystery."

"King Hiram's Lodge, baby. Chartered in 1795 by
Paul freaking Revere. I joined when I came back home
from Baltimore. Rudy brought me in. It was a way of
reentering the community, I guess. I haven't been to a
meeting in a long time, though." Coffin looked at his
watch. "Ever tried the Alden for lunch?" he said.

Lola frowned. "Following up on Carswell?"

Coffin stood and hitched up his chinos. "Yep."

"Gah," Lola said. "The sacrifices we make while in
the line of duty."

FIVE

On Friday and Saturday nights, even in the deserted depths of the off-season, the Captain Alden was usually crowded and loud. The bar was almost always busy, the pool tables in contentious use, the jukebox blaring the best of Led Zeppelin or the Stones, the window seats full of drinkers enjoying their fine view of Commercial Street and the foot of MacMillan Pier. The Alden offered many enticements on weekend nights: somewhat more than the usual amount of illicit drug dealing, as bars in Provincetown went; a fair number of single straight women between the ages of thirty and fifty with whom almost any reasonably ambitious male, regardless of age or appearance, stood a decent chance of hooking up; and frequent bar fights, which had a way of spilling out onto the sidewalk shortly before closing time, given a bit of expert, pants-hauling assistance from the two large bartenders, for whom "take it outside" was the one cardinal rule. There was, during the off-season, the added attraction of Friday night drag karaoke, which drew a large and raucous crowd. Sunday lunchtime, though, except at high season's manic zenith, was generally pretty dead.

"More flies than customers," Lola said, settling onto a bar stool. "Not a good sign." Except for Ticky, one of

Provincetown's semihomeless drunks, Coffin and Lola were the only patrons.

"That's cause most of the flies ain't tried the food," the bartender said, shoving a couple of greasy menus across the bar. He was a tall man with a considerable gut and a long, greasy ponytail. One of his front teeth was missing.

"That bad, huh?" Coffin said. He flipped the menu open. There was the usual array of Provincetown tourist food: burgers, lobster rolls, fried clams, Portuguese kale soup.

"I don't eat it," the bartender said, grinning, "and the boss gives it to me free."

Coffin nodded, closed his menu. "I'll drink mine," he said. "Walker Red, on the rocks. Pour one for yourself, if you want."

"Hey," the bartender said. "If the cops can drink on duty, why the hell can't I?"

"Just a Diet Coke for me," Lola said.

"Yes, ma'am," the bartender said. He took a pint glass from the rack, scooped it half full of ice, and spritzed it to the top with soda from the carbonated drinks gun. Then he dropped a few ice cubes into a pair of rocks glasses and poured triple shots of scotch into each of them. "Soda's on the house," he said.

"Thanks," Lola said, wiping a brown smear of lipstick off the glass with a bar napkin.

"So, who was working Friday night?" Coffin said. "You?"

The bartender nodded. "Me and Fat Tony," he said. "Big crowd Friday night. Kind of rowdy. Decent tippers, though."

"Do you know a guy named Stan Carswell?" Coffin said.

Lola took Carswell's picture from her breast pocket and slid it across the bar. "This is him."

The bartender shrugged. "He looks familiar," he said. "Sure. I've seen him in here a few times."

"Was he here on Friday night, for drag karaoke?"

The bartender rubbed his chin stubble. "Maybe," he said, gazing at the picture. "Me 'n' Fat Tony were both trippin' our balls off by about ten o'clock, so I couldn't say for sure. He would've been in drag, right?"

"Chartreuse wig and fake boobs under his shirt," Coffin said. "Singing 'Blue Suede Shoes.'"

"Maybe." The bartender looked at the picture again, head tilted, eyebrows raised. "I can't rule it out. I'd probably remember a chartreuse wig, though. A thing like that would be pretty intense if you were on acid."

"Got a number where we can reach Fat Tony?"

"Sure," the bartender said, retrieving a worn address book from behind the bar, "but I doubt he'll remember much. He was even more fucked up than I was."

Stan Carswell's psychiatry practice was in a newer building off Harry Kemp Way, a street named after a poet, novelist, and local fixture who lived much of his adult life in various shacks in and around Provincetown. Carswell's building was a low structure done in cedar shakes, just beginning to turn gray; its parking lot was surfaced with crushed oyster shells. In addition to Carswell's offices, the building housed a masseuse (Swedish, shiatsu, hot stone, and aromatherapy) and an acupuncturist/herbalist's called Feng Shui for the Soul.

In Carswell's outer office Coffin flashed his shield for the receptionist, a young Eastern European woman. She buzzed Carswell on the intercom. "Dr. Carswell," she said, in an accent that reminded Coffin of the Gabor sisters, "the police is here. Yes. Okay." Less than a minute later a nervous-looking client shuffled out of the inner office. "You can go in now, okay?" said the young woman. She was, Coffin thought, stunningly beautiful: dark hair and black eyes set deep above astonishing cheekbones. Such girls were everywhere in Provincetown, suddenly.

Carswell's office was better furnished than his house. A sectional sofa filled one corner; a mahogany desk dominated the center of the room. A leather armchair and an ottoman-style coffee table finished the seating arrangement. The rug was chocolate brown with a pattern of big pastel rings. It all looked to Coffin as though it had been ordered from the latest Pottery Barn catalog. The window overlooked a sunlit garden: scotch broom and beach rose, rampant.

"So," Carswell said, hands folded on his desktop. "You're back. How can I help you today?"

He looked nervous, Coffin thought. Dark circles of sweat were beginning to form under the arms of his shirt, a pale blue button-down worn with chinos, loafers, and no tie. A small faux stone fountain sat on an end table near Coffin's chair, its cord plugged into a wall outlet. The fountain gurgled in a way that was supposed to be soothing, but it sounded to Coffin like someone peeing down a shower drain.

"You lied to us, Stan," he said. "It doesn't look good, frankly."

Carswell's mouth opened, then closed. "There *was* someone there," he said. "I knew it."

Coffin shrugged. "Why didn't you tell us you were there the night before she died? Did you think we wouldn't find out?"

"I wasn't thinking," Carswell said. He blinked, then

swallowed, Adam's apple bobbing. "I was afraid it would make me look crazy."

"Stan," Coffin said, shaking his head. "Stan. When you lie to the cops, it makes you look *guilty*."

"Sorry," Carswell said. "I should have told the truth. I was scared, I guess."

The fountain tinkled companionably. "Nice fountain," Coffin said. "Very relaxing."

"Thanks," Carswell said. "My patients seem to like it."

"Does it ever make you feel like you have to pee?" Coffin said.

Carswell laughed, then squeezed his hands together, making a soft farting sound between them. "No," he said. "Not so far, anyway."

"Okay, so you went to Kenji's house Thursday night. Why?"

"To ask her to marry me. Again."

"Again? How many times would that have made?"

"Two."

"What did she say the first time?"

"She laughed."

"That's it? She laughed?"

"She told me not to be ridiculous. She said she had no intention of marrying anyone, but if she did it wouldn't be me."

"Who would it be? McCurry? Ed Ramos?"

"She didn't say." The fountain tinkled. Carswell made the little farting sound between his hands again.

Coffin frowned. "You thought you'd ask her to marry you again, just in case?"

"I was drunk. I convinced myself she'd been kidding the first time. Pathetic, I know."

"So you went to her house. Then what?"

"I let myself in the side door, through the kitchen."

"Why not the front door?"

"The side door's hidden from the carriage house. I didn't want that creepy Cavalo guy to know I was there."

Coffin looked at Lola. "He went in the kitchen door," he said.

"It's hidden from the carriage house," Lola said.

"Why did you care if Cavalo saw you?"

Carswell frowned, hands making rapid farting noises. "I'm not sure," he said. "It just seemed like he was always hanging around the periphery, watching. You'd walk out the door and he'd be sitting out there on his steps, pretending not to look at you. Creepy."

"Okay, so you went in the kitchen door."

"I went in the kitchen door. She wasn't downstairs that I could see, so I called her name."

"Kenjiiiiii!" Coffin called, doing his best Brando imitation. "Like that?"

"Probably not far off," Carswell said, smiling a tight little smile. "I was pretty looped."

"So then?"

"So then she came downstairs in this little see-through nightgown. God, she looked beautiful."

Lola looked up from her notebook. "What color was the nightgown?"

"White, I think," Carswell said. "Very sheer, like I said. She wasn't wearing any panties underneath. She'd do stuff like that, just to drive you crazy."

"Then what happened?" Coffin said.

"I tried to kiss her, but she pushed me away. That's when I figured out she was probably with somebody."

"Did that make you angry?"

"Sad. I wept. I begged her to marry me. She patted my hand like I was a hysterical schoolgirl. Told me to buck up. Buck up! Can you believe that?"

"Not quite what you wanted to hear," Lola said.

"No," Carswell said. "Not quite."

Coffin scratched his ear. "So then what?"

"I went down to the Old Colony. I stayed until closing time and drank a lot of Bushmills. I vomited twice,
walking home. I woke up with a screaming hangover."

"Did Kenji like to dominate you, Stan?"

Carswell's ears turned bright pink. His hands made
several rapid farts. "What do you mean?" he said.

"You know what I mean, Stan. Did she ever tie you
up, or spank you?"

Carswell looked down. "Once in a while, she liked
to play little games," he said. "Why not? It's a normal
variation, you know. All in fun."

"What about the strap-on? Was that all in fun, too?"

Carswell looked up, meeting Coffin's eyes. "Whatever Kenji wanted to do was fine with me," he said. "She
liked to try different things. So what?"

"You never felt humiliated?"

"I was ecstatic. She was with me, she had chosen me.
So whatever she wanted to do beyond that point was fine."

Coffin leaned back in his chair and tilted his head.
"Did you go to Kenji's house Friday night and kill her,
Stan? Because that's what it looks like to me."

Carswell blinked, then swallowed. "No," he said. "It
wasn't me. I was at drag karaoke, like I said. Ask the
bartender—Rick."

"We did. He was a little unclear about whether he'd
seen you or not."

"Oh, Christ," Carswell said. "He must have been
tripping."

"Was Kenji filming you?" Lola asked.

"Filming?" Carswell said.

"The things she liked to do to you—did she film
them?"

Carswell composed his face carefully and took a deep breath. "It's possible," he said.

"Possible? You don't know for sure?"

"There were times I felt she was posing me, almost. As if there were a hidden camera, maybe, and she wanted to make sure it had a good line of sight. There were times I felt as though we were being watched, somehow. I thought I was just being paranoid."

"You never saw a camera? Never saw any video?"

"No."

"Would it have upset you if she *had* been filming you?"

"No," Carswell said. "It would have turned me on."

Coffin stood. Lola was already waiting by the door, adjusting the tilt of her uniform hat.

"There's one other thing," Coffin said.

"Yes?"

"If you're planning on taking any trips out of town, you'll want to let us know ahead of time."

Coffin and Lola stepped into the outer office; Lola shut the door quietly. The receptionist was gone— probably worried INS was going to show up, Coffin thought. He stood and listened for a moment: Carswell fumbling with the phone, dialing, mumbling urgently for a minute or two. Coffin looked at Lola, who raised one eyebrow but said nothing.

"Who do you think he was calling?" Lola said, steering the Crown Vic out of Carswell's office parking lot. "His lawyer?"

"Unless he's a total idiot," Coffin said.

"As opposed to just a partial idiot?"

Coffin grinned. "Let's stop at the Yankee Mart," Coffin said, "and get a cup of coffee. Then I want to take another look at Kenji's house. This whole filming-of-the-boyfriends thing is getting interesting."

Lola put the turn signal on and turned left on Conwell Street. "Do you think Carswell did it?"

"It's possible," Coffin said. "He was acting pretty crazy around the time she was killed."

"Whenever you say something's possible, it means you don't really think it is."

Coffin grinned and rolled down the window. The town was filled with the musty scent of Scotch broom. "Okay, fine. I don't think he did it."

"You just want him to *think* you think he did it."

"Right."

"Because if he thinks he's a suspect he might be more inclined to come forward with information on the other boyfriends."

"Or tell us something about Kenji we don't already know. Or both."

"Maybe," Lola said.

Coffin looked for a long moment at Lola's profile: the straight nose, the firm chin. "What?" he said, finally.

"You *hate* it when people lie to you," Lola said. She turned in at the Yankee Mart and put the car in park. "You know that, right?"

Coffin got out of the car and stretched. He thought for a moment about the thin blue strip of harbor, just visible between the houses. Then he shrugged. "Who doesn't?" he said.

SIX

Coffin and Lola stood in Kenji Sole's bedroom suite. Nothing moved except the slow drift of dust motes in the window light. The room was an even greater shambles than it had been; Crime Scene Services had taken patches of carpeting, cut square samples of upholstery from chairs, and removed the sheets, blankets, mattress pad, and pillows from the bed and taken them all to the state crime lab in Sudbury for processing. Black fingerprint powder had been dusted onto every flat surface and smudged around light switches and doorknobs. The only sounds were the wind and an occasional car passing by on 6A.

"So," Lola said. "If you were Kenji Sole, where would you hide a video camera?"

"Could be almost anywhere," Coffin said. "You can get those little nanny-cams now that come inside teddy bears and clock radios." He picked up a potted ivy plant from the top of the dresser, peered into it, and set it down.

Lola shook her head. "What a world," she said.

"Tell me about it," Coffin said. He took off his shoes and climbed onto the bed. "We had a guy in Baltimore—murder victim—had his whole house wired with little spy-cams." He stood on the bare mattress, reached up, and began to unscrew the frosted glass bowl from the ceiling fixture.

"Anything?" Lola said.

"Not here," Coffin said, replacing the shade. "How many wires are coming out of that clock radio?"

The clock radio was small and white, with a blue LED. Lola picked it up. "Just one. Nothing on the face that looks like a lens."

"Maybe the smoke detector," Coffin said. He climbed down from the bed and picked up a wicker chair that had been toppled onto its side. He put the chair on its feet under the smoke detector, which was mounted high on the wall near the door.

"The smoke detector? Really?"

"Great place for a camera," Coffin said, stepping onto the chair. Its wicker seat crackled under his weight. "Completely invisible unless you're looking for it."

"Careful, Frank," Lola said.

"Let's just have a look," Coffin said, eyeing the smoke detector, then pulling it out of its white plastic bracket.

"Anything?" Lola said.

"Sometimes a smoke detector is just a smoke detector." Coffin stepped carefully out of the groaning wicker chair. He turned and rubbed his chin, then gazed at the dune-and-sunset print hanging crooked on the wall. "What do you think of that picture?" he said.

Lola followed his gaze. "The generic sunset-with-lighthouse print? I think it's godawful."

"Weird, isn't it?" Coffin said. "All the great ab-ex and color-field stuff in this house, and this is what she hangs in the bedroom?" He walked up to the print and peered at it closely. "Here we go," he said, pointing to the top of the lighthouse. "See that?" A tiny black lens glinted a half inch from his fingertip.

Lola stood beside him. "Wow," she said. "That's the lens?"

"They just need a pinhole," Coffin said. He lifted the print from its hanger and turned it around. A small white plastic box was mounted on its back, level with the lens; a six-inch wire dangled from the box.

"Battery pack, wireless transmitter," Lola said.

"Wireless," Coffin said. "Shit."

"I wonder what the range on this thing is," Lola said. "Fifty feet? A hundred?"

"Who knows," Coffin said. "If it's a hundred, the receiver and DVR could be anywhere in the house."

Lola sat on the bed. "If I were a DVR, where would I hide?"

"It would depend on what you were being used for," Coffin said. "We've got homemade porn in the bedroom and a missing computer in the study. Maybe you'd be in between?"

"Worth a shot," Lola said. "What's between us and the study?"

"Well, there's the Taj Mahal of bathrooms," Coffin said, "and a hallway." He poked his head out of the bedroom door and looked down the hall. "With what looks like a linen closet."

"I'll take the Taj Mahal," Lola said. "You do the closet."

The linen closet was a walk-in, lined in cedar. It contained a tall built-in cabinet with shelves above and wide drawers below. It had not been searched; perhaps whoever had done the searching hadn't thought to look there, or had run out of time. Coffin opened the cabinet doors, pulled the towels and sheets off the shelves, then slid the drawers out one by one. An electronic box was nestled behind the bottom drawer, which was about ten inches shorter than the other two, leaving a void inside the built-in plenty big enough for a DVR, a tangle of cables, and an electrical outlet. The DVR was warm to the touch. It had a green power light and looked like a large external computer hard drive. A smaller aluminum box was plugged into it.

"Pay dirt!" Coffin said. "Check it out."

Lola appeared at his elbow and peered into the drawer. "Wow, Frank," she said. "You're not as dumb as you look."

"Thank God for that," Coffin said. There was a third, medium-sized box behind the drawer. It was made of blue plastic and had two antennae sticking out of its top. Coffin tapped it with his finger. "Now, what the hell is *this* thing?"

"Okay, I take it back," Lola said, grinning. "You're still a throwback. It looks like a wireless router. You know, for the Internet. Must be pretty powerful to get a signal out of this cabinet. Mine barely hits the living room from under my desk in the bedroom."

"You kids today," Coffin said, unhooking the cables from the DVR, "and all your newfangled gadgets. If it wasn't for Jamie, I wouldn't even have dial-up." He fingered the small silver box; it also had antennae. "What about this critter?"

"Must be a wireless receiver," Lola said. "Quite a setup she had here."

"One receiver," Coffin said. "One camera?"

Lola nodded. "Makes sense. Too bad she didn't like to film herself in the living room."

Neither of them said anything for a few seconds. Coffin wanted a cigarette, but it seemed wrong to light one in the house where Kenji Sole had been killed.

"Jesus," Lola said, clutching the DVR against her chest. "What the hell are we going to do with this thing?"

"We can't take it to the office," Coffin said.

"Or give it to Boyle. Or Mancini."

Coffin scratched his ear. "Not until we've looked at whatever's on it. Which kind of leaves my place out."

Lola shook her head. "You're the only person I know who doesn't own a TV. What are you, some kind of Luddite?"

"When Mom's crapped out, I just never got around to buying a new one," Coffin said, walking around the beautiful blue-green rug and its large dark stain. "I haven't missed it except for the Red Sox games, and I can watch those at the bar."

Lola followed him out of the house. "Okay, that leaves my place," she said. "Man—just holding this thing's giving me the creeps. It's like it's got some kind of weird, freaky energy."

"Yesss, preciousss," Coffin said. "Let's get the fuck out of here, before somebody shows up."

On their way out, neither of them looked up. They did not look up as Lola climbed into the driver's seat, or as Coffin loaded the DVR into the trunk of the Crown Vic and then slid into the passenger's seat beside her. They did not look up, and did not see the curtains stirring in the front window of Bobby Cavalo's carriage house apartment, or the two men standing at the window, looking down at them.

"Well, now," Cavalo said, picking at a speck of dust on the curtain. "Look who found the Holy Grail."

"If I know Frankie," the other man said, "he'll keep it a secret till he knows what's on it. He's suspicious by nature." He was tall and broad, not quite sixty years old. He carried a large semiautomatic pistol in his jacket pocket.

"Where do you think they're taking it?" Cavalo said. "His place, or hers?"

"One way to find out," the other man said, lighting a cigarette. "The keys still in Kenji's Range Rover?"

At the bottom of the hill, Lola steered the Crown Vic onto 6A, heading back toward town center. "So, the guy in Baltimore," she said. "The one with all the cameras in his house. What happened to him?"

"He was a PI," Coffin said. "Did mostly divorce work. Very good at his job. Lots of high-end clients."

"But," Lola said.

"But. He was cutting it both ways. If the rich, philandering wife was good-looking, he'd approach her, show her some incriminating video of herself, tell her he could keep her secrets for a price."

"Nice," Lola said. "Talk about asking for it."

"Exactly. They'd do pretty much anything to keep him quiet, of course. They gave him money, slept with him, bought him fancy clothes, watches—cars even—you name it. He'd get them over to his house, screw their brains out, secretly film the whole thing, and then blackmail them some more."

"Who killed him?"

Coffin shrugged. "Beats me," he said. "He was shot at night, in his driveway, as he was getting out of his Mercedes. Three in the head." He tapped a quick rhythm on the dashboard—*bada-bing!* "Professional hit, no witnesses. The only physical evidence were the slugs that killed him, which were standard 9 millimeter. Could have come from any Wal-Mart on the eastern seaboard. Ballistics came up with a make and model on the weapon; nothing exotic, your basic Glock, hundreds of thousands in circulation. That was that, end of story."

"What goes around," Lola said.

Coffin nodded. "And then some," he said.

SEVEN

"Let's see if this thing works," Lola said. "Looks pretty simple to hook up to the TV."

"Got any popcorn?" Coffin said. Lola's apartment was a newer West End duplex on the inland side of Commercial Street—upstairs unit, one bedroom, generous living room, small kitchen, one bath. It felt like a midscale hotel; tidy, impersonal, everything color-coordinated.

"You've never been here before, have you?" Lola said.

"Nope," Coffin said. He pointed his chin at the big front window, which looked out on the harbor. "Nice view."

"I can't actually afford that view," Lola said, "but what the hell. You only live once."

"Unless you're a Hindu," Coffin said.

Lola was fiddling with the back of her wide-screen TV, borrowing the cable from her TiVo unit. "Popcorn's in the cupboard above the microwave. Next to the scotch."

"Now you're talking," Coffin said. "I'm not sure I can watch a dead woman having sex with a whole lot of hairy white guys if I'm not at least half in the bag."

"Better pour yourself a tall one, then, because here we go." Lola pushed the PLAY button and turned on the TV. The screen turned bright blue; she pushed another button, and it filled with snow for a moment before two figures appeared beside Kenji Sole's bed and started to undress each other.

"Weird," Lola said, "the way they just popped onto the screen."

"Must be the motion sensor in the camera," Coffin said. "There's a second or two delay, maybe, so you don't see them walking through the door. They just appear."

The picture was a bit fish-eyed from the spy-cam's wide angle lens, the action a bit herky-jerky, but otherwise the video quality was reasonably good. One of the figures was definitely Kenji Sole. The other was a man Coffin didn't recognize.

Kenji Sole and her lover had wrestled their clothes off. He lay on his back, and she turned and straddled his head, planting her backside firmly over his face, hips grinding while she stroked his erect penis with her left hand. There was no sound: The scene played out in jittery silence.

"What do you know," Coffin said, tilting his head. "A lefty."

"Frank?"

"Hm?"

"Shouldn't we watch the end first? You know, the part where the murder happens?"

"Hang on a minute," Coffin said. "Here comes the silk scarf."

"Frank?"

"And the paddle."

"*Frank.*"

"And there's the strap-on. Yeow—Cap'n Rory wasn't kidding. Look at the *size* of that thing."

Lola looked at him, eyebrows raised.

"Okay," Coffin said. "Fine." He knelt on the floor next

to the DVR and pressed the skip button. The next scene popped onto the screen, then the next: Kenji Sole with a silent procession of men—mostly middle-aged, mostly handsome, flickering into the big bedroom to be put through the same paces as the first one.

"There's Ed Ramos," Coffin said. He skipped through a few more scenes. "And Nick Stavros. Interesting tattoo he's got there. What is that—a butterfly?"

"Ew," Lola said. "When's he due back in town?"

"Tomorrow afternoon," Coffin said, pressing the skip button again.

"There's something very creepy about this," Lola said. "Creepy and sad. Are we almost at the end?"

"Yet it's weirdly hard to look away," Coffin said. "Holy shit." He pressed pause, squinted at the screen. "Is that *Boyle?*"

Lola covered her eyes, then peeked between her fingers. "God," she said. "I hope not. I already feel like I need a shower."

"I've *got* to watch this part," Coffin said. He pushed the DVR's fast-forward button. "Just for a minute, okay?"

"*Frank—*"

"Oh, come *on,*" Coffin said, sipping his scotch. "It'll be fun. Preston Boyle meets the Strap-on Queen. Imagine the watercooler hilarity!"

"Oh my God," Lola said, covering her eyes again. "I can't watch."

"Fine," Coffin said. "Suit yourself."

Chief Preston Boyle threw his clothes off, leaped onto the bed, and allowed himself to be tied, spanked, and violated by Kenji Sole at very high speed.

Coffin grimaced. "Do they still have the Hairiest Ass Contest at Carnival?" he asked. "Because I think we've got a winner."

He pressed the skip button. The screen went dark, grew bright again, and Kenji Sole flickered into the bedroom with another man. *Skip*, another man, *skip*, another. One of them was a corporate lawyer who flew his own plane to Boston five days a week. One of them, Coffin knew, owned a great deal of very expensive Provincetown real estate.

"It's enough to make you reconsider the erotic possibilities of the missionary position," Coffin said after a while.

Lola squinted. "Easy for you to say," she said.

"Hey," Coffin said. "It's McCurry." He pushed PLAY, and the video returned to normal speed.

"Look at that," Lola said. "No scarf. No paddle."

"No strap-on," Coffin said, scratching his chin, "but she's still on top."

"Different treatment for McCurry," Lola said.

"She liked him," Coffin said.

Lola nodded. "You can see it. There's real tenderness there."

"Except she's still filming him," Coffin said.

Lola's cell phone rang. She took it from her pocket and looked at the caller ID.

"Boyle," she said, looking up at Coffin. She thumbed the TALK button and held the small silver phone to her ear. "Winters," she said. "Yes, Chief. Yes. He's right here." She held the phone out to Coffin. "For you," she said.

Coffin took it. "Thanks," he said.

"Coffin?" Boyle said, his voice small and tinny in Coffin's ear. There was a surge of static. ". . . the fuck don't you get a fucking cell phone? How the fuck am I supposed to get ahold of you?"

"Cell phones don't work out here, Chief," Coffin said into another static blast.

"What?"

Coffin looked at Lola's phone. There were only two service bars showing. "Cell phones don't work out here!" he shouted.

"Jesus fucking Christ," Boyle said. "Are you trying to burst my fucking eardrum?"

"Sorry," Coffin said.

"I'm sure you're devastated," Boyle said. "Whatever. Where the hell are you?"

"In the car. On our way to interview one of the boy-friends."

"It'll have to wait. I need you and Winters to get your asses over to Town Hall, pronto. I've got an investigator here from the AG's office. As in attorney general." Boyle was from Ohio. He said things like "pronto" and "ahold."

"Tell me there's not another dead person," Coffin said.

"It's worse," Boyle said.

"Worse?"

"Child porn. They think your witness, what's his name—"

"Cavalo?"

"Right. They think he's been filming underage girls."

"Oh, for Christ's sake," Coffin said. "A woman got *killed* out here, remember? You want me to drop every-thing because one of Cavalo's Croatian girls was sev-enteen instead of eighteen?"

"You two get your asses in here. Stat," Boyle said. The cell phone crackled and went dead.

Coffin stared at the cell phone for a second or two, then closed it gently. "Strap-on Boy requires our pres-ence," he said.

"Thank God," Lola said. "I don't think I could have taken much more."

Coffin pointed at the DVR. "Before we go, let's hide this thing."

As Coffin and Lola climbed into the Crown Vic and pulled out of the parking lot, they did not see the two men slouched down in the seats of a red late-model Mustang parked a few cars away. The two men, both dressed unobtrusively in jeans and dark T-shirts, did not notice the Range Rover parked across the street as they levered themselves out of the Mustang's low-slung seats, walked up the two flights of wooden stairs to Lola's front door, and, without fanfare and in just under four seconds, pried her front door open with a short, wide crowbar specifically designed for that purpose.

"Son of a bitch," Cavalo said. "Who the fuck are *those* guys? Are we just going to let them take it?"

"Relax, *Colt*," the older man said. "We're not letting them take it. We're letting them *find* it. Saves us the trouble. They find, we take. Get it?"

"Okay," Cavalo said, after thinking it through for a moment. "If you say so—but who the fuck are they?"

"Cops, most likely," the older man said. He was big, with heavy-lidded eyes and gray close-cropped hair. He took a flask from his pocket and drank from it.

"Cops?" Cavalo said, after another pause for thought. "Wait—cops are stealing the DVR from other cops?"

"Right," the older man said. He put the flask back in his jacket pocket without offering Cavalo a drink. "Now we're going to steal it from them."

"What kind of cops?" Cavalo said, picking nervously at his seat belt. "Locals?"

The big man shrugged. "I didn't recognize them. Pretty slick, the way they popped the door. One way to find out, I guess." He climbed out of the Range Rover, took a pack of cigarettes from his pocket, tapped one out, and lit it. Then he sauntered across Commercial Street and into the parking lot next to Lola's building.

For Cavalo, watching Rudy Santos peer at the Mustang's license plate, then open its door and rummage through the glove compartment, was nerve-racking in the extreme. He slid down in the Range Rover's passenger seat as far as he could, eyes just level with the bottom edge of the window, expecting the two cops or whatever they were to come bursting out of the lesbian's apartment at any moment. "Come on, for Christ's sake," he muttered. Rudy closed the glove box, quietly shut the Mustang's door, and ambled back across the street.

"Well?" Cavalo said, as Rudy settled his thick hams into the driver's seat. "Who the fuck are they?"

Rudy took three items from the pocket of his suede car coat and set them on the console between the front seats: a set of car keys, a chunky semiautomatic pistol that Cavalo recognized as a Glock, and a cell phone.

Cavalo poked the gun with his index finger. "Holy shit," he said. "You stole their gun? And their *keys*? Holy fucking shit."

Rudy shrugged. "State of Massachusetts plates. If they're state police detectives, you'd think they'd be smart enough to lock their freakin' car, at least. Can you believe they left the keys in the ignition? Dumb-asses."

"State police? You stole from the *state police*?"

Rudy fixed Cavalo with a heavy-lidded stare. Cavalo half expected his eyes to blink from the side, like a snake's.

"This stuff doesn't belong to them, son," Rudy said. "It belongs to the taxpayers. You and me." He powered the window down and flung the set of keys into the bushes on the bay side of the street. "Besides," he said, "things will be a lot simpler if they can't follow us or shoot at us. Or call for backup."

"What," Cavalo said, "they don't have a radio?"

"Not anymore," Rudy said. He reached into his pocket and pulled out a black plastic radio microphone—the kind with a thumb-activated toggle switch—still attached to about six inches of coiled black cord.

Fifteen minutes later, the door to the lesbian cop's apartment opened, and the two men came out. One of them was cradling something in his arms: an object about half the size of a toaster, wrapped in a towel.

Rudy put a big hand on Cavalo's shoulder and shoved him down in his seat. "Here we go," he said. "Showtime." He climbed out of the Range Rover, approached the two men, pulled a very large pistol from his pocket, and pointed it at the crotch of the man on the left. The man on the right set the DVR carefully on the ground; then both men turned, put their hands on the Mustang's trunk, and allowed Rudy to frisk them. When he was done (having taken another gun from the man on the left), Rudy delivered a brief, finger-wagging lecture to the two men, who hung their heads like scolded schoolboys. Then he picked up the towel-wrapped DVR and walked back to the Range Rover as casually as a man bringing a six-pack of beer to a cookout.

"Jesus," Cavalo said, when Rudy had started the Range Rover and was accelerating rapidly down Commercial Street, swerving to avoid a clutch of German tourists on bicycles. "What'd you say to them?"

"I reminded them that stealing is wrong," Rudy said.

"I admonished them and suggested they try to behave less like thieving fucking scumbags in the future."

"Jesus," Cavalo said. "I am in *so* much trouble."

Rudy glanced at Cavalo for a second under his snake lids. "You don't know the half of it, son."

EIGHT

Cecil Duckworth sat perched on the edge of Boyle's desk. He was built like a fullback and had skin the color of low-fat cottage cheese. His smooth-shaved head flared now and then in the fluorescent light. He wore brown-tinted glasses with rectangular wire frames. Coffin had never met him before.

Duckworth stuck his hand out. "Well, now," he said. "The famous Detective Coffin. Very pleased to meet you."

Coffin shook his hand. It was slippery and dry in the way that snakeskin is both slippery and dry; it was also very large—like a catcher's mitt, Coffin thought.

"To what do we owe the pleasure, Trooper Duckworth?"

"The Cyber Crime Task Force has had its eye on this Cavalo cat for three months now," Duckworth said. "He's been running his own private Internet porn ring out here since last spring. We had a few complaints—some of the girls he's using appear to be underage."

"Cavalo's a witness in a homicide case," Coffin said, shaking the blood back into his hand. "You can't have him."

Duckworth unbuttoned his jacket and took a folded sheet of paper from the inside pocket. It was a big jacket, in a shade of pink Coffin couldn't quite name, somewhere between salmon and fuchsia, with an emerald green lining. Before Duckworth buttoned it again,

Coffin noted the handgun nestled under his armpit: a small semiauto in a web shoulder holster, probably standard issue. The stag-handled hunting knife Duckworth wore in a sheath at his hip was another story, Coffin thought. Definitely *not* standard issue.

"I don't want him," Duckworth said. "Not yet." He unfolded the paper and held it in front of Coffin's face. "Search warrant," he said. "Duly signed by Judge Samuel Hoskins of the Orleans District Court—I believe that's the proper jurisdiction, no?" He folded the warrant and slipped it back into his pocket. "To be executed immediately."

"Chief," Coffin said, "can we call the AG's office and verify this? Do they know Cavalo's one of our witnesses?"

Boyle's face was red. "Been there, done that," he said. "I just got off the phone with Poblano—he's out in Reno at some AGs' convention. He says we should assist Trooper Duckworth as requested."

Coffin pursed his lips and tilted his head. "What sort of assistance is Trooper Duckworth requesting?"

Duckworth giggled. "You're gonna hate it," he said.

"Gonna?" Coffin said.

"Two things," Duckworth said. "First, I could use a little help finding your boy Cavalo—his address doesn't show up on my GPS. Dorothy Bradford Lane ain't on the map."

"It's a private road," Coffin said. He shrugged. "Maybe it's not on the Geological Survey maps, or whatever they use for GPS. What's the second thing?"

"This is the part that'll tweak your nads: I need access to the Sole crime scene."

Coffin looked at Boyle. "Chief?"

"The AG has reason to believe there might be important video evidence there," Boyle said. "If he wants us to let Trooper Duckworth in, we let him in."

Coffin looked at Lola; she stood near the door, lips pressed tightly together.

"Interesting sidearm you've got there, Trooper Duckworth," Coffin said.

Duckworth slowly unbuttoned his jacket again and pulled it aside. "You mean Lucille here?" he said. He touched the knife's polished handle with his fingertips and smiled. "I picked her up in my Special Forces days. I mostly just keep her around for old time's sake, but you never know when you might find yourself in close with a bad guy."

"Get in close with a lot of bad guys in the Cyber Crime Task Force, do you?" Coffin said.

"A few," Duckworth said. "Although most of 'em are skinny little computer geeks." He looked at Coffin, then at Boyle. "That's a joke," he said.

Boyle stood. "I'll run Trooper Duckworth out to Cavalo's place," Boyle said. "In the meantime I might take a look at the crime scene myself, in case you two missed something."

"Always good to follow up on the work of your subordinates, right, Chief?" Duckworth said.

Boyle nodded. "Just doing my job."

"A bang-up job it is, too, Chief," Coffin said.

Boyle glared at him. "Are you fucking with me, Coffin?"

"No, sir."

"Good," Boyle said. "See that you don't."

"What a weird dude," Lola said as they trotted down Town Hall's broad front stairs. "He kind of gave me the willies."

"Was it the pink jacket," Coffin said, "or the hunting knife?"

Lola grimaced a little. "Both," she said. "That knife deal was definitely creeping me out."

"Think he's after what *I* think he's after?"

"I think he's after the DVR," Lola said. "I think Poblano sent him to look for it."

"I think you're right," Coffin said. They passed the World War I monument, its verdigrised soldier gazing out across the harbor. "How the hell does he even know it exists?"

"ESP?" Lola said, waiting for a pickup truck to pass before they crossed the street. "A hunch? A lucky guess?"

"Either that," Coffin said, "or somebody told him."

"Oh my God," Lola said, standing in the doorway of her apartment. "Holy fucking shit."

Coffin looked over her shoulder and let out a low whistle. "Whoa," he said.

The living room had been thoroughly trashed. The sofa was upside down, the cushions slashed and the stuffing removed. The upholstered easy chair lay on its side, disemboweled, stuffing flung around the room. The big-screen TV was still intact, but the electronics cabinet below it had been ripped open; Lola's TiVo and DVD player had been yanked from their shelves and thrown across the room with some force. The kitchen and bedroom were in similar shape: Every dish and glass had been swept from the kitchen cabinets and smashed on the floor; the silverware had been dumped from the drawers. It looked as though a bomb had gone off in the bedroom closet. Lola's clothes and shoes lay everywhere, mingled with tufts of pillow stuffing and smashed bits of nightstand. The dresser drawers had been emptied, too. A surprising variety of lingerie lay strewn across the buff-colored carpet. Coffin nudged a filmy pale green negligee with his toe. It reminded him of some delicate sea creature, stranded on the beach after a storm.

Lola followed his eyes. "What?" she said. "You think 'cause I'm a lesbian it's all jog bras and boy shorts, twenty-four seven?"

"That's another trick question," Coffin said. "I'm not going there."

"I can be girly when I want to, you know," Lola said, fists on her hips. "It pisses me off that people act like I'm not allowed to have a fucking feminine side."

"Fine," Coffin said. "Great. Just don't hit me."

"Christ. Look at this place."

"They work fast," Coffin said.

"They?"

"I've tossed a few apartments in my life," Coffin said. "One guy probably couldn't have done all this in such a short time."

Lola stuck her head into the bedroom closet. "They got it," she said. "It was behind the shoe rack."

"I had a feeling this would happen," Coffin said. "I just didn't think it would happen so fast."

"Jesus," Lola said, picking up a lace nightgown, dropping it again. "Jesus fucking Christ."

"Why don't you stay at my place," Coffin said. "Until you can get some new furniture."

Lola picked up her clock radio and put it on the windowsill. "Whoever did this better watch out," she said. "Because this shit *really* pisses me off."

Coffin looked at his watch. "Let's go have a drink," he said. "It's cocktail hour."

Lola hauled the mattress back onto the bed, picked up a shoe, and tossed it into the closet. "You go," she said. "I'm going to stay here and clean up."

"Come on," Coffin said. "You don't want to be here. We'll clean up tomorrow. You can take a personal day. Jamie and I can help."

"Frank," Lola said, brushing a strand of hair from her eyes, "you're very sweet, you know that?"

"I'm a lot of things," Coffin said, "but I am *not* sweet. Come on. Drinks are on me."

NINE

The Mews was one of the few fine dining establishments in Provincetown that stayed open through the off-season. It was perched on the harbor side of Commercial Street and had a gorgeous view of the water. The moon was just rising over Cape Cod Bay; a wrinkled avenue of light lay on the black water, stretching from the horizon to town beach.

It was Sunday night, and Dawn Vermilion was playing to a small but jovial crowd—mostly men sitting with men, tables of two or four, sipping large, colorful martini drinks. A few lesbian couples were there, too, and a scattering of straight tourists, but no children. It was not *that* kind of restaurant.

Dawn Vermilion was a handsome person of fifty or so. She sat at the piano in a tall crimson wig, playing selections from Cole Porter and Billy Strayhorn: "Let's Do It" followed by "Lush Life." Her eye shadow and fingernails were sparkly green. She wore a black cocktail dress with many sequins; it strained a bit across her broad back. Dawn's voice sounded like cigarettes, leather, and bourbon. The piano was only a little out of tune.

"She's on tonight," Lola said, sitting down at the bar.

"Pretty good crowd, too," Coffin said, catching the barmaid's eye. She was a young Eastern European woman, very pretty. She had the dark brows and high cheekbones of a Serb, Coffin thought.

"What can I get you?" she said.

Lola ordered Glenlivet on the rocks. Coffin ordered a vodka martini, very dry, and the tempura-sushi appetizer. He was hungry, he realized, and knew he shouldn't drink on an empty stomach.

The barmaid handed him a menu without smiling. "We have two hundred thirty-four different kinds of vodka," she said. *Wodka.* "Imports, flavors, whatever you want."

"What kind do you drink?" Coffin said, squinting at the menu in the dim light.

The barmaid raised an eyebrow. "You are flirting with me," she said, "or really wanting my advice?"

"The first thing," Lola said.

"I thought so," the barmaid said. She pursed her lips. "Tonight I would drink Stoli Elit. It's very smooth, and I'm a little upset."

"Upset?" Coffin said. "Why?"

"My boyfriend leaves me for another woman." The barmaid shook Coffin's drink with both hands, then poured it through a strainer into a chilled martini glass. Her fingernails had tiny sequins glued to them; they glinted in the dim light. "See?" she said, still not smiling. "I'm like an American now. I just meet you, I tell you everything about my life."

"Your boyfriend is a fool," Lola said.

The barmaid shrugged and poured Lola's scotch into a rocks glass. "Perhaps. I think this other girl is not so pretty as me, but maybe more sexier, I don't know."

"You said you were a little upset," Coffin said. "Why just a little?"

"He is not such good boyfriend," she said.

Coffin laughed and sipped his martini. It was perfect, with only a whisper of vermouth. A thin skin of ice floated on its surface. The Russian vodka was very smooth indeed.

"I am Yelena," the barmaid said. She stuck out a hand, offering it first to Lola, then to Coffin, who introduced themselves.

"Lola and Frank," Yelena said. "I say in American way: Please ta meet ya. You are couple?"

"No," Lola said. "We work together."

"We're police officers," Coffin said. "We're here to talk to Dawn."

Yelena lowered her voice. "She is in some trouble?"

Coffin shook his head. "No. Not at all. It's just a social call."

"That woman who was killed," Yelena said. "Kenji Sole. My friends clean her house."

"Zelenka and Minka?"

"Yes."

"That's not all they do," Coffin said.

Yelena shrugged. "You mean the pornos? They are stupid girls."

"I thought they were your friends," Lola said.

Yelena grinned. "They are not such good friends."

Coffin and Lola both laughed.

"Pornos, plural?" Coffin said. "They made more than one?"

Yelena nodded. "Is for Web site. It has stupid name—hungarianchicks.com—but no Hungarian girls. All from Croatia, Bulgaria. I guess nobody goes to Web site called bulgarianchicks.com."

"Whose Web site is it?" Lola asked. "Bobby Cavalo's?"

"I don't know his name." Yelena shrugged again. "They say he is handsome, pays good, cash. They try to get me to go, but I say no. For what? Few hundred dollars?" Her eyes flashed. "I like to make sex very much, but I don't do this for money. I am not prostitute."

When Dawn Vermilion had finished her set, she ambled over to the bar and sat next to Coffin. "Evening, officers. Buy a girl a drink?" She kicked off one of her size twelve pumps and wiggled her toes. "God. My feet are killing me. It's hell, getting old."

Yelena brought her a Grey Goose on the rocks. "Beautiful set, Dawn," Yelena said. "You are sounding just like Billie Holiday tonight." She moved a discreet distance away to shake up a couple of peach martinis.

"Nice girl, that Yelena," Dawn said.

"No kidding," Coffin said.

Lola nudged him with her elbow. "Easy there, cowboy."

"I thought you were spoken for," Dawn said, painted eyebrows lifted. "Don't tell me there's trouble in paradise."

"No," Coffin said. "Everything's fine."

Dawn sipped her vodka. "How's things on the baby-making front?"

"Good God," Coffin said. "Is there anything you don't know?"

"Not if it happened in P'town, honey," Dawn said. "If it's out there, I've heard it."

"What've you heard about Bobby Cavalo?" Coffin asked.

Dawn smiled and leaned close to Coffin's ear. "A lot," she said, "and it's all delicious. You know about the Web site, I assume?"

"Hungarianchicks.com?"

"Everybody knows about *that* one, honey," Dawn said, swirling the ice slowly around in her glass. "I'm talking about the *other* Web site."

"What other Web site?"

"Spycamdomme.com."

Coffin sat quietly for a moment, watching Dawn's face. She'd put on rhinestone-studded cat-eye glasses that sparkled in the dim bar light. "Spycamdomme.com," Coffin said finally. "Tell me about that."

"*Well*, here's the thing," Dawn said. "It doesn't exist. Not yet."

"What do you mean?"

"There's only one page with three or four video clips on it. All the faces are blurred electronically, but the action is *very* explicit."

"Like what? Whips? Leather?"

"I haven't actually seen it," Dawn said. "Pictures of straight people fucking give me the heebie-jeebies. No offense."

"None taken."

"But it's in that *realm,* apparently—and then some."

"So what's the connection?" Lola said. "How do we know Cavalo's involved?"

"*Well,*" Dawn said. "Apparently there's a way you can find out who owns a Web site: You can go online and check. Turns out, both hungarianchicks.com and spycam domme.com are listed under Bobby's name and address."

"They *are*?" Coffin said.

"How do you know all this?" Lola said.

Dawn lowered her voice to a raspy whisper. "I ordinarily *never* reveal my sources, *but*—Bobby's favorite boy-toy, Jordan, is good friends with my associate, Gordita Derriere," she said. "Gordita and Jordan got drunk one night over at the A-House, and Jordan spilled the beans. It's just amazing what people will tell you after six or seven Captain and Cokes."

Coffin looked at Lola. "I think we need to have another conversation with our friend Cavalo," he said.

"Assuming he's still in town," Lola said.

"Oh, he's in town," Dawn said. "I saw him myself at Al Dante's just a little bit ago, having cocktails with this *fascinating* man."

"Fascinating how?"

"About six-four, two-forty—bald, practically an albino, wearing the most *amazing* hot pink jacket. I thought about introducing myself, but you know me—I'm patho*log*ically shy."

The moon was high and almost full. Its light filtered through the big front window of Bobby Cavalo's apartment, glinting faintly on Cecil Duckworth's bald head, throwing his broad shadow across the studio floor. Duckworth smiled, touched Lucille's polished handle with his fingertips, and unsnapped her sheath's leather keeper. Bobby Cavalo groaned. He lay on the futon sofa, hands and feet duct-taped to the armrests at either end. Duckworth's favorite-mix CD was playing on the boom box: a snaky bachata thing that Duckworth was fond of, although he loved the tango best of all.

"Look, I told you," Cavalo said, voice quavering a little. "I don't know what *it* is. How can I tell you if I have it if I don't know what *it* is?"

Duckworth eased Lucille from her sheath. He felt her edge lightly with his thumb. "Do you have it, Bobby?" he said. "Seriously, now. No more fooling around. Do you have it?"

"I *don't know*," Cavalo said. "I don't know what *it* is. I swear to God—if I knew what it was, I'd tell you if I had it!"

Duckworth chuckled. He was wearing his favorite pink jacket and the lucky alligator shoes he'd bought in Mexico. ("Not so lucky for the alligator," he would say when women asked about them. It was one of his

favorite jokes.) "Well, let's just say for the sake of argument that maybe you *did* have it," he said. He peeled a
strip of duct tape from the roll and put it over Cavalo's
mouth. Then he held Cavalo's head still with his left
hand, and with his right he ran the pointed tip of Lucille's blade slowly and lightly down the side of Cavalo's cheek.

Cavalo tried to scream, but hardly any sound came out.

Duckworth smiled and watched the slow welling of
blood in the wound. He wore latex gloves: He was cautious with his health—he didn't want to catch anything.
"Let's just say," Duckworth said, "for the sake of argument, that we started to cut things off. Would you still
tell us you didn't have it?" He peeled the duct tape off
Cavalo's mouth.

"What?" Cavalo said, eyes brimming. "Don't have
what? I don't know what you *mean*—"

"Oh, we're not talking about cutting off anything
important," Duckworth said, putting the tape back over
Cavalo's mouth. He took his jacket off and hung it on a
chair. Then he smiled. "Maybe an ear, that's all. Then
if we're still not sure we believe you, a nose or a few
fingers. No big deal, really."

Cavalo's eyes got big. He made some muffled sounds
under the tape.

"So," Duckworth said, planting his hams on the edge
of the futon, near Cavalo's armpit. "Let's try again. For
keeps now. No more do-overs. Ready?"

Cavalo shook his head vigorously, grunting into the
tape.

Duckworth grabbed Cavalo's chin and held it still.
"Bobby?" he said. "Lucille's getting impatient. You need
to listen. Are you listening?"

Cavalo nodded, eyes wide.

"Last chance, Bobby," Duckworth said. The music thumped from the boom box—a peppy little salsa number now. "It's a simple question, Bobby. A simple yes or no. We're not dancing anymore." He leaned close, looking into Cavalo's eyes as he peeled the duct tape off. He waited a beat while he listened to the sound of Cavalo's rapid breathing. Then he leaned closer still, his nose almost touching Cavalo's. "Last chance, Bobby. Last. Chance. I *know* you know what I'm looking for. Do you have it?"

If anything, Kotowski's house was even more cluttered than usual. Stacks of books and newspapers covered almost every surface; a small outboard engine lay in pieces on the living room rug. Coffin could envision Kotowski in twenty years, unwashed, happy in his senescence, the house crammed with junk—trash bags full of beer cans and magazines piled to the ceiling, only narrow aisles left to walk through.

"There's one thing about this business I don't really get," Coffin said. He and Kotowski still played chess almost every week, even though neither of them played very well or liked the game very much.

"Really?" Kotowski said. "Just one?" He pushed a pawn, took it back, pushed it again.

A couple of Kotowski's new paintings stood propped against the wall: one with a figure who looked like Karl Rove as Dr. Frankenstein bringing a monstrous Dick Cheney to life; in the other a figure who looked like Dick Cheney with George W. Bush as a ventriloquist's dummy sitting on his knee, sharp little fangs in his mouth. Kotowski's rich new collector snapped them up as fast as he could paint them.

"Okay, more than one," Coffin said, eyeing the board.

"Didn't I take that knight of yours, like, three moves ago?"

"Are you accusing me of cheating, Coffin?"

"Yes."

"Fine," Kotowski said, taking the knight off the board. "You're such a stickler."

Coffin leaned back in his chair and pushed his fingers through his hair. "This whole thing with Kenji Sole tying up and spanking her boyfriends," he said. "What's the psychology there?"

"Don't forget the strap-on," Kotowski said. "That's the really amusing part."

Coffin sipped his beer. "I'm kind of a stranger to that whole world. I get the whole gay/straight/bi thing, I mean that seems pretty straightforward—"

"There's nothing straightforward about bisexuality," Kotowksi said, a small cloud of dust rising as he drummed his fingers on the arm of his chair. "Are you going to move, or what?"

"I sort of understand the transgender thing, and the cross-dressing thing—"

"The grass is always greener," Kotowski said, "when you're wearing lace panties. I'm planning to shoot myself when I turn eighty; could you move before then?"

"But the whole dominant-submissive thing—"

"Come on, Coffin," Kotowski said. "Don't tell me you've never given a woman a smack on the ass in the heat of passion."

"Well, sure, but—"

Kotowski threw up his hands and made a retching sound. "Oh my *God*," he said. "Too much sharing! I think I'm going to hurl."

Coffin moved his queen two spaces to the right. "Check," he said.

"Check?" Kotowski said, interposing a bishop. "You call that a *check*?"

"So, what?" Coffin said. "Does that make me, like, Dominant Guy now?"

"Dominant? *You?* Ha!" Kotowski said. "If you were any more vanilla, you'd be a freaking milkshake—though, you've had the impulse once or twice."

"So what's the difference?"

"If you were a real dom, you'd be more interested in the ass-smacking than the fucking." Kotowski drained his beer, stood up, and padded into the kitchen for another.

"Why?" Coffin moved his queen again. "That's the part I don't understand. How is smacking someone on the ass—or being smacked on the ass—better than sex?"

Kotowski plopped into his chair, a small cloud of dust rising around him. "How is anything better than sex?" he said. "It just is. Hell, at my age lots of things are better than sex."

"Really?" Coffin said. "Like what?"

"I was joking," Kotowski said. He looked at the board. "Did *you* cheat? You're not supposed to cheat."

"So it's a control thing, fine. Got it. What about the submissives? What's in it for them?"

Kotowski looked at him, eyes the color of wood smoke. "Trust," he said. He took a cigarette from Coffin's pack and lit it with Coffin's lighter. "And risk. You give control of your body to another person. You have to trust them not to push you past your limits. Not *too* far, anyway. Trust makes it possible. Risk makes it exciting."

"You'd still have a safe word," Coffin said. "So it's trust and risk with an escape hatch."

Kotowski studied the chessboard for a long moment.

"Fuck," he said. "How did you *do* that? Time for the Kotowski defense." Then he shook the board until all of the pieces fell over.

After Lola had dropped Coffin off at Kotowski's, she thought about going back to her apartment, then decided against it. Should she stay at Frank's? Sleeping on his mother's Victorian sofa was an even less appealing prospect than going back to her own ruined bedroom. She drove east on Bradford, away from her place. She turned onto Allerton, the last connecting street before Bradford and Commercial joined. She found herself in front of Kate's house—a pretty Cape Cod, one of the few affordable year-round rentals left in town. The lights were on. Lola put the Crown Vic in park, shut it off, and climbed out. It was very dark. The moon floated above the harbor, wreathed in yellow clouds. Lola flipped her cell phone open and dialed.

"Hey, you," Kate said after the second ring.

"Hi," Lola said. "I'm outside."

The living room curtains moved. Kate waved through the window. "So you are," she said. "Would you like to come in? I have a nice couch we could sit on, and I have bourbon . . ."

"I like bourbon and a nice couch," Lola said. The door opened. A shaft of yellow light fell across the grass. Kate stood in the doorway, tall and slim and smiling.

TEN

It was morning. Lola sat at Coffin's desk, picking through the papers in his in-box. "What's with the suit, Frank?" she said, glancing up. "Going to a funeral or something?"

The fat sewer pipe rumbled overhead.

"Yep," Coffin said. "So are you. Let's take separate cars—I've got to drive up to Boston later."

"Kenji's funeral's today? Thanks for the heads-up," Lola said, looking at her uniform. "I'm not exactly dressed for it."

"So change," Coffin said. "It doesn't start till ten o'clock. I'll meet you at the cemetery. Catholic section."

"Kenji Sole was Catholic?"

"Lapsed, I'm guessing."

Lola stood, pushing a loose strand of hair behind her ear. "Lapsed?" she said, already halfway out the door. "I guess that's one word for it."

After she was gone, Coffin thumbed through his in-box. There were two new cases: a break-in and a series of bad checks, all written by the same two people. They would have to wait.

The phone rang. Coffin picked up the receiver and punched line one. "Coffin," he said.

"Detective Coffin? It's Dr. Branstool at Valley View."

"Oh, for God's sake," Coffin said. "Don't tell me she's run away again?"

"I'm very sorry, Detective," Branstool said. "I really feel terrible about this. I mean, I know how bad it looks. We're a bit understaffed at the moment, what with the budget cuts and all—"

"Any idea how long she's been gone?"

"We're pretty sure she was in her room at midnight bed check."

"Pretty sure?"

"When we went to wake her this morning, we found that she'd stuffed some clothes and pillows under her covers, to create the effect—"

"What are you guys going to fall for next? A gun carved out of soap?"

"Well, we can't exactly strap her to the bed," Branstool said. "Not unless you sign a waiver."

"So that's the choice?" Coffin said. "Tie her to the bed or let her wander off?"

"We've sent a couple of attendants out to look for her," Branstool said, "but I thought it best to let you know."

"Thanks. Great job you people are doing up there." Coffin hung up. A drop of condensation from the sewer pipe splashed onto his desktop, just missing his coffee cup.

The gravesite was halfway up the hill, overlooking the access road and the low, sandy hills beyond it. In the middle distance, Shank Painter Road curved out to the highway. Beyond that was the beach forest, the National Seashore, and the Atlantic Ocean, all obscured at the moment by thin, swirling fog.

The usual canopy had been set up, thirty or so folding chairs in neat rows beneath it. The coffin—a monumental rosewood number—sat on a support frame over the newly dug grave, draped in a big bouquet of white roses. Four gravediggers stood nearby, smoking cigarettes and talking quietly. When the service was over, they would lower the coffin into the sandy ground.

As Coffin climbed out of the Fiesta, the heavy mass of cloud that had been rolling in all morning parked itself overhead and began to dispense a slow, chilly rain. The moss on the tombstones turned suddenly, impossibly green, fluorescing in the aqueous light.

Lola was already there. She wore a short charcoal-colored jacket, black trousers, and a black silk blouse, open at the throat. Her shoes were black, too—flats, good for walking on cemetery grass.

Coffin pulled up his jacket collar, then fished among the clutter in the Fiesta's backseat for an umbrella. He found one: It was small and half sprung, and when he opened it a dead mouse fell out, landing on the pavement beside his shoe.

"Ew," Lola said, regarding the desiccated mouse as it lay curled on the sidewalk. She hooked a thumb toward Coffin's car. "Any chance the DVR's in there somewhere?"

Coffin tried not to stare at her backside as she opened the Camaro's trunk and pulled out a sleek black umbrella, popping it open just before the rain began in earnest.

The funeral was sparsely attended. Kenji Sole's father was there, sitting under the canopy, looking old and frail in a black suit and no socks. Priestess Maiya sat beside him, wearing a slim black evening gown, black sunglasses, and a broad black hat with an ostrich plume. Gracie, the monkey, sat on her shoulder. A wide black bow was tied around her neck.

"Oh my God," Lola said. "It's Holly Golightly in mourning."

A few chairs away, Stan Carswell wept openly. A young woman Coffin recognized as a reporter for the *Cape Cod Times* stood at the periphery, taking notes. A middle-aged priest in a wrinkled cassock stood by the coffin, stuttering a bit as he recited the canticle: "*R-r-r-requiem æ-t-t-ternam dona ei, D-d-d-omine* . . ." Father Kevin? Father Keith? Coffin couldn't remember. He hadn't been to church in years.

"Not much of a crowd," Lola said.

"I guess all the boyfriends are busy trying to patch up their marriages," Coffin said. "It's always interesting to see who shows up at these things—and who doesn't."

Lola looked at Coffin, head tilted a bit. Her eyes were more gray than blue in the muted light. "Is that why we're here? To see who shows up?"

"It's a question of appearances—in domestic cases especially. If you've killed your girlfriend, say, and you don't show up and pretend to be sad, people will start to wonder. Of course, if you show up and can't keep it together, that's risky, too. Quiet dignity is what you want—no throwing yourself on the casket. A strained expression, maybe a couple of tears that you dab with a handkerchief."

"So what's your read on Carswell?" Lola said.

Stan Carswell was sobbing audibly. Coffin watched him for a minute, then gazed at Lola's umbrella with envy. His was leaking. "The reaction fits the story," he said. "He was in love, she's dead, he's sad."

"Or acting. Or he's overcome by guilt."

"Maybe," Coffin said. "Or he's worried about getting caught. Or he misses all the Kenji-drama."

"I wasn't expecting to see Priestess Maiya."

"Because you thought she didn't do it? Or because you thought she did?"

"The first thing. Now I'm not so sure."

Coffin rubbed his mustache. It was almost entirely gray; he was pretty sure it made him look old. "There could be layers of meaning here," Coffin said. "Maybe it's for J. Hedrick's benefit. Playing the supportive girl-friend and all that."

Lola nodded. "Maybe it's some complicated gender thing: woman-plays-drag-queen-plays-woman goes to funeral. Maybe she's going to have sex with the priest when the service is over."

"Right," Coffin said. "Her camera crew will jump out from behind a mausoleum and film the whole thing."

"It's a lovely spot here, really," J. Hedrick Sole said when the funeral was over. They walked together slowly through the cemetery, between the mossed and tilting rows of eighteenth- and nineteenth-century gravestones that always reminded Coffin of bad Victorian teeth. "If one has to be buried somewhere, one could do a lot worse."

Coffin wanted to say that if it was him, he'd prefer to be a bit farther above sea level, but he stopped himself. Instead he said, "I wish we had better news for you about the investigation."

"Not going well, eh?" J. Hedrick said. "I feared as much."

"We're still trying to sort out who might have been with her the night she died," Coffin said. "It's a very complicated picture."

"She was a very complicated subject," Priestess Maiya said, giving Gracie a peanut. Gracie shelled the peanut with her nimble little hands, ate it, and chittered for another.

"I suppose you could say that," Coffin said. "Yes." He stopped walking. Lola, J. Hedrick, and Priestess Maiya stopped, too. "Have you read her dissertation, by any chance?"

"Me? No," J. Hedrick said. "Couldn't make heads nor tails of it. Maiya has."

"You have?" Lola said.

"Don't act so surprised," Priestess Maiya said. "It's actually quite good. Kenji was very bright, in her way. It's a discussion of porn as a coercive art form. The coercive aspect, from Kenji's point of view, is what makes porn interesting to viewers, and ultimately to critics."

"Coercive how?" Coffin asked. He ran his hand over the head of an alabaster dog lying forever at the feet of its master, one Captain Jeremiah Slocum. The dog was scabbed in pale green lichen, but its eyes were eerily blank.

"Both in the making and in the viewing. Although I take issue with her argument that all of the actors are coerced. It may not be everyone's dream job, but it's better than digging ditches."

"Isn't it true that a lot of them *are* coerced?" Lola said. "Pimped into the business by their boyfriends? Or even sold into it as sex slaves in some countries?"

"What if you just can't find a better job?" Coffin said. "Could that be considered a form of economic coercion?"

"Right on both counts," said Priestess Maiya. "In fact, for a lot of viewers the idea of coercion is part of the excitement."

"Bah," said J. Hedrick. "Liberal claptrap. Nobody has to do *that* for a living. Not in the United States of America."

"So the act of viewing is coercive how, again?" Coffin said. "I mean, the film's already been made, right?"

"Right," Priestess Maiya said, "but what if, as an actor, you've had second thoughts? What if you've moved on with your life, had children, say, gone to college, gotten a job? Anyone who wanted to could, in theory, find those movies of you having sex and watch them over and over again, without your permission. There's nothing you could do about it."

"Nonsense," J. Hedrick said. He coughed, then spat a stringy gob into the grass. "No one makes them sign the contract. No one makes them take the money. They could just as easily work at McDonald's and never have a thing to be ashamed of."

"My brother worked at McDonald's for a couple of years," Lola said. "He smelled like French fries all the time, even after he'd showered."

The wind hissed softly in a tall row of cedars at the cemetery's edge. Coffin started walking again, and the others followed.

"So just by viewing porn, by being part of the market for it, you're participating in the coercion of the actors?" Coffin said.

"It's an oversimplification, but that's basically the idea," Priestess Maiya said, giving Gracie another peanut.

Coffin raised an eyebrow. "That's why people get off on it?"

"Right. It's not the sex, it's the act of coercion that's at the heart of the voyeuristic impulse. That's the standard psychological reading, anyway."

"That was something that Kenji was concerned about?" Lola said. "As a social justice issue?"

Priestess Maiya shrugged. "I suppose so," she said. "Or she pretended she was."

"Pretended?" Coffin said.

"Appearances are everything," Priestess Maiya said. "Especially in academia."

"You make a good point," Coffin said. Lola shot him a look.

J. Hedrick coughed and spat again, wiping his mouth with the back of his hand. "How so?" he said.

"If Kenji was concerned about the coercive aspect of voyeurism, why would she have filmed her lovers with a hidden camera?"

"What?" J. Hedrick said. He turned on Coffin, eyes bulging. "*What* did you say?"

Priestess Maiya took his arm. "He said that Kenji filmed her lovers with a hidden camera, dear."

"That doesn't seem to surprise you," Coffin said.

"No," Priestess Maiya said. "It would have surprised me if she hadn't been up to something like that. I mean, no one really bought her interest in porn and voyeurism as a purely academic exercise. Why study porn if you're not *into* porn?"

J. Hedrick's face was very red. His breath was coming in little gasps. "I think I'd better sit down," he said. "Have you got my pills?"

"Of course, dear," Priestess Maiya said, catching some of his weight as he lowered himself onto the base of a tall column with a marble globe at its top. The column marked the grave of Coffin's great-grandfather, Captain Ephraim Coffin, who had hanged himself in the cupola of his Commercial Street mansion in the 1880s.

"I'm sorry," Coffin said. "Perhaps I shouldn't have said anything."

"You shouldn't have," Priestess Maiya said, "but you did." She looked at Coffin with her hard black eyes. "I suppose that makes you no better than the rest of us, Detective."

Coffin nodded. "I suppose it does," he said. The rain had started again in earnest, and Coffin was getting very wet. "I'm sorry for your loss," he said, and he and Lola turned to walk back across the cemetery to their cars.

ELEVEN

Coffin absently steered the moldering Fiesta, trying not to stare too long at the gray harbor and, in the middle ground, the magenta bursts of beach rose flickering between the rows of tiny cottages as he drove out Route 6A, through Beach Point on his way off-Cape. There was something almost heartbreakingly romantic about those cottages, he thought—all built in the thirties or forties, some a bit run-down now, but still booked solid every summer with tourists who didn't mind the high prices and cramped conditions, as long as they were waterfront and kid-friendly. At night, the view from Beach Point back toward Provincetown was lovely—moonrise over the harbor, the twinkling lights of Commercial Street—but now it was daytime, early afternoon. Coffin was driving up to Boston to meet with Kenji Sole's private investigator, one D. Towler, who had refused to discuss anything to do with Kenji over the phone.

For the moment, the Fiesta seemed to be running reasonably well. The heat gauge was only slightly above normal; the transmission was sluggish but shifting; all the tires had air in them. Coffin turned left off of 6A after passing the old Days' Cottages, then paused at the stop sign before turning right onto Route 6, the "new" highway, four lanes for the next few miles, until the exit for Truro Center. As he waited for a truck to pass, the Fiesta shuddered, then stalled. He turned the key in the ignition. The Fiesta farted a blue plume of oil smoke before rattling back to life. The engine sounded like a garbage disposal grinding up a stainless steel fork. As Coffin pulled onto the highway, two women rode by on matching mountain bikes. They turned in their seats, pointed at Coffin's car, and laughed.

The drive from Provincetown to Boston could take anywhere from two and a half hours in the off-season to four-plus hours on busy summer weekends; most of the P'town natives in Coffin's circle avoided it except in cases of absolute necessity. To those who had never lived anywhere else, anyplace off-Cape seemed almost as foreign and distant as Turkmenistan or Tierra del Fuego. Even for Coffin, who had lived off-Cape (in exotic Baltimore) for almost ten years, Provincetown and the Outer Cape had a kind of gravitational pull that kept him close; leaving was always a big deal.

The rain started again as Coffin neared the turnoff for Wellfleet Center; he flicked on the windshield wipers, which groaned—somehow the right wiper blade had adhered to the windshield—and then suddenly flapped into action. The blade that had been stuck was now torn; part of it hung loose from the wiper like a ragged black ribbon, slopping back and forth across Coffin's field of vision. He turned the wipers off. *At least it's only a drizzle,* he thought. A fork of lightning zagged out of the clouds as he passed the Wellfleet Drive-in, and the sky seemed to open up as the Fiesta labored into the storm, the drizzle becoming a torrent in an instant. The rain roared on the Fiesta's roof, and Coffin could see nothing through the windshield except rain and more rain. He turned on the wipers again, cranking them up as fast as they would go. The torn blade flapped back and forth a few times, then flew off, disappearing into the storm. The wiper's metal arm screeked shrilly across the windshield, the blade clip grinding a large, curved scratch into the glass.

Coffin gritted his teeth. "Christ," he said. "*This* is fun." He was thinking about pulling over at one of Eastham's several Route 6 gas stations and trying to buy a new wiper blade when the rain stopped almost as abruptly as it had started, the clouds parting to reveal blue sky directly ahead. Coffin turned on the radio, but the reception was bad all across the dial. The only station that came in clearly was right-wing talk, some blowhard grumbling about how the U.S. was winning the war in Iraq, but the media refused to report the truth. The blowhard seemed more dispirited than outraged to Coffin, as though he were just going through the motions, saying what he was paid to say.

Coffin turned the radio off and kept driving, through Eastham's congested roadside commercial zone, two or three miles of clam shacks and package stores and mini golf for the tourists, and then through the Orleans rotary, one of those New England engineering oddities known elsewhere as a traffic circle. The rain started again, wind-driven and hard, just as Coffin's Fiesta entered the two-lane stretch between Orleans and Dennis that everyone called Suicide Alley.

Suicide Alley was one of the most dangerous stretches of highway in New England, despite the installation of a raised center divider (about six inches wide by three inches high and topped with slender, three-foot plastic pylons), meant to discourage those who were foolhardy enough to try to pass slower vehicles in Suicide Alley's thirteen miles of blind curves and hidden on-ramps. It usually wasn't too bad in the off-season: You might get stuck behind a slow-moving truck, or a local senior citizen motoring along at forty miles per hour with his left turn signal on, but there was also a decent chance that you'd sail straight through from Orleans to Dennis unobstructed and at a reasonable speed. During the season, though, there was no escape—Suicide Alley would suck you into its long alimentary canal, and there'd you'd be, slowly digesting in your own juices until the mid-Cape was done with you and you popped out the other end. This time of year—with the first real flow of tourists and preseason renters just beginning to appear—traffic was heavier than Coffin expected, though it still moved faster than the high-season crawl. The Fiesta was nestled between an eighteen-wheeler and a humongous SUV, with a long tail of traffic strung out behind. Oncoming traffic was sparse and moving fast in the heavy rain, passing cars and trucks kicking up explosive, blinding sheets of water from the road surface.

Coffin's left shoulder and shirtsleeve were getting wet. It was confusing at first—the window was all the way up—until he realized that the door seal was leaking. "Wonderful," Coffin said, wiping at the wet spot with his right hand. "Fabulous."

Then the Fiesta jerked hard to the left and half-jumped the center divider, plowing over a dozen of the tall plastic pylons (*thwapthwapthwapthwapthwap* against the front bumper) before Coffin's brain could compute what was happening. The road seemed to have melted into rubble—the stuttering left front tire rapidly losing pressure and starting to shred. Coffin braked and tried to steer back into his lane, but the big SUV behind him blasted its horn, not giving way. Coffin found himself driving down the centerline, half into oncoming traffic, barely able to steer on the one bare rim, headlights bearing down. A horn blared and a big delivery van in the oncoming lane swerved around him, two wheels on the narrow shoulder, spewing a curtain of spray, horn blasting, the driver leaning down to give Coffin the finger and mouth the word "asshole." Coffin swerved left again, between two oncoming cars and onto the eastbound shoulder, before he braked the Fiesta to a skidding, sideways stop.

"Holy shit," Coffin said, still gripping the Fiesta's wheel, the little car standing still at last, off-kilter, facing the wrong way on the eastbound shoulder, the smell of melted rubber seeping in through its rusted floorboards. The rain pelted the Fiesta's roof. Coffin lit a cigarette, hands shaking a little. He wasn't sure if he had a spare tire—he'd never checked. A state police cruiser pulled onto the shoulder in front of him, blue lights flashing.

The trooper took his time running Coffin's plates before he got out of his big Crown Vic, put his hat and his rain slicker on, and walked around to Coffin's side of the car. Coffin rolled down the window.

"I was three cars behind you when your tire blew," the trooper said. "Lucky you didn't kill us all, driving a piece of shit like this on a state highway." He was young and seemed to be working at projecting an air of authority.

"I'm glad you're okay," Coffin said, handing the trooper his shield along with his license and registration.

"Well, looky here," the trooper said. "Detective Coffin, from Provincetown. You made the collar on that serial killing out there, a couple years ago."

"Not me," Coffin said. "My partner."

"Well, nice going anyway."

"Thanks."

The trooper pursed his lips and peered into the Fiesta's fogged interior. "They outfit all you P'town detectives with fine vehicles like this one? Or are you undercover or something?"

"As what?" Coffin said.

"I don't know. I see a lot of Eastern European guys driving piece of shit cars like this nowadays. One of them, maybe."

"I *bought* this car from an Eastern European guy. Croatian, I think."

The trooper kicked meditatively at the Fiesta's flat tire. "Wow," he said. "You paid money for this thing?"

"Look," Coffin said, "I've got to get to Boston. I'm not sure I've got a spare."

"I'll call a wrecker for you," the young trooper said. "Shouldn't take him but a few minutes to get here. I'll tell him to bring a doughnut, which ought to get you into the nearest service station. Hey—are you working on a case right now? That rich broad that got stabbed?"

"That's the one," Coffin said.

"Any leads?"

"Too many."

"Gotcha," the trooper said. "Well, good luck gettin' this piece of shit to Boston." He rapped twice on the Fiesta's roof, then strode back to his cruiser.

The tow truck arrived ten minutes later. The driver was a tall, wiry Eastern European man with a thick mat of black hair and Cyrillic letters tattooed across his knuckles. He looked at Coffin's car and laughed. "Haw haw," he said. "I know this car." His accent was heavy.

"Hey," Coffin said. "Great."

"It belong-ed to my cousin, Zoran," the driver said, pulling a jack and a lug wrench from behind the seat of his truck. He wore no hat and no raincoat. His T-shirt was already soaking wet. "He sell it. Piece of shit, this car. You buy this stupid car from Zoran?"

"That was his name," Coffin said. "Zoran."

"Haw haw," the driver laughed, loosening a lug nut, then another. "That Zoran. I ask-ed him, who would buy this piece of shit car?"

"It was the only one I could find in my price range," Coffin said.

"What," the driver said, jacking up the Fiesta with a few quick pumps of his long, muscular arm, "you don't have job?"

"I'm a cop," Coffin said. The rain drummed on the Fiesta's roof. "Out in Provincetown."

"You are cop! Haw haw," the driver said, putting on the small temporary spare. "You crack me up, buddy. You should drive tow truck like me. Make good money. After work, drink some beers, meet some nice girls."

"Sounds pretty good," said Coffin. "I'll give it some thought."

"All set," the driver said, lowering the jack. "Where you want old tire?"

"Backseat, I guess," Coffin said. "The trunk's kind of small."

"You go two exits, back to Brewster—turn left, stop at Exxon. They sell you new tire. Retread. Very good price."

"What do I owe you?" Coffin said.

The driver shrugged. "Nothing. Maybe someday I'm in P'town, you do *me* a favor."

"I'll do that," Coffin said. "What's your name?"

"Zoran." The driver grinned, his teeth wolfish and sharp. "Like my cousin."

The Fiesta handled even worse with the spare than it had on its four bald tires. At forty-five miles per hour, the front end started to shudder; at fifty it bucked and jerked as though the wheels were falling off. Coffin slowed to about forty and drove back toward Orleans, a long line of traffic crawling along behind him. Just before he reached the Harwich exit, the red battery light next to the speedometer flickered on.

"Uh-oh," Coffin said. He tapped the clear plastic over the gauges with his fingernail, but the light stayed on. "What the fuck does that mean?"

He passed the Harwich exit—feeling the barbed hatred of the drivers behind him—intending to follow Zoran's directions to the Brewster Exxon station. After two or three miles his windshield wipers started to slow perceptibly and the engine temperature gauge began to rise, trembling just below the red zone. The steering grew even worse—stiff and heavy, as though the Fiesta were driving through a shallow lake of glue. He pulled over onto the narrow shoulder as far as he could. The Fiesta died completely about two hundred yards from the Brewster exit.

"Motherfucking fuckball," Coffin said. He lit a cigarette and waited, traffic streaming past on his left. The rain had almost stopped.

Ten minutes later the young state trooper appeared again, lights flashing in Coffin's rearview mirror. Coffin got out of the Fiesta and walked over to the cruiser as the trooper was typing something into his dashboard computer. The trooper looked up.

"Looks like you busted your serpentine belt," he said.

Coffin looked. A thick black loop of rubber hung from the Fiesta's engine compartment like an intestine. "Ah."

"Not your day, I guess."

"Not so far," Coffin said. "It doesn't want me to leave."

The trooper's blue eyes flicked up to Coffin's face. "What doesn't want you to leave, Detective?"

"The Cape. It's not letting me leave. Ever have that happen?"

"Nah. I live in Buzzards Bay. Other side of the bridge. You said you were headed to Boston?"

"I was," Coffin said. "Doesn't look like I'm going to make it, though."

The trooper looked at his watch. "I go off duty in exactly seven minutes. Hop in. I'll give you a ride."

TWELVE

The Ramos house felt cramped to Lola, even for a Provincetown saltbox. The ceilings seemed unusually low, the doors exceptionally narrow. The furniture was early rumpus room, all vinyl and plaid. Plastic Fisher-Price toys occupied most of the living room floor space.

"Once a cheater, always a cheater," Mrs. Ramos said. "That's what they say."

Sophie Ramos was a large, tired-looking woman with hair the color of butterscotch. She sat on her plaid sofa, entirely surrounded by plastic toys. The two-year-old, little Ronnie, was parked in front of the TV set watching *Bob the Builder*. The rest of the kids were at school.

"Should we be talking about this here, Mrs. Ramos?" Lola said, tilting her head in little Ronnie's direction. "Maybe we should step into the kitchen for a minute or two."

"Nah," Mrs. Ramos said, dismissing the suggestion with a wave of her meaty paw. She wore a nubbly terry-cloth bathrobe. Her fingernails were painted bubble-gum pink; the polish was chipped at the edges. "We had a big blowout about it last night. The kids know everything. No way to keep secrets in this teensy little house."

"Okay," Lola said. "If you say so." She lowered her

voice. "Are you saying your husband's had other affairs?"

"Uh, *yeah*," Mrs. Ramos said, letting the inflection rise a little. "With me. He was married when we first got together. I hired him to install some cabinets, and I guess you could say one thing led to another. He was a hottie, you know? We've always been under that cloud, in a way."

"You never really felt you could trust him," Lola said.

"Yup," Mrs. Ramos said. Tears welled in her eyes, and she dabbed at them with a Kleenex. "I just figured maybe I could keep him busy, you know? Things cooled off after I had little Ronnie here, though. I guess I kind of lost interest, after three kids in five years. I'm like, you know, can we give it a rest, already?"

"Daddy been bad," said little Ronnie, still staring at the TV.

"So after little Ronnie was born, things changed between you and your husband?" Lola asked.

Mrs. Ramos nodded her head. She looked like a sad bear in a housecoat. "I started noticing some stuff. Like the way he looked at other women, you know? It seemed different. Like there was purpose to it—not just curiosity. Then I guess one of them looked back and liked what she saw."

"Kenji Sole."

"Yeah," Mrs. Ramos said, lower lip trembling. She dabbed at her eyes again.

"Me hateses Daddy," little Ronnie said. On the TV, Bob the Builder and a talking steamroller were fixing a hole in a sidewalk.

"You shouldn't say that, honey," Mrs. Ramos said.

"Daddy been *bad*," little Ronnie said.

"This is a hard question for me to ask," Lola said,

looking down at her notebook, "but where was your husband on Friday night, Mrs. Ramos?"

"Here with me and the kids," Mrs. Ramos said. "For a change. He came right home from work and never left the house."

"For a change? That was unusual for him?"

"Yup. Especially on a Friday night. Usually he'd go out and have some beers at the Old Colony. You know, unwind a little."

"So why not this Friday?" Lola said.

Mrs. Ramos shrugged her thick shoulders. "I don't know. He said he was tired and felt like staying home. I was happy about it. I made his favorite dinner."

"Which is what?"

"Steak and french fries," Mrs. Ramos said. "Eddie's a red meat kind of guy."

"Me likes french fries," little Ronnie said. "Yum."

The conference room of D. Towler Investigations was located on the third floor of a narrow brick building on Warrenton Street, in the middle of Chinatown, above a street-level porn shop and a second-floor dim sum restaurant. The conference room smelled like ginger and pork grease. Coffin realized he was hungry.

"I was damned sorry to hear about Kenji," Towler said, propping his elbows on the stained conference table. He was a slender man in his late fifties with an accent that Coffin couldn't quite pin down—West Virginia or Kentucky, maybe. He wore a soup-strainer mustache, a gray pin-striped suit, and brown cowboy boots. His red-gray hair was pulled back into a short ponytail. "She was a nice lady."

"She had lots of friends," Coffin said. "Men, mostly."

Towler shot him a look. "Well, she sure as hell didn't

deserve to get stabbed to death, whatever else you might think of her."

"No," Coffin said. "She didn't." He tapped the green file folder that lay, closed, on the conference table in front of Towler. "Tell me about Priestess Maiya."

Towler pulled a pack of Pall Malls from the inside pocket of his sport jacket. "Smoke?" he said, tapping a cigarette halfway out of the pack and offering it to Coffin.

"Thanks," Coffin said.

The conference room was narrow, with carpet the color of bread mold and two high windows overlooking the busy street. The overhead fluorescents buzzed in their fixtures. A tall, wan ficus tree stood forlornly in the corner.

Towler dug in his jacket pocket, pulled out a kitchen match, and popped its head into a sulfurous yellow flame with his thumbnail. He reached across the table and lit Coffin's cigarette before lighting his own. "I tried smokin' those all-natural ones, you know—the kind without all the chemicals in 'em. They taste pretty good, I guess, but after a while I realized the chemicals were the best part." He flipped open the folder. "Priestess Maiya, a.k.a. Ruth McGurk. Can't say I blame the girl for changing her name. Twenty-six years old. Father an associate dean at UMass Amherst, mother writes and publishes romance novels under the name of Rebecca Kayne. Very successful, apparently—got twenty-some books still in print." He tapped the ash from his cigarette into a large green glass ashtray.

"Not what I expected, somehow," Coffin said.

"Not exactly trailer trash, if that's what you mean," Towler said. "Ruth went to a fancy all-girls prep school and graduated near the top of her class. Went straight on to college at Brown and almost immediately became involved in an affair with a tenured English professor—guy named Porter Jenkins. Ruth was seventeen at the time."

"Whoops," Coffin said.

"No shit, whoops," Towler said. "Professor Jenkins lost his job, his wife, and most of his property and almost went to jail. Attempted suicide right after they de-tenurized him. Not sure where he's at now; two years ago he was teaching at a community college in Akron, Ohio, but he's not there anymore."

"Ruth landed on her feet, I'm guessing."

"Yep," Towler said, flipping a page. "She wrote three chapters of a tell-all memoir about the trauma of it all, found a fancy New York agent, and sold the book—get this—for half a million. Evidently there was quite a little bidding war."

"Lucky Ruth. Next stop, Oprah."

"Except the book never came out. Turns out the publisher wasn't happy with the draft she turned in. Allegations of plagiarism, counterallegations of undue editorial interference, lawsuit, settlement. Ruth has to give back the lion's share of the advance."

"Except she doesn't."

"Bingo. She declares bankruptcy. Claims she had to spend the whole half million on living expenses and research for the book. Apparently she and the professor traveled in high style during the course of their affair, all paid for on his credit cards. She thought it necessary to retrace their steps—"

"In order to refresh her memory," Coffin said.

"Bingo again. You're getting good at this. Publisher's lawyers threaten this and that, Ruth sues for harassment—"

"And wins?"

"You're three for three. Judge rules she doesn't have

to pay back the advance, but she gets nothing on the harassment deal. Any guesses as to the name of the law firm representing the young lady?"

"Scrooby, Sammitch, and Sole," Coffin said, smoothing his mustache. It was bristly and coarse.

"You're a damn genius, Detective. For once the papers got it right."

"So . . . ?"

"So she doesn't finish college, needless to say. She drops out of sight for a while, then reappears in about a year as the star of an 'art' film directed by a friend of hers from Brown." Towler pulled a grainy eight-by-ten photograph from the folder and pushed it across the table to Coffin.

Coffin looked at the photo. A younger version of Priestess Maiya lay sprawled on a green divan, naked, hair in blond curls. She held a mandolin loosely in her right hand. A white dog looked out a window in the background. In the foreground, a cat crouched in a chair. An older man stood at an easel, painting a picture.

"Interesting," Coffin said, eyebrows raised.

"The movie's about a French painter, guy named Balthus. He made a career of painting young girls without their clothes on. Evidently he was one weird dude. The movie was kind of an avant-garde hit."

"Go figure," Coffin said.

"Yeah. Go figure," Towler said. "She made a couple more movies after this one—same director. Both were basically artsy-fartsy porno movies as far as I could tell. Lots of on-screen sex that didn't look all that simulated. Both got crappy reviews. That's right about the time she appears to have gotten herself involved in the meth scene. Somewhere between the last movie and when she changed her name to Priestess Maiya and started doing the performance art deal."

"I'd like to see one of those performances," Coffin said.

"You and me both. Apparently there's videos of 'em on the Internet."

"She still a tweaker?"

Towler leaned back in his chair. If there'd been a brass spittoon, Coffin thought, Towler would have spat in it. "Hard to say. She's been in and out of rehab a couple times. Any guesses as to who picked up the tab?"

"J. Hedrick Sole," Coffin said. "Of course."

"Of course. Then a funny thing happens."

"Funni*er*," Coffin said.

"J. Hedrick gets picked up by the cops, wandering the streets near his town house in Cambridge. They think he's senile or a drunk or both. He's incoherent and combative, doesn't know his address, appears to have pissed himself. They take him to New England Medical Center. The ER folks work him up and decide he's had a stroke. Routine blood work comes back, lo and behold, turns out the old guy's a meth head, too."

"The family that smokes together," Coffin said.

"Has strokes together," Towler said. "At least they do if they're in their seventies."

"Kenji know about this?" Coffin said.

Towler nodded. "That's the sticky part. She came in about a week before she was killed, and I walked her through pretty much the way you and I just did. I make a point of presenting sensitive information to clients in person. I don't trust the telephone all that much. You never know who's listening these days."

"How'd she react?"

"She was enraged. She got very protective."

"Of her father or his money?"

Towler pursed his lips for a moment. "I guess it'd be

fair to say both. She wanted to call the cops, have Ruth charged with everything from drug dealing to attempted murder. I suggested she get back in touch with her attorneys first—that if her father was bankrolling Ruth's meth habit, he'd likely be the one who'd ended up getting busted on drug charges."

Coffin picked up the photo of the naked Ruth McGurk and peered at it, allowing himself to admire her slim hips, the upward tilt of her nipples. "What do you think, D. Towler—did Ruth kill Kenji Sole?"

Towler shrugged. "I've been asking myself the same question. I've not actually met the young lady, but everything I know about her suggests that she's greedy, opportunistic, fundamentally dishonest, and sexually promiscuous to the point of making a career of it. She's pretty enough to be a model, and all indications are she's reasonably smart—she got a four-point-oh in prep school—but she'd rather suck some guy's dick in a low-budget art movie than get a real job."

"Mad at her parents," Coffin said. "Where were all the girls like her when I was in high school?"

Towler wrinkled one side of his face into a half-smile. "I've known one or two like that in my time," he said. "Fun on a date, but then the next day you're pissing broken glass and their boyfriend's looking to beat the shit out of you."

"The boyfriend you didn't know they had," Coffin said.

Towler nodded. "What they wanted was to pull as many people as they could into their drama. Made 'em feel important. I think that's Ruth, in a way. I don't think she killed Kenji—she was having too much fun pushin' her buttons. If anything, Kenji had it in for Ruth."

There was a sudden fusillade of what sounded like small-caliber gunfire from the street. It went on with

considerable intensity for a minute or so, a blue cloud
of smoke drifting past Towler's windows.

"Insurrection?" Coffin said, eyebrows raised.

"Firecrackers," Towler said. "Old Mr. Chin must have
had another grandson. He's the guy who owns the porn
shop downstairs."

"What do you mean, Kenji had it in for Ruth? Ruth
said she threatened her."

"It was a little worse than that. After Kenji left my
office that last time, she came back about an hour later,
very agitated. Know what she wanted to ask me?"

"Where to hire a leg-breaker," Coffin said.

Towler rotated his mustache slightly to the left and
eyed Coffin for a moment. "Bingo," he said. "She danced
around it a little bit, but yeah—pretty much."

"What'd you tell her?"

"I told her what you're supposed to tell people when
they ask you damn fool questions like that: that I wouldn't
be a party to a criminal conspiracy to commit murder,
and that if I believed she was serious about going ahead
I'd be forced to contact the police, despite our privileged relationship, as required by law. She got a little
pale and apologized, but who knows where she went or
who she called after she left my office."

"You didn't call the cops?"

"I didn't think she was serious. Last I heard she was
working with her attorneys to try to get the old boy
declared incompetent."

"Any idea who might've killed her, if not Ruth
McGurk?"

Towler shrugged. "I figure it was somebody out in
P'town. A jealous boyfriend, maybe. All those stab
wounds don't seem like woman's work."

Coffin stood and stuck out his hand. "I appreciate
your time, D. Towler," he said.

Towler's handshake was dry and firm, exactly two shakes up and down. "My pleasure. Like I said, I liked Kenji."

Coffin squinted one eye. "I don't mean to be nosy," he said, "but."

Towler grinned. His teeth were long and yellow. "*But* no, I never had sex with her. She was good-looking and all, but not really my type."

"Too skinny? Too rich?" Coffin said, genuinely surprised.

"Yep," Towler said. "You're nosy, all right. Kenji was a little too Anglo. I seem to have developed a preference for full-blooded Asian girls. Maybe it's the neighborhood."

"One more thing," Coffin said. "You ever eat at a noodle place around here called Phó Bo?"

Towler tucked the green file folder under his arm. "Sure, I've eaten there. It's just around the corner. Take a right at the porn shop, then another right."

"How is it?"

"Not bad. The competition in this neighborhood's pretty fierce, so almost all of these little Asian joints are okay. They all pay off the health inspectors, and they all serve reasonable chow." Towler crossed to the door and pulled it open, letting Coffin step out into the hallway ahead of him. "They all got pretty little waitresses, too," he said, face wrinkled into its half-smile. "Fresh off the boat."

Phó Bo was a cramped ten-table affair with a dirty linoleum floor and a big window around two sides. Coffin sat near the door, and a small, pretty waitress handed him a menu without smiling.

"What you want to drink?" she said. She was about five feet three and very slender. She wore tight black jeans and a white cotton blouse, open one button more than was strictly necessary.

"How about a Vietnamese beer," he said.

"Saigon or 333?"

"Saigon," Coffin said, scanning the menu. "And a small bowl of phó. With flank steak."

"No tendon? No tripe?"

"No," Coffin said. "Thanks."

"Ha," the waitress said. "One gringo special. No sense of adventure."

Coffin watched her walk away, noting her slenderness again, the slight rotation of her hips. When the kitchen door had swung shut behind her, he looked out the big wraparound window and observed the traffic on Washington Street: the cars and trucks moving sullenly through the light rain; pedestrians hustling down the sidewalk—mostly Asian men and women, a few white people in lab coats or pale green nurses' scrubs, coming from the big New England Medical Center complex a block away. *Jamie would like it here*, he thought. The big city with its throbbing energy and sheen of rain—horns honking, rainbow slick of oil in the road. This noodle joint, too, almost empty except for a table full of doctors and a couple of Asian families, the big window, the smell of beef broth and steam. Coffin realized he missed her—had been missing her for days now. The miscarriage and all the trouble they'd been having trying to conceive again hung over the relationship like a little blue anxiety cloud. The sex was no longer just sex—in fact, there was something a bit grim in Jamie's determination to have a baby, Coffin thought; what had once been carefree in their relationship was now freighted with purpose.

So he missed her. Missed her as she'd been before the miscarriage, missed her as she was now—the same, mostly, but with the slight, anxious edge of a woman whose plans are on hold, whose biology isn't behaving entirely as planned.

A fly landed on Coffin's fork and rubbed its forelegs together. He waved it away. *No one likes being thwarted*, he thought.

The waitress came back with his bottle of beer, poured it into a glass, and plunked the glass down on the table. "Saigon," she said. "I be right back with your noodle."

The beer in the glass was mostly head. Coffin sipped at the foam. It was yeasty and tasted slightly skunked. Coffin didn't mind. He waited a minute for the head to settle and poured more beer into the glass. The waitress came back again with a tray full of food.

"Phó with flank steak," she said, placing a large white bowl on the table.

"That's a small?" Coffin said.

The waitress turned and pointed at an Asian man sitting in the corner. "See what he got? That a large," she said. The bowl in front of the Asian man was the size of a bathroom sink.

She took a plate from the tray and put it on Coffin's table, next to the bowl of soup. "Bean sprout, basil, slice chili pepper, and lime," she said. "You put inside."

"Inside?" Coffin said.

The waitress rolled her eyes. "Inside the soup," she said. "I show you." She set her tray down on Coffin's table, frowning a little, and started to pluck leaves from the sprig of basil and drop them into Coffin's phó. She was very pretty. Coffin watched her small, quick hands use chopsticks to scoop the mung bean sprouts into his soup, and then add a few slices of jalapeño. When she was through, she squeezed the lime wedge into the soup, too. "All set," she said. "You can put chili sauce inside, too, you like."

"Thank you," Coffin said. The soup smelled delicious. The thin slices of flank steak were cooking in the broth as he watched.

The waitress shrugged. "No big deal," she said. "Slow now. It busy, you on your own. You want another beer?"

"Sure," Coffin said. "Let's try a 333 this time." The waitress went back to the kitchen, but this time Coffin didn't watch. He took a slurp of broth. It was wonderful: rich and complex, the aromatic wilt of basil leaves, a slight bite from the jalapeño slices. He set his spoon down and picked up a bean sprout with his chopsticks: It was crunchy and tasted like water. He used both spoon and chopsticks to lift a slithery clump of noodles to his mouth. He slurped them, as he'd seen the other customers doing. They were soft and mild and oddly satisfying. Vietnamese comfort food. He picked up the squeeze bottle of chili sauce (there was one on each table, like ketchup in a diner) and squirted some into his soup, stirring the broth a bit with a chopstick. The broth changed color, from amber to a rich light orange. He sipped it, and a slight sweat started on his forehead. He picked up a slice of meat and popped it into his mouth: It was tender and perfect and tasted like beef and broth and chili sauce. Coffin finished his beer and wiped his mustache with a paper napkin.

The waitress came back with a bottle of 333. "How you like?" she said, pouring his glass half full of foam again.

"It's great," Coffin said.

"You got to try tendon next time," she said. "That my favorite."

"Not the tripe?"

She shrugged. "It's okay. I like the tendon."

"Do many gringos order the tripe?" Coffin asked, slurping noodles.

"Nah. You kidding me? Only Vietnamese people."

"Only? Gringos *never* get the tripe?"

"Well, sometime they try to impress their friends, but they never finish. Eat a little bit, that's all. Very bad, waste food like that."

Coffin took a photo of Priestess Maiya from his jacket pocket. Lola had printed it from her Web site. Priestess Maiya was dressed in a peasant blouse and lots of bangles. Her makeup was dramatic, her hair pulled up in a dark, cobwebby swoop. Coffin showed the picture to the waitress. "How about her?" he said. "She ever come in and order tripe?"

The waitress frowned. "Dude. You a cop or something?" she said.

Coffin showed her his shield. "Police detective. From out in Provincetown."

"Why a P'town cop come here, ask questions in Chinatown?"

"The woman in this picture may be a suspect in a murder case. In P'town."

The waitress took the picture from Coffin's hand. She frowned at it. "Yeah, I know this girl," she said. "She come in here sometimes. Always try to talk Vietnamese. Very funny. Crack everybody up, back in the kitchen."

"Do you remember her coming in back in April, with an older man and a blond-haired Asian American woman?"

"Sure, I remember. Blond girl about thirty, right?"

"Right."

"They having a big fight. Yelling back and forth—freak out other customers."

"Who was doing most of the yelling?" Coffin asked. He tapped the picture of Priestess Maiya with his finger. "This one or the blond girl?"

"Funny you ask," said the waitress. "Blondie shout a lot. Old man shout at blondie. Trashy girl just sit there smiling, kind of." The waitress put a fingertip to her temple. "I think to myself, how strange."

"Did anybody make any threats?"

"Sure. Blondie says she gonna cut trashy girl's tits off."

"That was it?"

"Dude—that not enough?"

Coffin gave the waitress one of his cards, which she slid into her front pocket. Then he opened his notebook and asked for her name and phone number.

"You call me, ask me out? That why you want my number?" she said.

"No," he said. "I promise. It's in case we need to ask you any more questions."

"Okay," she said, bending down, writing the information in Coffin's notebook while he tried very hard not to look down her blouse. "Who knows, maybe I go out with you, you call me. I like older guy sometimes—body not so great, but always take you someplace nice, pay for everything, real polite."

Coffin could see her entire left breast. It was very small, and the nipple was brown and erect. The waitress glanced up from her writing, and Coffin knew he'd been caught looking, but she didn't pull her blouse together or act annoyed. Instead, she bent close to his ear and lowered her voice to a near whisper. "Young guy just want a quick fuck, you know? Wham bam, thanks a lot. I like older guy better. Take more time."

Coffin looked at his notebook. Her name was Lang Nguyen.

"Lang—that's nice."

"It mean 'sweet potato,'" Lang said, straightening up, thumbing a strand of black hair behind her ear.

"Sweet potato?"

"My mother have eight daughters," Lang shrugged. "She run out of names."

Coffin grinned. "If I didn't have a nice girlfriend back in P'town, I think I would ask you out."

Lang grinned and poked Coffin in the arm. "Your girlfriend so nice, how come you looking down my shirt?" She turned and walked back to the kitchen. "We go out, you got to lose the mustache, dude. It's so, like, *eighties*."

Outside Phó Bo, Coffin stood on the sidewalk in the drizzle, trying to hail a cab. The few that whisked past on their way to New England Medical Center all had passengers. He looked at his watch; it was getting late. Pedestrian traffic was heavy, and the sidewalk was narrow. A man in a gray suit bumped Coffin's arm with his shoulder bag, nearly pushing him into the street.

Coffin waved at another cab, wondering if he looked like a rube from the Cape in his bomber jacket and flannel shirt. The cab passed, the driver pointing to the OFF DUTY sign in the windshield. Then a green minivan pulled up, an Asian man at the wheel. The rear passenger door slid open on its greased track.

"Yo, dude," the Asian man said. He was about twenty and very thin. "You need a cab?" A large orchid was tattooed on his left forearm. It was a Taiwanese gang tattoo, Coffin knew. In Baltimore, the Purple Orchids had been at war with the Tiger Boys for a time, the bodies of young Asian men popping up all over the city. In the end, the two gangs had nearly wiped each other out.

"No thanks," Coffin said. "I'll walk." He felt something hard nudge into his lower ribs.

"Get in the van, motherfucker," a voice said. The
voice sounded like it was coming out of a tin can.

Coffin half-turned, saw no one. The hard thing
prodded him low in the ribs again.

"I said get in the van, or I shoot your motherfuckin'
lungs out."

Coffin looked down. A Chinese midget was poking
him with a very large pistol. The midget was barely four
feet tall. He scowled at Coffin. Coffin climbed into the
van. The midget climbed in after him, followed by another young Asian man of normal size. The van's passenger door slid shut.

THIRTEEN

Tommy McCurry's wife was named Alecia. She was the second palest human being Lola had ever met, after Cecil Duckworth. She was like a woman from a Flemish painting: Her hair was pale, her eyebrows were pale, the faint down on her upper lip was pale, even her lashes were pale. Her skin was so pale it seemed transparent, a faint mapping of veins underneath. Her eyes were very pale gray; her lips were pale, too, colored only with a thin smudge of pale pink gloss. She wore a pale blue jumper and a pale yellow blouse. The couch was pale beige. A pale wedge of sunlight fell on the pale green rug.

"I knew he was seeing someone," Mrs. McCurry said, dabbing a tear with a wilted Kleenex. "What could I do? Divorce him? I've got five kids. I haven't had a job since 1993, for God's sake."

The McCurrys lived in a modest saltbox near the high school, on Mozart Avenue. The house had three small bedrooms and a single bath the size of a closet. Lola had a hard time imagining what it must be like when all five McCurry children were home from school. She scratched her ear with her pen cap. "So you did nothing, then?"

"What I did," said Alecia McCurry, "is I kept my

mouth shut. I hoped it wasn't serious. I had twins. Then I got depressed and went on Prozac."

Lola tried not to stare at the pointed tip of Alecia McCurry's nose, which wiggled slightly as she talked. "How did you find out?" Lola said.

Alecia McCurry rolled her eyes. "God. It was obvious. Every Wednesday night he'd say he was going out to the Old Colony Tap for a few beers with the boys—his big night out. A few hours later he'd come back smelling like he'd just gotten out of the shower. Have you ever been in the Old Colony Tap?"

"A few times," Lola said. "To break up fights."

"Well then, you know what it smells like in there." Alecia McCurry's lower lip quivered; then she shook her head, her short, pale hair bobbing around her face. "When you get married, you never think you'll end up praying for your husband to come home smelling like cigarettes, stale beer, and urinal mints—but every Wednesday night, that's what I did."

Lola patted her hand. "This must be very hard for you," she said. "This whole business."

Alecia McCurry straightened her back and breathed in through her nose. "I'll live," she said. "The rage is kind of keeping me going right now. How *dare* he drag us into this, you know?"

"Did you know who he was sleeping with?" Lola said.

Tommy McCurry's wife nodded her pale head. "I followed him a few times when he left the house. If the sitter showed up in time, I'd get in my car and follow him with the lights off. I'd park down on 6A below her house. Sometimes I could see them through that big front window, all foreshortened because I was looking almost straight up at them. I'd sit down there as long as

I could take it, then I'd go have a few drinks somewhere until it was time to go home."

"Where were you and your husband last Friday night? The night Kenji Sole was killed?"

"We were here at home, watching TV. Well, I was watching TV. The kids were in bed. Tom was in his recliner, snoring loud enough to rattle the windows. Mr. Excitement, when he's with me."

"What were you watching?"

Alecia McCurry ducked her head, embarrassed. "*Law and Order*," she said. "I'm addicted. Doesn't it seem like it's *always* on?"

The green minivan turned down a narrow side street, passing a row of porn shops and Asian markets. The rain fell harder. The driver turned on the stereo; disco music thumped softly from the speakers, a girl's voice singing in Cantonese.

The midget frowned and waved his gun at Coffin. It was a chrome-plated revolver with a short barrel and a bore the size of a dime. "Okay, *sei gwai-lo*. What you want with my girl?"

"Your girl?" Coffin said. "You mean Lang?"

The midget and the driver laughed. The other young man was wearing headphones. His eyes were closed. He seemed to have fallen asleep in his seat.

"That what she tell you her name was? Lang?" the midget said. "That's pretty funny, dude."

"Look," Coffin said, a cold trickle of sweat in his left armpit. "I think we've got a misunderstanding here."

"Misunderstanding?" the midget said. "You round-eye motherfuckers up in here all the time, hitting on my homegirls? Shit." He poked Coffin in the ribs again. "Misunderstand *this*, motherfucker."

"I'm a cop," Coffin said. "Lang's a potential witness in a homicide investigation. I had a few questions to ask her."

"You don't look like no cop," the driver said over his shoulder.

"Yeah, motherfucker," the midget said in his tin-can voice. "You a cop, let's see some ID."

"Fine," Coffin said. "It's in my inside pocket. I'm going to reach in and get it out. Don't shoot me."

"Do it slow, bitch. Two fingers."

Coffin fished the ID from his inner jacket pocket and flipped it open. "Detective Coffin," he said. "From Provincetown."

"What the fuck, Lenny," the driver said, looking over his shoulder again. He had a thin, droopy mustache. "Dude's a cop."

"Lenny?" Coffin said.

"Yeah, so what?" the midget said. "You never heard the name Lenny before?" He set the pistol on the seat beside him and rubbed a small hand over his face. "Fuck, man. A fuckin' cop. What I'm gonna do with a fuckin' cop?"

"How about giving me a ride?" Coffin said. "I'm late for an appointment."

"You serious?" Lenny said. He picked up the pistol and absentmindedly scratched his ear with the barrel.

Coffin put his shield back in his pocket. "Why not?"

Lenny pondered for a moment, then shrugged. "Sure. Why the fuck not? Where to?"

Coffin told him the address. "There's one other thing. A question."

Lenny pointed the pistol at Coffin's heart. "Shoot," he said. Then he grinned. "Just fuckin' wit' you, dude." He put the pistol in his jacket pocket. "Ask away."

"How'd you know I was talking to Lang? She tell you? It had to have happened awfully quick after I left the noodle shop."

Lenny waved a small hand. "No, man," he said. "She'n't tell me nothin'. I saw it on the camera, dude."

"What camera?"

"The security cam. The monitor's in the kitchen, case somebody tries to rob the place."

"You work there?"

"Shit. Work there? Fuck no. My uncle owns the place, man. I just hang out 'cause I like the food. I'm a fuckin' engineer."

"Engineer?" Coffin said.

The young man with the headphones opened his eyes and looked at Coffin for the first time. "Lenny's a senior at MIT," he said. "Four-point-oh, baby."

Lenny touched his head, then held out his hand. "*Mens et manus*, motherfucker," he said.

Lenny and his friends dropped Coffin off at the offices of Kenji Sole's lawyers, Torkel, Baldritch, Nash. They occupied all three floors of a beautifully restored brick town house on a quiet street near Boston Common. Coffin looked at his watch: He was five minutes late for his appointment with Sarah Baldritch. He pulled the polished oak door open and walked in.

The reception area was hushed and seemed dark, even compared to the gray late spring afternoon. The walls were finished in dark oak wainscoting below hunter green wallpaper. There was a Persian rug in reds and blues on a dark oak floor. The chairs were leather and cherry; a dark marble table held sober magazines: *Forbes* and *Architectural Digest*. The receptionist sat at an oak desk under the room's only bright light. She wore a charcoal gray suit and black glasses with trendy rectangular frames. Her blond hair was cut short and parted on the side. There was something cool and almost artificial about her, as though she might have been made of surgical steel and whirring servos beneath a sleek vinyl skin.

Coffin felt a bit self-conscious in his chinos and flannel shirt. "Frank Coffin," he said. "I have a meeting with Sarah Baldritch."

"Ah," said the receptionist, running a frosted fingernail down the open appointment book. "Here we are. Detective Coffin, from Provincetown."

"Yes," Coffin said.

"Ms. Baldritch is on an overseas call, Detective. She'll be right with you. Would you like coffee or a mineral water while you wait?"

"No thanks," Coffin said. "I'm fine."

The receptionist smiled faintly, and Coffin imagined the bright steel mandible working beneath the pleasing contours of her face.

"If you need anything, just ask. My name's Stephanie."

"Nice to meet you, Stephanie," Coffin said.

He sat in one of the dark leather chairs and picked up a copy of *Architectural Digest*. The cover article was about the exotic homes of extremely rich people. There were glossy photos of "infinity edge" swimming pools surrounded by rattan furniture and palm trees. The pools appeared to be suspended above bright blue oceans. None of the pictures had any people in them.

The receptionist—Stephanie—picked up her phone and spoke into it briefly before hanging up. "Mr. Coffin?" she said. "Ms. Baldritch can see you now." She stood. "Please follow me."

Stephanie either had surprisingly long legs or her gray pin-striped skirt was surprisingly short. *Or both,* Coffin thought. She wore two-inch heels, and something in the weave of her stockings glittered slightly in the dimly lit hallway. Coffin imagined the servos purring beneath her vinyl skin. She stopped at a large oak door and knocked.

"Come in," said a woman's voice.

Stephanie pushed the door open and said, "Detective Coffin, Ms. Baldritch." She waved Coffin in with her left hand. The door closed silently behind him.

"Well, Detective Coffin," said Sarah Baldritch, rising from her desk chair and sticking out a hand. "A pleasure to meet you."

Sarah Baldritch was the anti-Stephanie. Stephanie was tall, but Sarah Baldritch was short—barely five feet, Coffin guessed. Stephanie was slender, but Sarah Baldritch was stout. Stephanie was pretty, but Sarah Baldritch was plain in the big-nosed, small-eyed manner of human plainness. Stephanie was young; Sarah Baldritch was fifty or so. Stephanie appeared to be a robot, but Sarah Baldritch was very clearly composed of lumpy human flesh.

Coffin shook her hand. "Quite a place you've got here," he said. The office walls had been papered in sage green silk. The desk was massive, carved from burl walnut. The rugs, antique Persians, had no doubt been knotted by the nimble fingers of Shi'a slave children.

"It'll do," Sarah Baldritch said, grinning. "Have a seat." She opened a rosewood humidor and offered it to Coffin. "Care for a cigar?"

"No thanks," Coffin said, settling into the buttery leather guest chair. "I only smoke cigarettes, and I can barely stand them."

"Mind if I indulge? I just bought some great Cohibas, and I haven't had a chance to try them yet."

"By all means," Coffin said.

Baldritch made a show of clipping off the end of her

cigar and lighting it carefully with a small propane torch. Then she leaned back in her chair, smoke rising in blue billows over her head.

Coffin lit a cigarette in self-defense.

"I was glad to hear you'd taken on the investigation into Kenji's murder," Baldritch said. "I liked her a great deal. She was one of my favorite clients."

"Then you won't object to letting me look at the letters you sent on her behalf."

Baldritch stuck the cigar into the corner of her mouth and squinted at Coffin through the smoke. "You'll have to be more specific than that," she said. "I sent a number of letters on Kenji's behalf."

"The ones regarding her father's competence," Coffin said. "Of course, if there are others that might shed light on the investigation, I'd like to see them, too."

"There's a matter of attorney-client privilege in play here, you know," Baldritch said, making a little steeple of her index fingers, then pointing it at Coffin. "Client's death notwithstanding. It's my feeling that most of the legal correspondence we prepared for Kenji Sole is not relevant to her murder. There may be a couple of avenues, however, that might be relevant, and I'm prepared to discuss them with you. The first, as you say, is the issue of her father's competence." A black leather folder lay on her desktop. She opened it, extracted a sheet of paper, and pushed it across the desk with her fingertips. "I wrote this letter at Kenji's request." She tapped the letter on the left. "This one, in February, shortly after Kenji's father was picked up by the police after having a stroke."

"I heard about that," Coffin said. "I met with Towler about an hour ago. He told me the whole story."

"Then you know that at the time of his stroke, J. Hedrick Sole had methamphetamine in his system."

"Yes," Coffin said. He read the letter. It did not seem like a routine inquiry to him. It was, he thought, a strongly worded demand for an extensive physical and psychiatric evaluation of J. Hedrick Sole, by physicians of his daughter's choosing. "Would you call this a routine letter of inquiry?" he said when he'd struggled through the three dense paragraphs of legalese.

Sarah Baldritch snorted. "Hardly," she said. "It's a broadside, an open threat. Jerry Sole knew exactly what it meant—and knew it was the precursor to his daughter's petitioning of the family courts for a competency investigation and hearing. Damned if he does and damned if he doesn't."

"Damned if he allows himself to be examined and fails, and damned if he refuses because it makes him look crazy?"

"Exactly."

"So what was his response?"

"He told us to fuck off."

"In so many words?"

Baldritch shook her head. "He said what a guy like Jerry Sole *would* say: He would not submit to his daughter's demands, and if she persisted he could produce affidavits from a dozen medical specialists all verifying that he was in excellent mental and physical health, and any further discussion of the matter would result in her immediate and total disinheritance and a countersuit for harassment."

"So then what? What was the next step?"

"The next step was that Kenji got stabbed to death with a chef's knife."

"Do you think Kenji's murder was related to her issues with her father?"

Baldritch shrugged. "There was a lot of money involved. You'd be a fool not to entertain the possibility, at least."

"That wasn't my question."

Baldritch squinted at Coffin, then scratched her nose with a blunt fingertip. "Do I think J. Hedrick or his attention-whore of a girlfriend murdered Kenji Sole? No on J. Hedrick, maybe on the girlfriend. She have an alibi?"

Coffin stroked his mustache with his fingertips. It needed trimming and still smelled like phó. "Sort of. It leaves room for skepticism."

"I think we'd all be wise to be skeptical of little Ruth McGurk," Baldritch said, leaning back in her chair.

"What's the other avenue?" Coffin said.

Baldritch removed another sheet of paper from the leather folder and pushed it across the desk.

"This is Kenji's will," she said. "You know, of course, that she was very wealthy."

"Am I reading this right?" Coffin said.

"If you can read, then you're probably reading it right," Baldritch said.

"The P'town Heritage Museum gets *how* much?" The Heritage Museum was located in a small stone building near the foot of the Pilgrim Monument. It was a curious enterprise, even for Provincetown: Its prize exhibits were a stuffed polar bear and one of the world's largest scale models of a Grand Banks schooner. Coffin had gone to the grand opening with Jamie, his first and only visit.

"The bulk of the estate. About sixty percent. The rest goes to establish a foundation so we can continue to do good work in Kenji's name, la la la."

"So how much is sixty percent?" Coffin said.

"You'd have to talk to the accountant to get the current

number, but the last time I checked it would have been around twenty million."

"The *Heritage Museum* gets twenty *million*?"

"Yep." Baldritch eyed her cigar, then lit it again with the torch. "That's about the size of it."

"Do they know that?"

"We haven't notified them, if that's what you mean. All the notification letters go out at the same time; we'll probably send them Monday."

"Holy crap," Coffin said. "Twenty million."

Baldritch scratched her ribs. "I heard you had a little car trouble getting out here. How you planning on getting home?"

"Towler called you?"

"We stay in touch."

Coffin nodded, not surprised. "I was going to take a cab to the bus terminal," he said.

"The bus? Why not take the ferry? It's forty-five minutes."

"I don't like boats," Coffin said.

Baldritch raised a bristly eyebrow.

"Long story," Coffin said.

She waved a hand. "Well, the bus is out of the question," Baldritch said, picking up the phone. "Stephanie? Detective Coffin needs a lift back to Provincetown. Call Edward and tell him to warm up the Cessna." She paused, chewing on her cigar. "And a Town Car to Logan, yes. Thank you, Stephanie." She put the phone back in its cradle. "You okay with airplanes, Detective?"

"As long as they don't crash," Coffin said.

Baldritch stood and stuck out her hand. Coffin shook it.

"Nice meeting you, Detective," she said. "Let me know if there's anything else we can do for you."

* * *

Pre-rush-hour traffic was heavy between the offices of Torkel, Baldritch, Nash and Logan Airport, but the liveried driver of the firm's sleek Town Car didn't seem to mind. He swerved deftly around honking semis and made creative use of the breakdown lane when passing herds of SUVs. Coffin turned and looked out the rear window, half-expecting to see a river of wrecked cars in their wake—but there was nothing back there but the usual Boston gridlock.

"Clearing up, finally," the driver said, peering up at the sky as he passed a truck pulling a huge pleasure boat on a trailer, the speedometer needle rising past eighty miles per hour.

"Good," Coffin said, gripping the gray leather armrest. "Small planes in bad weather. Not fun."

"You're flying out to P'town, right?" the driver said. "I got a sister in P'town. Nice place. I try to get out there a couple times a year. She runs a guesthouse, puts me and the wife up in the bridal suite."

"Yeah?" Coffin said. "Which guesthouse?"

"The White Orchid," the driver said.

"Your sister," Coffin said. "Is her name Julie?"

"No," the driver said, looking at Coffin in the rearview mirror. "That's her partner. My sister's name is Angela. What, you know the place?"

Coffin shrugged. "I live in P'town. The White Orchid's about three blocks from my house."

The driver flicked his eyes up to the rearview mirror again. "It's mostly lesbians that stay there," he said. "It took me a while to get used to it, I guess. Now they just seem pretty much like anybody else."

"Pretty much," Coffin said.

"It's not like we didn't know about Angela early on," the driver said, passing a convoy of school buses on the right.

Coffin looked at the speedometer: It was quivering just above ninety.

"She was always a tomboy," the driver said. "Some aunt or uncle would give her a doll for her birthday and she'd take it back to the store the next day, get herself a frickin' catcher's mitt instead."

"How'd your parents handle it?" Coffin said, trying not to look out the window. He was gripping the arm-rest hard enough to leave nail marks.

The driver shrugged. "They were perplexed. They talked to the priest about it. Father Mickey, we called him, on account of he was always tryin' to show us boys his package. He told 'em the usual—say a few Hail Marys, light a couple candles, blah blah blah. Suffice it to say, it didn't do shit."

"I guess not," Coffin said.

"I wasn't surprised," the driver said, pulling up in front of Logan's main terminal. "Even then, I had no belief in the supernatural. If a freak like Father Mickey could make a living off religion, then I figured the whole thing had to be a racket."

Flying from Provincetown to Boston could be harrow-ing even in good weather. The flight path into Logan Airport took you overland almost the entire way, more or less following Route 6 over a crazy quilt of woods, golf courses, residential neighborhoods, salt marshes, and mall parking lots, all of which heated and cooled at different rates during the day. The resulting updrafts and downdrafts could be brutal; even in clear weather the half-hour flight from Provincetown to Logan could feel like an endless and terrifying roller-coaster ride. The twin-engine, ten-passenger Cessnas flown by Cape Air bucked, dipped, and rattled nauseatingly for almost the entire trip before turning north and then west over Boston Harbor for the final descent.

In good weather, though, the flight from Boston back to Provincetown was both beautiful and serene. Over water the entire way, the flight afforded spectacular views of the South Shore coastline and the deep gray-green of Cape Cod Bay, the Cape itself like a flexed arm extending out from the mainland, the clenched fist of Truro and Provincetown rising slowly up from the horizon as the plane drew near. From the air the Cape always reminded Coffin of a big Italian *vaffunculo*, swinging arm, fist up, the gesture a larger and more expressive version of the American middle finger.

Coffin was the only passenger. He sat in a roomy leather captain's chair, bottle of Evian in the cup holder, copy of *Newsweek* on his lap. He was looking out the window at the miles of deep, green water below them. His grandfather had drowned in Cape Cod Bay in shallow water off Herring Cove; his father had been lost on the other side of the Cape, miles from shore in the cold North Atlantic, thrown overboard while making a drug run in his fishing boat, the *Nora Jean*.

The pilot made an announcement over the PA system. "Looks like we got whales at four o'clock. Let's go take a look." Coffin gripped the armrests as the Cessna banked and dove toward the water, which came up at the window with alarming speed.

"There's three of 'em right out your port window," the pilot said, the plane tilted on its side, still descending. "We'll go down to about a thousand feet so you can get a good look."

"Thanks," Coffin said, knuckles turning white. He looked out the window. Three humpbacks churned the water to a pale, frothy green below his window. They were surrounded by a trio of whale-watch boats. The whales breached and spanked the water with their tails, unperturbed. Two hundred years ago, humpbacks this close to shore would have been pursued and slaughtered with dogged efficiency by Coffin's Yankee ancestors. Would the whales of 1808 have been similarly relaxed as men with harpoons rowed toward them in their fragile boats?

The Cessna leveled, then began to climb again. Coffin sat back in his seat and took a deep breath. The sun was going down behind them. The thin, high scrawl of clouds to the east glowed pink, reflecting the sunset's fuchsia throb. Ahead, Provincetown and the curve of the Outer Cape crawled over the horizon: pale shoulder of beach, shawl of scrub pine. The Pilgrim Monument and the water towers sprouted in the distance; Coffin picked out MacMillan Pier and the dark mass of Town Hall's slate roof. The Cessna banked again, starting its descent. Coffin could see the pilot through the open cabin door, talking emphatically on his headset radio. He pulled back on the throttle and the Cessna climbed, passing over the airport at maybe two hundred feet. The intercom crackled.

"We've got five or six deer on the runway, looks like," the pilot said. "Ground crew's gonna run down there with a Jeep and chase 'em away. We'll be landing as soon as I can get us turned back into the wind." The plane banked twice, then twice again, making a loose rectangle in the air. Then they descended, floating over the runway, wingtips dipping and righting before the wheels touched, bounced, then touched again.

The Cessna's passenger door swung open at the top and bottom, like a big aluminum clamshell. Coffin climbed down the steep, short set of passenger stairs. His shirt was damp at the armpits, and he realized he stank a bit. He felt like kissing the ground.

Lola was standing on the tarmac, wearing her uniform. "You don't look so good, Frank," Lola said. "Tough flight?"

"That's it," Coffin said. "I'm never leaving the Cape again."

"So," Lola said, driving the big Crown Vic back out Race Point Road toward town center. "What'd you find out?"

"Princess Maiya and J. Hedrick are both tweakers, hidden cameras are everywhere, and the word for 'sweet potato' in Vietnamese is *lang*."

Lola grinned. "Not a bad day's work. That it?"

Coffin looked out the window. On both sides of the road the forest of scrub pines was broken by new development, much of it sitting abandoned, half-finished. "If you're going to take a road trip in an '84 Ford Fiesta, wear a crash helmet."

"What about those routine inquiries from Torkel, Baldritch, Nash?"

"Routine for Gitmo, maybe. How was your day?"

They passed a brace of young men Rollerblading along the bike path. They were all muscular and tan, dressed in shorts and muscle shirts, even though the evening was cool and damp. Lola told him about her interviews with the wives. "Also Stavros called," she said. "There's a message on your desk. He wants us to meet him at his house tonight, around six."

"Fine," Coffin said.

"So now what?" Lola said.

"Home for a shower," Coffin said.

Lola wrinkled her nose and glanced at him under lowered lids. "Good plan. And then?"

"A drink and a nap," Coffin said, "and then we'll go talk to Boyle."

When Lola dropped Coffin off in front of his house, the battered red Fiesta was parked at the curb. A tall, lanky Eastern European man leaned against the fender; a man who could have been his brother sat in a late-model Dodge truck, idling a few feet behind the Fiesta.

"You are Officer Coffin?" the first man said.

Coffin nodded. "That's right, and that's my car."

The man took two steps away from the Fiesta, then turned and regarded it, lips pursed. He had strong features and dark brows. He was thin, but his arms were long and corded with sinew, his hands big and powerful and black with grease. "This car is some piece of shit," he said. "Not safe. Front bearings on both sides shot. Fucking wheels fall off, you die. Seriously!" The man leaned toward Coffin and pointed his two fingers at his eyes, then at Coffin's, then back at his own. "Look at me," he said. "I'm telling you."

"I can't believe you drove it up here from Brewster," Coffin said. "What do I owe you?"

The man stuck out his hand. It was like shaking hands with a big pair of pliers, Coffin thought.

"I am Bojan," the man said. "Zoran the tow-truck man is my brother." He pointed to the man in the car. "This is also my brother, Drago."

The man in the car waved; Coffin waved back.

"Zoran my cousin should not sell this car to you," Bojan said. "He did not know you were police man. I buy it back now, okay?" He took a roll of bills from his pocket and peeled six hundreds off the top.

"I only paid five for it," Coffin said.

"Ah," Bojan said. "Extra hundred for your trouble.

No problem!" He tucked the bills into Coffin's shirt pocket.

Coffin fished them out and handed them back. "How much do I owe you for the tire and the delivery?"

"You sure?" Bojan said.

"I'm sure."

Bojan shrugged. "Okay. Is your funeral. No charge for tire; is cheap retread anyway. I replace your serpentine belt, too—also no charge. Car is maybe okay to drive around town." He wagged a long finger in Coffin's face. "But not on highway," he said. "No, no, no. Okay?"

"Okay," Coffin said. "Thanks for the heads-up."

Bojan shook his narrow head and climbed into the passenger seat of his brother's pickup. "I tried, right? I tried, but you said no."

"Right," Coffin said. "You did your best."

"Okeydokey, smokey," Bojan said, giving Coffin a big thumbs-up as Drago dropped the pickup into drive and pulled slowly away from the curb.

FOURTEEN

Mancini sat at Boyle's desk, fiddling with a glass paperweight. It was a clear globe with a tiny three-dimensional village inside. When you shook it, a blizzard of fake snow swirled around the little buildings.

"That's *it*?" Mancini said. "That's all you've got?"

Coffin looked at his notebook, flipped a page, and pursed his lips. "It's not nothing. Lots of boyfriends, lots of wives, Daddy's nasty girlfriend—big inheritance goes to none of the above. Some kind of porn angle that we haven't entirely put together yet. Plenty of people with motive, but not much useful physical evidence so far." He looked up at Boyle. "What were you expecting after three days? The killer, on video?"

Boyle was perched awkwardly on the corner of his desk, where Duckworth had been sitting the day before. His face flushed bright red, but he said nothing.

"So what's the next move?" Mancini said. "We keep checking the boyfriends' alibis? Dig deeper on the porn angle?"

Coffin's eyes felt gritty from lack of sleep. His left lower eyelid twitched once, then again. "We?" he said, rubbing his eyes. "This whole thing would be a lot easier if we could just get the DVR back."

"What the hell are you talking about, Coffin?" Boyle said.

Coffin could almost see the steam rising from Boyle's bald spot. He imagined cracking an egg on Boyle's head and watching it fry. "The DVR our guy was looking for. After he murdered Kenji Sole. We had it, but it got stolen before we had a chance to see what was on it."

"Stolen by who?" Boyle said.

"Whoever it was," Coffin said, "they did a pretty professional job on Sergeant Winters's apartment."

"Should we bring in CSS?" Mancini said. "Check for prints and fibers and whatnot?"

Coffin shrugged. "If you want to," he said, "but I doubt there'd be much point."

"So you don't have this DVR?" Boyle said.

"No."

"And you didn't see what was on it."

"We saw a few minutes toward the beginning, but then we were interrupted. By the time we got back, Lola's apartment had been broken into and the DVR was gone."

"Interrupted?" Mancini said. "By what? Your girlfriend drag you off to the fertility clinic again?"

Coffin leaned back in the vinyl chair. "Well, no, actually," he said.

"It doesn't matter what interrupted him," Boyle snapped. "What matters is that he screwed up and lost a vital piece of evidence because he didn't follow proper procedure."

Coffin leaned back a bit and met Boyle's eye. "You might want to think twice," he said, "before you go that route."

Boyle's eyes bugged. "Is that some kind of *threat*, Coffin?"

Coffin imagined the egg growing crisp around the edges, firm in the center.

Mancini shook the paperweight. The snow fell again on the little village. "You said 'he.' You think it was a man?"

Coffin shrugged. "They usually are," he said. "It's not easy to stab someone to death. It's messy. You usually have to stab them a bunch of times before they die, and it's not like they're holding still letting you do it. A lot of the time they try to get away, or they put up a fight; you have to either corner or subdue them. You have to be pretty strong to stick a knife in someone's rib cage, too—especially a big butcher knife like the one that killed Kenji Sole."

Mancini peered at Coffin through the swirling miniature snow. His eyeball looked huge. "I thought it was a man from the get-go," he said.

"Could have been a woman," Coffin said. "Maybe. If she was really pissed off. Or crazy."

"Not *crazy* crazy," Mancini said. "Five or six stab wounds, not thirty or forty. The killer stabs her in the heart on the sixth try, she dies, the killer stops. No mutilation or any psychotic shit like that."

"Who *isn't* crazy?" Boyle said. He levered himself off the desk, walked to the window, and raised the venetian blind. "Hell, half this *town* is out of its fucking mind. God only knows what they're capable of."

"Tell me about this DVR," Mancini said. "Are you saying there might be a video recording of the murder?"

"Kenji had a hidden camera in her bedroom," Coffin said. "It was a pretty elaborate setup. The camera connected wirelessly to a DVR, which was in the linen closet, in a secret drawer. The DVR was connected to a wireless router, which sent video to Kenji's computer. Whoever killed Kenji took the computer but left the DVR. An amateur's mistake, but not that surprising."

"Oh ho!" Mancini said. "A boudoir-cam. I guess we know what was on it."

Coffin nodded. "She liked to watch herself having sex. Some people use a mirror. Kenji used a hidden camera."

"My," Mancini said, setting the paperweight down on Boyle's desk. "Our Miss Kenji was a *bad* girl. If you were a married guy involved with a freaky-deaky broad like that, and you found out she was filming your ass—"

"You never really know what people will do when the going gets weird," Coffin said, watching Boyle's face. Boyle's ears were crimson. His mouth worked, but he said nothing.

"She must have been something," Mancini said. "Sack-wise, I mean. All these guys who should've known better, selling their souls for a little sniff."

Coffin shrugged. "*C'est l'amour,*" he said.

"Ha," Boyle said, lips twisted into a tight little sneer. "*L'amour* my ass."

Mancini knitted his fingers, leaned forward. "What's your gut telling you, Coffin? You've met the major players—the boyfriends, the father, his little squeezola. Did one of them kill her?"

Coffin thought for a moment. "Probably," he said.

"For fuck's sake, Coffin," Boyle said. *"Probably?"*

Outside, the sky was the color of slate. Gulls orbited above MacMillan Pier, yelping like small, sorrowful dogs.

"Probably," Coffin said. "It's probably a man. It's probably someone she was involved with. That leaves us something like ten suspects, including Cavalo. Of course, I could be wrong about it being a man."

Mancini leaned back and laced his fingers on top of his head. "Got the prelim report from CSS, if you're interested."

"I'm interested," Coffin said.

"They found a bunch of different hair samples—in the bed, in the rugs, in the shower trap. Like, ten different samples, not including the victim's. Weeks and weeks of fun with DNA."

"Fascinating," Coffin said. "That it?"

"They also found an impressive collection of strap-on dildos and other sex toys, including a couple of paddles. That jibe with what you know about her?"

"Pretty much. We've had a couple of witnesses mention it." Coffin glanced at Boyle, who was staring blankly out of his office window.

"What about the hidden camera? Any video of her playing dominatrix?"

Coffin nodded. "Yep. It seems to be a recurring theme."

"A recurring fucking *theme*," Boyle said, still staring out at the harbor. "That's one way of putting it."

"Well," Mancini said, looking at his watch. "If there's nothing else, I'd better get back to Barnstable. You should see the frickin' pile of paperwork on my desk."

"Paperwork," Coffin said. "Damn. It sucks being you."

"Fine," Mancini said, standing. "Very funny. What would you recommend for dinner?"

"Try the Captain Alden," Coffin said. "Great clam rolls."

Lola gave Mancini a thumbs-up. "The best," she said.

"Huh," Mancini said. "Who knew?"

When he was gone, Boyle settled into his desk chair. "All right, Coffin," he said. "Say what you have to say."

"I think you already know," Coffin said.

Boyle smirked. "I'm not playing your guessing game, Coffin."

Coffin looked out the window. The harbor lay flat and grey in the twilight. A beat-up panel truck rattled down Commercial Street, loaded with junk. "You're on the DVR," Coffin said. "You're one of the boyfriends."

Boyle said nothing. A patch of fluorescent glare shifted on his bald spot. His face squirmed and twitched; he was very red. Coffin wondered if he was having an aneurysm.

"So?" Boyle said at last.

"So we need to ask you where you were the night Kenji was killed," Coffin said.

"Friday night?" Boyle said.

Coffin nodded.

"I was at home, alone. My wife was in Boston on a shopping trip with friends. I heated up a frozen pizza in the oven—pepperoni. I drank two beers, watched a John Wayne movie on TCM—*The Searchers*—and went to bed."

"What time?"

"A little after eleven o'clock."

"You never left the house? Nobody saw you?"

"Right."

"Did you make or receive any phone calls? Send any e-mail?"

"No and no."

Coffin rubbed his chin, looking out the window. A small blue sailboat was passing the breakwater, sail bulging with wind. "Not much of an alibi, Chief," Coffin said.

"No shit, Sherlock," Boyle said. "So now what do we do?"

"I'd recommend voluntary DNA testing," Coffin said.

"Assuming you're not a match for the semen in Kenji's vagina, it could go a long way toward clearing you."

Boyle waved a hand, dismissing the idea. "Screw that, Coffin. What I meant was, how do we keep my wife from finding out? If she finds out what I was doing with Kenji Sole, she'll divorce me so fast it'll make your head spin. There goes the house, the car, the boat—the whole deal."

"You own a boat?" Coffin said.

"Yes, Coffin, I own a freaking boat. Have you got a problem with that?"

"To each his own," Coffin said. "I guess."

"Jesus fucking *Christ*, Coffin," Boyle said. "Can we try to stay on topic here?"

Coffin looked blank for a second.

"Chief Boyle was hoping his wife wouldn't find out," Lola said.

"I'm afraid it's probably too late for that, Chief," Coffin said. "I mean, even if your involvement is limited to just the affair with Kenji, and even assuming you didn't get called to testify in court—"

"I know all that, Coffin. All I ask is that you be as discreet as possible. As a personal favor. There's no reason to go blabbing all over town, is there?"

"No, sir," Coffin said. "What should we do about Mancini?"

"Look," Boyle said. "Look at me, all right?"

Coffin looked. Boyle's eyes were bulging like a Boston terrier's.

"I didn't kill her. I had an affair, but that doesn't make me a killer. Okay?"

"When was the last time you saw her?"

"Early last week. Monday, I think."

"How long had the affair been going on?"

"Almost four months. Since late January." Boyle looked at Coffin, then at Lola. "She came on to me, Coffin. She came on to *me*. Can you believe that?"

"Sure," Coffin said. The blue sailboat was now just a pale dot on the horizon. "Sure I can."

FIFTEEN

Nick Stavros lived in a big house in the Heights, Provincetown's exclusive—and still wildly expensive—gated community. The house had a nice view of the West End, the breakwater, and the tidal salt marsh. If it had been lighter, Coffin could have seen the roof of Kotowski's house out the big front windows.

"So how long had you been in a relationship with Ms. Sole?" Lola said. She was sitting on the couch, a massive sectional in lime green silk.

"About two years," Stavros said. Twenty years ago—even ten—he would have been strikingly handsome: He still had the square chin and straight nose of a movie star. Now he was probably sixty, with a mane of silver hair and the beginnings of jowls. He wore a white suit and a bright green shirt, maybe two shades lighter than the couch. His voice was scratchy and thick; he spoke with a slight Mediterranean accent. "I was very fond of Kenji. She was an extraordinary woman."

"Extraordinary how?" Coffin said.

Stavros leaned forward. "Well, she was highly intelligent, for one thing, and funny—she had a lively sense of humor. I enjoyed her company a great deal. I'll be frank with you, officers. Sex with Kenji Sole was a transformative experience for me. I would have done anything she asked."

Coffin thought for a second. "What sorts of things did she ask you to do?"

"Well," Stavros said, adjusting his glasses, "I suppose that's a fair question. Experimental things, I'd say—at least for me. Light bondage, that sort of thing."

"Who was in charge? Kenji or you?"

"Kenji was. She was very definite about that. She had no interest whatsoever in playing the submissive role."

"That was all right with you?" Lola said.

"It was a revelation." Stavros leaned back, tapped a cigarette from the pack on the coffee table, and lit it. "It unlocked a whole side of my sexuality I never knew was there."

Coffin's left eyelid started to twitch. He touched it lightly with his fingertips. "Did you know she was filming you?"

"No," Stavros said, glasses glinting under the recessed lighting. "Not until Friday evening, when I found the note in the front seat of my car."

"Can we see it?" Lola said.

Stavros nodded. "It's in the bedroom," he said. "I'll be right back."

When he'd left the living room, Lola raised her eyebrows a bit. "Nice place," she said, half under her breath.

"He owns a ton of real estate in town," Coffin said. "Two hotels, a bunch of summer rentals, a restaurant, you name it. P'town's answer to Donald Trump."

"With much better hair," Lola said.

Stavros appeared in the doorway, holding a folded sheet of paper. "It's quite crudely done," he said. "Childish, almost. That's part of what makes it so creepy." He handed the paper to Coffin.

"'Check out spycamdomme.com,'" Coffin read. "'Password: avocado. Wait for more.' Written in bright orange crayon."

"That's it?" Lola said. She stood, looked over Coffin's shoulder.

"That's it," Stavros said.

"So you checked it out," Coffin said.

"I did. After nearly having a heart attack."

"The password," Lola said. "That was Kenji's safe word, right?"

"Right," Stavros said. "Not that I ever used it."

"So after you read the note—" Coffin prompted.

"After I read the note I went straight to my study—in a cold sweat, I don't have to tell you—and found the Web site. The first page was blank, just a black background and a box to type in a password."

"So you typed in 'avocado,'" Lola said.

"Right."

"And there you were?"

"There I was, along with five or six other guys, all these little film clips. My face was blurred out—all the faces were, including Kenji's—but of course I recognized myself right away."

"Recognize anybody else?"

"Honestly? I couldn't bring myself to watch the other clips."

Coffin rubbed his eyes. They felt gritty from lack of sleep. His eyelid twitched a few times, then settled down. "So there you were. Then what did you do?"

"Well, I was stunned. I didn't know what to do, honestly. I mean, at first I couldn't believe Kenji would do something like that. I felt so betrayed, you know?" Stavros's movie-star chin was quivering.

"Of course," Coffin said. "So then what? Did you call her? Drive out to her house?"

"I called her, though I had no idea what I was going to say. I mean, what *would* you say? It just seemed so crazy. I called her house and no one picked up. So I tried her cell."

"And?"

"No answer. So I left a frantic message, as you can imagine."

"That's it? You didn't drive out to confront her?"

"Well, that's the funny part. I did."

Coffin's eyelid twitched furiously. "You did?"

Stavros nodded. "I paced back and forth for a while, trying to decide what to do. I poured myself a scotch, smoked a couple of cigarettes. Ordinarily I'm not particularly averse to conflict, but the idea of confronting Kenji was very daunting somehow. Then, when I'd worked up my courage a bit, I got in the Porsche and drove out there."

Coffin nodded. People who owned Porsches always referred to them as "the Porsche," in his experience—never as "the car." "Okay," Coffin said. "You drove out there."

"I stopped at the bottom of the hill and pulled onto the shoulder. It was starting to rain, and the Porsche's top was down—like an idiot, all I could think of was the interior getting ruined. I hit the button; then I looked up at Kenji's house as the top was closing. All the lights were on. The place was just blazing. I'd never seen it like that before, I don't think. By then I was already having second thoughts—it was very unlikely she was alone. What would happen if I knocked on the door and she refused to answer? I'd feel like a fool. What if she *did* answer—could I still confront her if one of her other lovers was there?"

Coffin wanted to poke Stavros with a stick. Instead he said, "Go on."

"As I was driving up the hill I noticed a weird thing. There was a car parked on the side of the road, two wheels in the ditch. It's a very narrow drive—and steep. An awkward place to park. It struck me as odd, so I remembered it."

"What kind of car?"

Stavros shrugged. "I don't know the make. Some kind of sedan. Very anonymous looking—like a rent-a-car."

"Okay, so you drove up to Kenji's house . . ."

"Right. There was another vehicle in the drive—you know, between the house and the garage—and this one I did notice."

"A second car."

"Yes. A black one. A big Mercedes. Very impressive car."

Coffin's eye twitched. "So you saw the sedan parked on the hill. You saw the Mercedes. All the lights were on. Then what happened?"

Stavros chewed his lower lip. "I chickened out," he said. "I never even got out of the Porsche. I turned around in the drive and went home."

"Why didn't you contact us earlier?" Coffin said. "Surely you knew this was important information?"

"I thought it might be," Stavros said, "but I had hoped I might be able to save my marriage."

"So why now?"

"My wife left me after she found the second note." Stavros took his glasses off, rubbed a hand over his face, and put them back on. "Christ," he said. "I'm sixty-three years old. I've lived in Provincetown thirty-five years, almost. *All* my friends are gay, you know? Lovely people, all of them. Sometimes I think I'm practically gay myself, but I can't keep away from the pussy. It's my great weakness."

"The *second* note," Coffin said, eye twitching madly. "What second note?"

Stavros pulled a folded piece of paper from his shirt pocket. "This was left in my mailbox when I was out of town. My wife brought it in with the mail yesterday. Naturally, when I got home today, she wanted an explanation. I didn't have a very good one, I'm afraid."

"So she left?" Lola said.

"First she threw a very valuable pre-Columbian figurine at my head. Then she packed her bag and drove off in the Ferrari."

Good for her, Coffin wanted to say. He unfolded the paper. Unlike the first note, it had been printed on a laser or ink-jet printer. It was a detailed set of instructions that began "If you want your identity on spycam domme.com to be kept secret, you will bring fifty thousand dollars in cash to Herring Cove tomorrow night."

"I can see how this would be problematic for your wife," Coffin said.

"Tomorrow night?" Lola said. "Your wife got the note yesterday?"

"Right," Stavros said. "So tonight."

"Is that feasible? Could you raise fifty K overnight?"

"I could, yes," Stavros said. "I'd call the bank, order the cash, then go in the next day after the Brinks truck came and pick it up. I can't speak for any of the other gentlemen on that Web site, though."

"Not the world's most sophisticated blackmail operation," Lola said.

"Not if by leaving the note they cause the target's wife to leave him, no," Stavros said. "Not exactly."

"The drop's *tonight*," Coffin said. "At Herring Cove. 'Leave it in the trash at the far end of the parking lot,' it says. 'Exactly 10:30 P.M. Come alone. No cops.' It's like every blackmail operation on every bad detective show ever made."

"Yes."

Coffin leaned forward, slid a cigarette from Stavros's pack, and lit it. "You could redeem yourself somewhat, Mr. Stavros," he said, "if you were willing to help us catch your blackmailer."

Stavros smiled. His teeth were startlingly white. "Oh, hell yes," he said. "What do I have to do?"

Outside, in the Crown Vic, Lola started the engine, then turned and looked at Coffin. "Dude," she said. "What's up with your eye?"

"You can see it?" Coffin said. His eyelid twitched twice, then twice again.

"Uh, yeah," Lola said, "and it's freaking me out a little."

Coffin reached up, turned the rearview mirror, and peered at himself. "Jesus. I look like the crazy chief inspector in the old Pink Panther movies."

"If you say so," Lola said. "What's going on, do you think?"

"I don't know," Coffin said. "Stress, maybe. I haven't been sleeping very well."

"Uh-oh. More dreams?"

"You're pretty smart, you know that?" Coffin said. "Not the same ones, though. These are about the miscarriage. *A* miscarriage."

Lola put the Crown Vic into reverse and backed down Stavros's long, steep driveway. "I'm going to drop you off at your house. Your job is to get a couple hours of sleep. I assume we're going out to Herring Cove later tonight?"

"Absolutely. I'll call Tony and see if we can borrow his camper."

"We're going in a camper?" Lola said.

Coffin nodded, eyelid still twitching frantically. "Think of it as camouflage," he said.

SIXTEEN

There were two connected parking lots at Herring Cove: one large, more or less square lot that sat between the dunes and Province Lands Road, and one long, narrow lot just north of it that ran between the dunes and the beach. For most locals, the long, narrow lot was "the lot at Herring Cove"—the place they would go to sit in their cars and watch the occasional winter sunset, or to which they might sneak off late at night for an illicit tryst. It was also a popular spot in which to commit suicide, particularly during the long, dark days around the winter solstice, when Provincetown's population had shrunk to three thousand or so and it was dark by 5:00 P.M. Once or twice in a typical year, some forlorn visitor from off-Cape would drive to the far eastern end of the continent, park in the Herring Cove lot, and, as the sun sank into the blood red waters of Cape Cod Bay, put a pistol into his mouth and pull the trigger. Not that they were always from off-Cape: At the height of the AIDS epidemic in the late eighties, there had been a suicide every couple of months at Herring Cove for a period of several years. Almost all the Herring Cove suicides were clear-cut and routine, and almost all were cleaned up by Park Service rangers, a fact for which Coffin was mightily grateful.

On a Tuesday night in May, the lot was almost completely deserted; a few early tourists had parked their RVs near its midpoint, intending to do a bit of surf-casting at land's end (the water was still too cold for swimming, except for the hardiest of souls). Their campfires—for which they were required to have permits—wavered in the bay breeze. Twenty feet away, the small waves sloshed in the dark.

The far northern end of the lot was deserted and very dark. There was only one way out by car—back through the long, narrow lot and out the main entrance. It was a terrible place for a drop, Coffin knew. He tapped his fingers on the wheel of the battered motor home he'd borrowed from his cousin Tony: a boxy twenty-foot Travelcraft, circa 1977—the cabin still done up in the original sunflower yellow and avocado green. Lola sat next to him, fiddling with the night-vision binoculars she'd brought.

"Cavalo's a danger to himself and others," Coffin said. "This is the worst drop site ever."

"Assuming it's Cavalo," Lola said.

Coffin nodded. "Could be somebody else that has access to the video. Or somebody pretending they do."

"Either way," Lola said. "You'd have to be an idiot to set up a drop with only one exit. It's like they want to get caught."

Coffin looked at her. "Interesting thought," he said. "We'll see."

"How's your eye?"

"Fine," Coffin said, covering his eye with his hand.

"Move your hand."

"No."

Lola grinned, then looked at her watch. It was a chunky men's TAG Heuer, bought at an army PX in Germany. "T minus two minutes," she said.

A car turned at the parking kiosk and pulled into the

lot, rolling slowly over the speed bumps and past the half-dozen RVs and campers. It was a dark blue Porsche convertible.

"There's Stavros," Coffin said. "Right on cue."

Lola scanned the beach and dunes with the night-vision binoculars. "Still no sign of anybody lurking in the dunes. Bet you they just drive in and make the pickup."

"If they're idiots," Coffin said.

"I think we've already established that," Lola said.

Coffin picked up the handheld radio. "Jeff?" he said.

Officer Jeff Skillings was waiting just off the bike path, about ten yards into the dunes. He was dressed in bike shorts and a helmet; his mountain bike lay next to him. "Frank," he said, voice a low whisper.

"Anything?"

"Nope. Not a soul."

"We've got the drop," Coffin said, watching as Stavros parked the Porsche next to the trash can, removed the lid, placed a plastic grocery bag stuffed with what could very well have been cash inside, replaced the lid, got back into his car, and drove slowly away.

"Okeydoke," Skillings said.

"Frank?" Another voice crackled over the radio. It was Coffin's cousin Tony, stationed in the bushes on the far side of the outer lot. "We got a car coming in. Looks like a Range Rover."

"Got it," Coffin said as a pair of headlights swung into view at the entrance to the north lot.

Coffin and Lola scrunched down in their seats as the Range Rover passed behind them, slowed for the three big speed bumps, then rolled to a stop at the far end of the lot.

"Jeff," Coffin said, "I'll need you in about twenty

seconds. I'm going to let him get back in the vehicle before we move."

"On my way," Skillings said.

A man climbed out of the Range Rover, walked five steps to the trash can, lifted the lid, and removed the stuffed grocery bag. The man looked over his shoulder, paused, then climbed back into the Range Rover and started the engine.

Coffin turned the key in the RV's ignition. The starter ground; the engine coughed but failed to catch. "Fuck," Coffin said. "Come on." He pumped the gas, turned the key again, and the engine rumbled to life before stalling out.

Skillings appeared on his bike at the mouth of the trail and paused for a second, not sure what to do. The Range Rover was turning around at the end of the lot.

"Frank?" Lola said.

"Fucking *Tony*," Coffin said, eye twitching furiously as he turned the key again. This time the engine roared to life, and Coffin backed out, the RV's nose pointing north. The Range Rover was coming at them, taking the speed bumps effortlessly at about twenty-five miles per hour. Coffin dropped the RV into drive and goosed the accelerator a bit harder than he wanted to, closing the distance to a hundred yards in a hurry. Skillings was back on his bike, pedaling toward them.

Then, for the first time, the man driving the Range Rover seemed to realize he'd made a mistake. He swerved hard to his left, swung the Range Rover into a fast 180-degree turn, and then floored it, heading north again toward the beach—narrowly missing Skillings as he went by. Skillings went down in a heap, and Lola grabbed the radio.

"Tony Tony Tony!" she yelled. "Jeff's down! Call

rescue and backup and get your ass over here! We've got a Range Rover heading north on the beach! Jeff, you okay?"

"Fucking shit," Skillings said, scrambling back onto his bike. "I'm okay, but did you see that? The fucking guy almost killed me."

"Done," Tony said. He sounded out of breath, hoofing it to the cruiser concealed in the beach rose bushes at the edge of the south lot. "They're on their way. Fuck—I was taking a leak!"

"Fucking *fuck*!" Coffin said, stomping on the gas, hitting the speed bumps at forty-five, his head nearly banging the ceiling as the RV jounced and rattled over them, stowed pots and pans clanging in the small galley. "He had to be driving a fucking *Range* Rover!"

The Range Rover slowed a bit at the end of the parking lot, climbed a concrete curb as though it weren't there, then accelerated again down the beach, heading toward Hatch's Harbor. The tide was up; there were only about ten feet of beach between the water and the steep, loose rise of the dunes. Coffin slowed to a near stop, hoping the RV wouldn't bottom out as it waddled over the curb, frame groaning. When the back wheels cleared he punched the gas again, already two hundred yards behind the Range Rover with little hope of catching up.

"He's going to run out of beach pretty soon," Lola said. "Once he gets to Hatch's Harbor there's no place to go but into the dunes."

"If he can drive that thing he might be able to make it out to the road," Coffin said, his voice coming out quavery and strange as the camper jounced over the rutted beach.

"Doubtful," Lola said, hanging on to the armrest, left arm braced on the dash. "Most people can't drive for shit."

The Range Rover's brake lights glowed suddenly red, and then brake lights, taillights, and all vanished abruptly.

"There go his lights," Lola said. "Think he turned them off?"

"If he's a moron," Coffin said, hoping the top-heavy camper wouldn't bog down or roll.

"Idiot. Moron," Lola said. "Same thing, right?"

"Here we go," Coffin said. The camper's weak headlights had picked up the Range Rover: It lay half in the water on its side, wheels still spinning. The man was trying to climb out of the passenger door but was having trouble levering himself up and out with the grocery bag clutched in one hand.

Coffin tromped on the brake, and Lola jumped out as the camper slid to a clattering stop. She had her .38 pointed at the man's head and the safety thumbed off before Coffin's boots hit the sand.

"Police," Coffin said. "If you try to run away again, Sergeant Winters will shoot you."

"Oh, thank God," the man said, dropping the bag and putting his hands up. He was slender and very blond. "I thought you were that fucking maniac Duckworth."

"You're Jordan?" Coffin said when the man was sitting cross-legged in the sand, hands cuffed behind his back. "Cavalo's boyfriend?" He clicked off Tony's flashlight and tucked the man's ID back into his wallet.

Tony was still bent over, trying to catch his breath. He'd bogged the cruiser in the sand just north of the parking lot and run the half mile or so to the edge of Hatch's Harbor. Skillings and Lola were searching the inside of the Range Rover.

"I don't care who the fuck he is," Tony said, wheezing a little. "I'd like to kick his ass for making me run all the fucking way out here in the sand. My calves are killing me."

"We've got a gun!" Lola said. "Big-ass Colt in the glove compartment."

"What were you doing with a gun, Jordan?" Coffin said.

Jordan sniffled faintly. "I told you—I was worried that lunatic Duckworth would show up. God. I'm in a lot of trouble, aren't I?"

"Oh, yeah," Coffin said. "Big-time."

SEVENTEEN

"Cigarette?" Coffin said when they'd installed Jordan in the PPD's only interrogation room: a windowless, fluorescent-lit space slightly bigger than a closet, with scuffed green linoleum on the floor and just enough room for a steel-legged table and three chairs.

"Oh, God yes," Jordan said. Lola had just removed his handcuffs; his wrists were chafed and red.

Coffin slid a pack of Camel Lights across the table. Jordan tapped one out, and Coffin lit it for him.

"Thanks," Jordan said. "I don't suppose there's any chance of a cocktail to go with it?" He had a soft, slow accent that was half Deep South, half Brooklyn. New Orleans, Coffin thought.

Coffin took a pint of vodka from his jacket pocket and set it on the table. "We'll see," he said. "If you're good."

"Oh, I'm good," Jordan said, exhaling a blue stream of smoke. "I'm very, *very* good." He was five foot six or so, very slender. His hair was dyed yellow-blond. The Range Rover's air bag had blackened his left eye and bruised his cheek when it deployed.

Coffin put his elbows on the table. He watched Jordan for a long minute. "Why are you so afraid of Duckworth?" he said finally.

"Well, sweet baby Jesus," Jordan said, hand shaking

a bit as he took a long drag from his cigarette. "Have you seen him? Have you actually looked into his eyes? That mofo's one extra crispy bucket of crazy, and that's no joke."

"That's it? His eyes?"

"That and that pig-sticker of his. It wasn't just me: Bobby was scared of him, too. Real scared."

"Was?" Lola said. "Past tense?"

Jordan's unblackened eye widened a bit. The unbruised side of his face went pale.

"Has something happened to Bobby?" Coffin said.

Jordan's face crumpled; he started to cry. "I don't know," he said.

"What do you mean, you don't know?" Lola said.

Coffin twisted the cap off of the pint of vodka and slid it across the table. "Tell us the part you *do* know, Jordan."

"Right," Jordan said. "Good idea." He took a swallow of vodka. "I saw Bobby and Duckworth together. Last night, in Bobby's apartment."

"What were they doing?"

"Dancing."

Lola frowned. "*Dancing?* That's what you saw?"

"Yeah—some kind of Latin dancing. Salsa or something. I saw them through the window."

Coffin frowned. "*Dancing?*" he said. "You saw dancing and immediately suspected foul play? What—you never saw Bobby dance before?"

Jordan nodded rapidly, then shook his head. "No. Right. Exactly."

Coffin and Lola both raised their eyebrows.

"*Never?*" Coffin said.

Jordan frowned. "What is that, like a stereotype? All gay men just live to disco?"

"Sorry," Lola said.

"Bobby *hated* dancing," Jordan said. "You couldn't get him out on the dance floor if you held a gun to his head—I don't care how drunk he was. No way, no how. That's how I knew something weird was going on."

"So, what, you went to his apartment—"

"I went looking for him—he wasn't picking up his phone, so yeah, I went to his apartment. Thinking maybe we'd go out for a nightcap or something. I was on his front porch, about to open the door. There was music on inside, loud—like, *Latin* music. That was weird, too. So I looked in the window."

"And Bobby and Duckworth were dancing?"

"Well, sort of. Part dancing, part Bobby getting tossed around like a rag doll. Part Bobby looking miserable—and scared. I never saw him look scared before, really. It made *me* scared."

"Then what did you do?"

"I ran. *Ran* down that fucking hill to my bike—in flip-flops! I almost killed myself! I rode back into town as fast as my little legs would pedal. I was spooked, I don't mind telling you."

"And then?"

"Well, I didn't know *what* to do. Call the cops? Tell them what? I decided I should get the hell out of Dodge, but I didn't have any money. Like, none, practically." Jordan shook his head. "God. I suck at blackmail."

"Probably a good thing to know about yourself," Lola said.

"Let's back up a minute," Coffin said. "You were ready to skip town because of what, exactly?"

Jordan took another drink. "I got mixed up with a bent cop in New Orleans, when I was a teenager. He beat me up a few times, raped me. Then he turned me out. I tricked from one end of the Quarter to the other for almost a year; damn near killed me."

"You were a prostitute?" Lola said.

"That's right, honey," Jordan said. "I was a teenage rent-a-boy. I had a hell of a time getting away from that son of a bitch. I still have nightmares. When I saw Duckworth dancing with Bobby that way, and the fear in Bobby's eyes, it was like déjà vu all over again. I figured if it could happen to Bobby, it could sure as hell happen to little old me."

"Okay," Coffin said. "I get it now. Then what happened?"

"I went back to my room real quick and typed the note. Then I left it in Stavros's mailbox. I had a few drinks in town and spent the night at a friend's place. The rest is history."

"Did you think of checking on Bobby? I mean, you were worried, right?"

"I did. I rode out there around noon."

"And?"

"He was gone. I mean *gone* gone. His suitcase was gone, too—and a lot of his clothes. Like he'd just thrown a few things in a bag and boogie-oogie-oogied."

Coffin and Lola exchanged a look.

"That when you picked up the Range Rover?" Coffin said.

Jordan nodded. "The keys were in it." He paused, then shrugged elaborately. "I mean, hey—you can't blackmail somebody on a *bicycle*, right?"

"Tell me about spycamdomme.com," Coffin said. "How did Cavalo get the video?"

"He pretty much had the run of Kenji's house," Jordan said. "He'd house-sit when she was out of town, which was a lot. He'd poke around on her computer when he was over there. Kind of like going to somebody's house and looking through their medicine cabinet—not that he didn't do that, too. He must have stumbled across her porn stash."

"He saw an opportunity?" Lola said.

"Bingo," Jordan said. "Bobby had kind of a moral blind spot, if you know what I mean. If he saw an opportunity to make some money, he'd exploit his own mother. So he burned some of Kenji's dominatrix stuff onto a DVD and took it home. He called me right away."

"Then what? You went over to his apartment and helped him set up spycamdomme.com?"

"I went over to his apartment and tried to talk him out of it."

"Why's that?"

Jordan's eyes teared up again. "Because it seemed like a good way to get yourself killed. We were doing fine with hungarianchicks.com—there was no need to get greedy."

"But Bobby insisted?"

"Yeah, man. He kept saying what a gold mine it was going to be—that we could have five or six guys paying us off for years."

"How many of those notes did he send out? The crayon ones?"

"Three or four. He delivered them. Except for the one to the attorney general—that one he mailed."

Coffin's eyebrows went up. "Attorney general," he said.

Jordan nodded. "Art Poblano—attorney general for the state of Massachusetts," he said.

"So Bobby delivered them. When?"

"Friday. He left them where he thought only the targets would find them."

"He delivered all of them the same day?" Lola said. "What was he thinking?"

Jordan shook his head. "I don't know. He was crazy. Maybe not so smart, like you say. He wouldn't listen to anybody."

"Cavalo was going to blackmail the attorney general?" Lola said.

"Not by himself," Jordan said. "That crazy Rudy was helping him."

"Why did he need Rudy's help?" Coffin asked.

"Bobby was no brainiac, but he had enough street smarts to know when he was out of his league."

Coffin and Lola exchanged a look.

"Or not," Coffin said.

Lola tapped her pen against the legal pad. "How did you know Duckworth's name?" she said.

"I met him," Jordan said. "He came to Bobby's apartment—he was with the police chief, what's his name. Red-faced guy."

"Boyle," Coffin said.

"Right," Jordan said. "Boyle." He took a last, long gurgling drink of the cheap vodka and set the bottle down carefully on the table. "Maybe I'm just really, *really* paranoid," he said, "but I don't think so. That Duckworth guy is creepy as hell. I mean, have you seen that pink jacket of his? Who would *wear* that, even in P'town?"

Bobby Cavalo's apartment was dark inside; the blinds had been lowered. When Coffin knocked, no one answered. The door was unlocked. Coffin pushed it open.

Lola felt for the grip of her .38. "Pretty fucking creepy," she whispered.

"No kidding," Coffin said, stepping into Cavalo's living room. He flipped the light switch but nothing happened.

Lola slid the Maglite out of her utility belt, switched

it on, and swept its focused beam slowly around the living room. The apartment was tidy, almost unnaturally clean. It smelled faintly of bleach, Coffin thought.

"Trying to make it look like he skipped town," Lola said. The night had grown humid; her shirt was spotted with sweat on the back.

Coffin stuck his head into the bedroom; again the light switch did nothing. "Yep—but Duckworth got it wrong. Cavalo was a slob. He wouldn't have left it this way."

Lola trained the flashlight beam on the bed: It was neatly made. The wicker trash can had been emptied. They checked the bathroom. Cavalo's toothbrush and razor were gone, as though he'd packed them for a trip.

"Frank," Lola said, when they'd checked the bedroom and hall closets. She was standing in the living room, shining the Maglite on the futon. A quilt had been spread over its wooden frame, a cluster of throw pillows neatly arranged at one end.

"No mattress," Coffin said, a high, sharp whine starting in his left ear. He pushed the pillows onto the floor and pulled off the quilt. The bleach smell was strong. "Put your light on the wall for a second," Coffin said. He pointed. "See here?"

"That part's lighter than the rest," Lola said. "Like somebody scrubbed something off the paint."

"Right," Coffin said.

"Not good," Lola said, lips pressed tight.

Coffin's vision was starting to blur. "No," he said. "Not good. Not good at all."

When Mancini arrived, Coffin was sitting on Cavalo's front steps, smoking a cigarette. Lola was inside the apartment. She'd found a working floor lamp and was taking digital pictures of the futon frame, the wall, and the flecks of blood they'd found along the baseboard. Her preliminary search for a weapon had turned up a number of possibilities—kitchen knives, a hatchet in the wood-box by the fireplace—but nothing conclusive.

"You don't look so good, Coffin," Mancini said, climbing out of his Lexus. Pilchard, the state police detective, climbed out on the passenger side. He was wearing a brown suit, brown shoes, a brown patterned tie, and light brown socks.

"Thanks," Coffin said, "for pointing that out. I thought I looked a little like George Clooney in *O Brother, Where Art Thou?*"

"Kind of," Mancini said, "but greener and a lot less handsome."

"Where's your girlfriend?" Pilchard said.

Coffin looked at him blankly. "Girlfriend?"

Pilchard leered. "You know. Lesbo the Super Cop."

"Do you work at being a dick," Coffin said, "or does it just happen all by itself?"

"So am I understanding this right?" Mancini said, gelled hair hardly stirring in the night breeze. "You think the pretty-boy tenant got whacked?"

"Looks that way," Coffin said. "We have a witness in custody that says Duckworth did it."

"Duckworth?" Mancini said, cocking his head. "The AG's investigator? Why the fuck would he kill Cavalo?"

"If I had to guess," Coffin said, "I'd say he was after the DVR."

"This *is* getting complicated." Mancini frowned and scratched his head.

"Careful," Coffin said. "You'll ruin your do."

Later, Coffin sat on his screen porch listening to the small late-spring night sounds: the wind in the neighbor's arborvitae; a june bug flinging its hard pellet of a body against the screen. Jamie was in bed—asleep, he hoped. It had been a long day, and he wasn't sure he was ready for another urgent bout of baby-making sex. What he wanted, more than anything, was to sit alone in the dark on his quiet screen porch, drink Johnny Walker, and concentrate his full attention on the faint mustiness of the Scotch broom blooming in his garden and the throat-gripping sweetness of the wisteria wrestling his neighbor's porch. He wanted to not think about babies, or miscarriages, or Lola having hot lesbian sex, or his mother, or dead women lying naked and bloody on their living room rugs. He lit a cigarette, yawned, and kicked off his boots.

A large, dark shape reared slowly up from behind the tangle of roses on the trellis. "Ssst! Frankie!" it said.

Coffin jumped. "*Fuck*."

"It's me," the shape said in a harsh stage whisper. "The little woman in bed?"

"Rudy," Coffin said. "Christ, you scared the crap out of me." He stood and pushed the screen door open.

Coffin's uncle Rudy stepped onto the porch. He was a big man, hulking and thick through the chest and neck. He was almost sixty; his leather jacket smelled like sweat and marijuana smoke. "Surprised to see me?" he said. "You shouldn't be. Got any more whiskey?"

Coffin went to the kitchen, dropped a couple of ice cubes into a glass, and grabbed the bottle of scotch. When he got back to the porch, Rudy was sitting in his seat, rolling a joint on the end table's warped top. "Thanks, Frankie," Rudy said. "Fill 'er up, there's a boy."

Coffin poured. "Okay, I'm done being startled," he said. "What brings you to town? Things a little slow down in Key West?"

"It's a business venture," Rudy said, lighting the joint. The screen porch filled with the sharp cat-funk of marijuana smoke. "A potential gold mine, as a matter of fact."

"Is it legal?" Coffin said.

"What is it with you?" Rudy said. "Why do you always ask me that?"

"Well, is it?"

Rudy took a long toke from the joint, held it, then let the smoke seep slowly from his mouth. "Well, no. Not technically. But what does legal have to do with anything? It's legal for Bush to eavesdrop on law-abiding citizens or torture kids in some Iraqi prison, but if you or I smoke a little weed we go to jail? That's the system you judge things by? That's some fucked-up shit, Frankie."

"Count me out," Coffin said.

"But Frankie—"

"No."

"What if I told you I've got what you're looking for?"

Coffin put his glass down. "*What?*"

"The video thingy. You want it, I've got it."

"You trashed Lola's place? Man, is she gonna be pissed at *you*."

"Ha," Rudy said, licking his fingertips before he snuffed the joint between his thumb and forefinger. "Think she can take me?"

"In a fair fight, yes."

"Who said anything about fair? But no, I didn't trash her place. Didn't have to."

"So who did?"

"The two knuckle-draggers I stole that fancy VCR from, obviously. Jesus, Frankie—try to catch up, already."

"Okay," Coffin said. "Let's slow down for a minute. You just happened to be outside Lola's apartment—"

"You could say that, sure," Rudy said. "I just happened to be parked across the street there, minding my own business, and right after you and the Amazon princess left, these two apes get out of their ride and let themselves into the apartment. I had a look at their plates just for the hell of it: state government, baby."

"Whoa," Coffin said. "So they were what? State police?"

"Maybe," Rudy said. "I didn't ask, and they didn't tell."

"You robbed the state police?"

Rudy rolled his eyes. "Robbed. See? There you go again with your value judgments."

"What, they just gave it to you?"

Rudy pulled a slim leather wallet from his pocket and flipped it open. "After I showed them this, they were happy to oblige." He shrugged. "Okay, maybe happy's the wrong word."

Coffin looked at the badge inside the wallet. "U.S. Marshals? You told state police detectives you were a *U.S. Marshal*?"

Rudy shrugged. "They believed me, that's their problem. Besides, what were they going to do? They figured they were lucky I didn't bust them for B and E."

Coffin tapped the badge. It was gold and appeared to be genuine: a five-pointed star set inside a circular band, Department of Justice eagle at the center. "Where did you get this?"

Rudy shrugged. "I found it."

"*Found* it?"

Rudy's nostrils flared. "That's right, Frankie—I *found* it. As in, it was lying on the floor and I picked it up. As in, the *opposite* of stealing."

"Keeping something that somebody lost is the opposite of stealing?" Coffin said.

"You know what I mean."

"So whose floor was it lying on, exactly?"

Rudy grinned. "I can't tell you that, Frankie. Privileged information."

They sat for a long moment in silence. A june bug fizzed against the screen.

"Why would the state police trash Lola's place and steal the DVR?" Coffin said finally. "How did they even know we had it?"

"They stole it because they wanted what was on it," Rudy said. "Or because they wanted to protect somebody. They knew you had it because they saw you take it out of Kenji's house. Either that, or somebody else saw you and told them."

Coffin rubbed his chin. He hadn't shaved since early that morning; his beard stubble was mostly gray now, its texture spiky and dense. "How did they know it existed in the first place?" he said.

"Frankie," Rudy said, patting Coffin on the shoulder. "Seriously. Try to catch up. Who do the state police work for? Who would have the authority to send them out on little errands like this?"

"The governor. The attorney general. The DA's offices. Various officers within the state police. That's about it." Coffin hit himself in the forehead. "Poblano?" he said. "Poblano sent them?"

"Poblano. Mancini. Who knows?" Rudy said. "You understand what I mean now when I say this thing is a potential gold mine. Somebody powerful wants it, and they want it bad."

"But you're going to give it back to me," Coffin said. "Why? And in exchange for what, exactly?"

Rudy draped a heavy arm around Coffin's shoulders and gave him a rough squeeze. "Frankie. Buddy! We're family, you and me. We've gotta stick together!"

"You've already copied all the video to your own hard drive, haven't you?" Coffin said.

Rudy sighed. "Frankie. This hurts me. We're blood, for God's sake."

"You're my father's sister's ex-husband," Coffin said. "We're not blood."

"Whatever. You're such a stickler. Your old man and I were like this." Rudy held up two crossed fingers.

"What do you want, Rudy?" Coffin said.

"Twenty minutes in Kenji's house. Alone."

"For what?"

"Can't tell you."

"Forget it," Coffin said. "Absolutely not."

"Have you watched the part of the video where the guy trashes Kenji's bedroom?" Rudy said. "I gave it two thumbs up."

Coffin finished his scotch and poured another half inch into his glass. "Three conditions," he said. "First, you get five minutes, not twenty."

"Frankie," Rudy said, "I could just break in if all I needed was five minutes. You think PPD's going to get a cruiser there in five minutes, if the alarm even goes off?"

"Okay. Ten. Not a minute longer."

"Fine."

"Second, if you take anything out of that house that's relevant to my investigation, I will personally put you in jail for breaking and entering, theft, and tampering with a crime scene."

"Ha! You don't have the stones."

"Watch me," Coffin said. "My word against yours."

"What's number three?"

"Whatever it is you're after, once you get your mitts on it, you never, ever tell anyone where it came from."

"Done," said Rudy.

"All right," Coffin said, standing up, dusting a few specks of wisteria pollen from his pants. "Let's go before I come to my senses."

EIGHTEEN

The night had grown cloudy and still; a thin fog hung at about roof height outside Kenji Sole's house. Back across the harbor the lights of the town center seemed to twinkle and shift in the slight wind. All the lights were out in Kenji's house; Bobby Cavalo's windows were dark, too. It was very quiet, except for the small sounds of the harbor and the occasional car whooshing by on 6A.

Coffin drummed his fingers on the Fiesta's steering wheel. He peered at his watch. Rudy had been gone for almost seventeen minutes, and Coffin was beginning to worry. Big, affable, dangerous Rudy; Rudy the loose cannon. There was no telling what he was searching for in there: Bricks of heroin? A stash of blood diamonds? More video of God knows what? Coffin lit a cigarette and blew a thick stream of smoke out the window. "Come on, Rudy," he said under his breath. "Let's get the fuck out of here, already."

As if on cue, Rudy's big head appeared in the passenger window. "Got it," he said. He was cradling something flat and rectangular in his big arms: It was wrapped in a towel, and about the size of a small flat-screen TV. Coffin reached across and opened the passenger door, and Rudy climbed in. "You won't regret this, Frankie," Rudy said. "Just so you know. I owe you one."

"What is it?" Coffin said, starting the car. "Or do I not want to know?"

"This?" Rudy said, giving the towel-wrapped object a gentle shake. He pursed his lips. "It's a Pollock."

"A pollock? Like the fish?"

Rudy shook his big head. "Frankie," he said. "I swear to God. You need to move back to Baltimore. Living in this town is making you stupid."

"A *Jackson* Pollock? A painting?"

"Bingo. The real deal. This thing is legendary. Worth several hundred large, minimum. When I spotted it in the video I knew I had to get in and grab it before that scumbag DA figured out what it was."

"What do you mean, it's legendary?"

"Pollock used to hang out here in the forties. That was when he first started doing the drip thing, but he wasn't famous yet. He was broke most of the time, and he liked to drink and play cards. If he owed you money, he'd give you a small painting to make good on the debt. That's where this baby's from."

"How do you know all this?" Coffin said, turning right on 6A and heading toward the town center. "What, you're an art historian now?"

Rudy grinned. "Like I said, this thing is legendary. Pollock owed a couple hundred bucks to Stinky Mayo—lost it to him in a poker game. Couple hundred bucks was a lot of money in '47. Pollock gives Stinky the painting, they call it even. Stinky doesn't know squat about art, though—thinks the painting's the ugliest fucking thing in the world. Ends up trading it to Bucky Morales for doing some work on his boat. Bucky loves the thing—he sees the genius of it, puts it up on the wall of his house. Then *Life* magazine does a feature on Pollock, and suddenly the painting's worth some serious cash. Dealers show up at Bucky's house, trying to buy it. He won't part with it, no matter what. Then, about a year later, Bucky's house catches fire and pretty much burns to the ground with him in it. Bucky gets incinerated, and everybody thinks the painting does, too. There's even a piece in the *Cape Cod Times* about it."

"But it doesn't get burned up," Coffin said.

"Nope," Rudy said. "It doesn't. The fire starts in Bucky's room—smoking in bed, probably. It doesn't spread to the kitchen where the painting is until later. One of the firemen sees the painting, has an idea what it is, and lifts it before the whole place goes up in flames."

"Jesus," Coffin said. "Some story."

"Yeah," Rudy said. "People don't like to think about firemen looting shit out of burning houses, but it happens all the time. Know who that fireman was?"

"I'm afraid to ask," Coffin said.

"As well you should be," Rudy said. "It was my father, your great-uncle Manny Santos, who you never met but who was a fucking pistol, I don't mind telling you."

"So how did Kenji end up with it?"

Rudy shrugged. "Pops was no fool. He knew somebody who knew somebody who was willing to buy it under the table. Probably only got a fraction of what it was worth, but it was still a pretty good chunk of change. Then it moved around from rich asshole to rich asshole until it wound up with Kenji Sole. The way I see it—"

"Don't say it, Rudy," Coffin said, fingers tightening on the steering wheel.

"No, seriously. The way I—"

Coffin pressed down on the accelerator. The Fiesta responded with a loud backfire. "If you say that painting is rightfully yours I'm going to wreck this car, I swear to God."

Rudy looked at Coffin and put his seat belt on. "That painting is rightfully mine. My father stole it, it belongs to me. Until I sell it, of course."

Coffin said nothing for a long minute. It was almost 3:00 A.M., and there was no traffic on Bradford Street. The Fiesta's one working headlight flickered, went out, came back on. Overhead, the clouds were moving out to sea in a hurry, herded along by a freshening wind.

"Rudy?"

"Yes?"

"You knew where the painting was, right?"

"Yep. Hanging in the bedroom, over the dresser. Just like in the video."

"You were in there for seventeen minutes. What took you so long?"

Rudy shook his head. "Frankie," he said, "we've got to talk about the lack of trust here. It hurts me, it really does." He fished his flask from his jacket pocket, uncapped it, and took a long swallow. Then he offered it to Coffin.

"This is my scotch, isn't it, Rudy?" Coffin said, taking a drink.

"Yeah. I don't know why you buy this fucking blended stuff," Rudy said, taking the flask back from Coffin and emptying it in one long swallow. "Life's too short to drink cheap booze, Frankie."

Coffin slowed, then pulled the car off the road into the parking lot of the Tennis Club. He killed the lights but left the engine running. "I must be losing my fucking mind, Rudy," Coffin said. He sat back in his seat and looked at his uncle under lowered brows.

"Uh-oh," Rudy said, lighting a cigarette. "Must be serious if you can't talk and drive at the same time."

"How did *you* know about the DVR, Rudy? The state cops knew, but so did you. How?"

"Educated guess." Rudy shrugged. "Based on what I'd heard from Cavalo."

"Cavalo? What's your connection to Cavalo?"

"WitSec. He thinks I'm his minder."

"Wait a minute," Coffin said, holding up both hands, palms out. "Just hold on. Cavalo's in the witness security program?"

"Check."

"The *federal* witness protection program."

Rudy nodded. "Right. He got mixed up with some mob boys out in Vegas. Saw some stuff he shouldn't have seen, ended up testifying in federal court."

"He thinks you're a federal marshal assigned to his case?"

"Right again."

"Why does he think that, Rudy?"

Rudy spread his big hands. "Because that's what I told him," he said. "The badge helped."

"The one you found," Coffin said.

"Right. Cavalo's no fucking Albert Einstein. Doesn't get a lot of blood to the brain, if you know what I mean."

"And you knew he was in WitSec because . . . ?"

"I hear things, Frankie," Rudy said. "People talk in this town. What else is there to do in the off-season?" He put a hand on Coffin's shoulder. "Which reminds me—how's the fertility thing going? Any luck?"

"You're freaking me out a little," Coffin said.

"Good," Rudy said. "I like to maintain an air of mystery."

"So you heard Cavalo was in WitSec and what, you figured you could exploit him?"

" 'Exploit' is such an ugly word. Besides, you've got it all wrong. I heard about his porn operation, then I heard about WitSec, *then* I figured maybe he needed a business partner." Rudy pointed at the keys dangling from the ignition, then tapped his watch. "Can we drive now? I've got an appointment with a young lady."

"At 3:00 A.M.? An appointment? What kind of young lady are we talking about here?"

Rudy looked at him, eyes glinting in the dark car.

"Forget I asked," Coffin said. He restarted the Fiesta and pulled out of the parking lot onto Bradford.

"I've been thinking about this whole deal with the hidden camera," Rudy said after a minute or two. "If it wasn't about outright blackmail, it was probably a control thing—do what I say, or I'll expose you. If not control, security. She wanted to have something on them. The whole crew."

"Security?"

"She must have known she was playing a dangerous game," Rudy said. "People have feelings—they get jealous, they get angry, they do crazy shit. Hell, I can't even manage one relationship, let alone twenty."

Coffin passed Conwell Street and the Yankee Mart, then turned right on Standish. "So she wanted them on tape because she couldn't trust them?"

"Something like that. Or maybe it was just a trophy-taking thing. She wanted to have a personal record of her conquests. People do that shit, you know. Another notch in the bedpost, or whatever. I mean, she was into porn in a big way. Why not make some of her own?"

"So she filmed the same scenario over and over—"

"Because that's the thing that turned her on."

Coffin pulled up in front of his house and turned the engine off. The Fiesta shuddered and clanked for a few seconds before it finally died.

"So what *were* you doing in there, all that time?" Coffin said.

"That's what I love about you, Frankie," Rudy said, squeezing Coffin's shoulder. "Always asking questions." He dug his thumb into the pressure point hard enough to make Coffin's eyes bulge, then opened the door and levered his broad frame out of the Fiesta's passenger seat, the towel-wrapped painting under his arm. "Well, it's been fun, Frankie. *Hasta con carne.*"

"Rudy?"

"Yo."

"The DVR. Hand it over."

Rudy grinned. "Right. Almost forgot." He crossed the street, unlocked the blue Chevy pickup truck he'd borrowed from his son, Tony, and put the painting inside. Then he reached into the passenger seat and pulled out a cardboard box. "Here you go, Frankie," he said, setting the box down on the Fiesta's hood. "If I was you, I'd skip to the end and watch the last ten minutes or so. Tonight, before somebody else steals this thing."

Coffin stood on the screen porch, fumbled a bit with his keys, and unlocked the front door. He had been born and raised in Provincetown and had been back for almost fourteen years now after living in Baltimore for a decade. In Provincetown he had never locked his house, even at night—nor had his parents nor anyone he knew—but ever since the incident two years ago with Duffy Plotz, whenever he left Jamie home alone at night he made sure to lock the door.

When he let himself in, the living room was dark. A small bronze clock ticked on the mantel. The stuffed goat's head leered down from the shadows, yellow-eyed, deranged. He set the cardboard box on the coffee table. Something stirred beside him, and Coffin turned the hair on his arms prickling.

"Frank?" It was Jamie. She'd fallen asleep on the sofa. She sat up slowly, pushing her hair away from her face. She was wearing one of Coffin's white T-shirts; her nipples showed dark through the thin cotton "What time is it? Where were you?"

"It's late. After three. Let's go to bed."

Coffin held out his hands; Jamie took them, hauled herself off the couch, then collapsed slowly into Coffin's arms. "Bed," she said, nuzzling into Coffin's neck; on her tiptoes she stood three inches shorter than he "Good thinking."

Coffin's hand grazed her hip. She wasn't wearing any panties.

Jamie looked up at him and placed both of his hands firmly on her backside. "But seriously," she said. "Where were you?"

"Out," Coffin said. "With Rudy."

"Oh," she said, nibbling Coffin's earlobe. "Jesus. Rudy."

"Yeah," Coffin said, leading Jamie up the stairs. "You know things are about to get weird when Rudy shows up."

"Weird*er*," Jamie said. She pinched Coffin's buttock "You know, you're still pretty perky for an old guy."

"Thanks," Coffin said. "Thanks a lot."

At the top of the stairs, Jamie put her arms around Coffin from behind and began to unbutton his shirt. "I was wondering," she said, "if you had any plans at the moment." Her hands were slender, the fingers long and articulate.

"You were?"

Jamie unbuckled Coffin's belt. "I was."

"I thought you might be."

"I'm predictable like that," Jamie said, unbuttoning

Coffin's khakis with one hand, sliding the other into his boxer shorts.

"There is one thing," Coffin said.

"Really?"

"That box in the living room—"

Jamie grazed the head of his penis with her fingernails. "You didn't just say that, did you?"

"Me? No." Coffin said. He turned, kissed her on the mouth, then grabbed a handful of her T-shirt and pulled her into the bedroom.

Fifteen minutes later, Jamie looked over her shoulder at Coffin as he knelt behind her. "Everything okay back there, cowboy?"

"Sorry," Coffin said, giving her rump a pat. "Just getting a little leg cramp." He shook his leg a bit. "There— all better."

Five minutes after that, Jamie turned and looked at Coffin again. "Another leg cramp?" she said.

"Sorry," Coffin said. "I must be tired."

Jamie wiggled her backside against his pelvis. "Come on, little man," she said. "Give me your sperm."

"Maybe we could try a different position."

"No, no, no," Jamie said. "How many times do I have to tell you? Doggy-style makes boy babies. Everyone says so. Now giddyup—my eggs aren't getting any younger, you know."

Three minutes later, Jamie turned and said, "You *must* be tired. Need a little jump-start?"

"I need sleep," Coffin said, flopping onto his back. Outside, the sky had paled at the edges; birds were waking up, whistling back and forth in the trees.

"Apparently so does this guy," Jamie said, rolling onto her side, stroking his slack penis lightly with her index finger.

"Sorry," Coffin said. He took a cigarette from the pack on the nightstand and lit it; they were Jamie's organic brand—the kind that weren't supposed to kill you as quickly.

Jamie smiled. "You should be," she said, turning onto her belly, "but I forgive you. This time."

Coffin blew a stream of blue smoke toward the ceiling. "Ever been curious about the whole dominant-submissive thing?"

"Mmmmm," Jamie said, rolling her hips a bit. "School-girl outfits and riding crops? When do we start?"

"Really?"

"Oh, yeah."

"I had no idea."

"Well, you never asked me until now. A girl doesn't just volunteer these things, you know."

"What about the other way around?"

Jamie laughed. "You mean if *you* were wearing the schoolgirl outfit? Is there something you'd like to tell me, Frank?"

"Not *me* in particular," Coffin said. "What I mean is, would it excite you to be the dominant one?"

Jamie propped herself up on her elbows. "Maybe. If I could keep a straight face. Would I get to wear a leather bustier and thigh boots?"

"Sure. Why not?"

Jamie jiggled a cigarette out of the pack, looked at it, and put it back in. "Actually, no. I don't think so."

"How come?"

"It's complicated," Jamie said. "For me, I think it's kind of about control—it's exciting to let go of that for a while, but I'm not really interested in controlling anyone else. You know? It just seems like too much work, somehow."

Coffin told her about Kenji Sole, how she'd filmed the same scenario over and over with a dozen different men. "It was obsessive," Coffin said. "Like a test they had to pass."

"That's pretty weird," Jamie said. "Like she was hazing them, almost. But why did she film them? Why did they let her?"

"Mostly I think they didn't know." He sat up and stubbed out his cigarette in the art deco glass ashtray he'd inherited from his father: a naked girl in a bathtub, knees up, breasts floating, head thrown back. "I'm not sure why she filmed them. Rudy thought it was a control thing. Either that or trophy-taking."

"The first thing makes the most sense to me," Jamie said. "It comes back to control. If they didn't do what she wanted them to do, she'd expose them."

"So it was her way of keeping them on a leash, you think?"

Jamie rolled onto her back, and pulled up the covers. "I think it was her way of keeping them," she said, closing her eyes. "Period."

"Frank! Frank! Oh my God!"

It was Jamie. Coffin tried to get out of bed, but his arms and legs felt rubbery and weak. "What is it?" he said. "Jamie? What's wrong?"

"Oh my God! It's everywhere!*"*

Coffin lurched down the hallway. The floorboards rippled and warped under his feet. "Jamie? Jamie, are you okay?"

She stood in the bathroom, nightgown pulled up above her waist. The light was impossibly green. She was covered with blood. Blood on her legs, on her belly. Blood in the toilet. Everywhere, blood. "Oh my God!" Jamie sobbed. She seemed unable to move. "Frank! Oh my God!"

Coffin was dizzy; the side of his face tingled. He reached for one of the white towels on the rack. The towel seemed to shrink from his hand. When he touched it, a dark spot of blood welled through the cloth. "It's okay," Coffin said, trying to mop the blood from Jamie's legs. The more he mopped, the more blood there seemed to be. It pooled on the floor, spattered the walls. Everything he touched began to bleed: the doorknob, the faucet, the sink. "It's okay," he said. "It's okay."

Coffin woke up early. He had slept only an hour or two. Something was wrong with his face, he realized: His lower left eyelid was twitching. Jamie lay on her back, sound asleep and snoring a little. More than anything he wanted to stay in bed with her, wake up slowly, make love, eat a late breakfast, go for a walk. He got up as quietly as he could, pulled on a pair of sweatpants and a T-shirt, and went downstairs.

Outside, a damp fog hung between the cedar trees. The neighbor's laundry drooped on the clothesline, empty and vague at the edges. Coffin dropped a filter into the coffeemaker, spooned in an overdose of espresso roast, filled the carafe at the sink. Poured it in. Flipped the switch. Remembered the cardboard box in the living room.

"Rudy," Coffin said, left eyelid twitching. He walked out to the living room and sat down on his mother's Victorian sofa. The box sat on the coffee table where he'd left it. He pulled the flaps open. The DVR was not inside. *"Rudy,"* Coffin said. There was a thick paperback book in the box instead. Coffin reached in and took it out. It was called *Overcoming Male Infertility: Understanding Its Causes and Treatments.* The authors were Drs. Leslie R. Schover and Anthony J. Thomas Jr.

Coffin's face felt hot. His eye twitched furiously. He stood, stalked barefoot across the living room, unlocked the front door, and walked through the screen porch and into the fog-damp yard, the screen door slapping shut behind him. "Rudy!" He yelled. "God damn it—*Rudy!*"

No one answered. The Long Point foghorn skwonked in the distance. Three starlings pecked in Mrs. Rivera's yard.

Coffin looked up. Mrs. Rivera was looking at him out of her upstairs window.

Coffin waved. "Hi, Mrs. Rivera," he said.

Mrs. Rivera frowned, closed her window, and pulled the shade.

Coffin could hear a phone ringing, faintly, inside someone's house. Then he realized it was his and ran inside.

"Detective Coffin? Are you all right? You sound a little out of breath."

"I'm fine, Mr."—Coffin said, checking his caller ID—"Attorney General. Just ran in from outside. What can I do for you?"

"I'm partly just checking in," Poblano said. "Wondering how things are going out there. But I'm also a little concerned." He had a deep, smooth voice: If it had a color, Coffin thought, it would be chocolate brown.

"Concerned, sir?" Coffin said.

"We seem to have lost touch with Trooper Duckworth. Haven't heard from him in a couple of days, and his cell phone appears to be out of service. I was wondering if you'd been in touch with him at all."

Coffin paused for a moment. Strange, Poblano calling him at home. "Not since the day before yesterday, no, sir."

There was a brief pause. "Well, I hope he's all right," Poblano said. "If you hear from him, could you have him give me a call?"

"Yes, sir," Coffin said. "Will do."

There was another pause. "All right, then," Poblano said. "Good-bye, Detective."

"Good-b—" Coffin said, but Poblano had already hung up.

"Is there coffee?" Jamie said from the top of the stairs.

"Yes," Coffin said. "I think so."

"I heard yelling," Jamie said. "Then the phone rang." She'd thrown on one of Coffin's flannel shirts, a red and white plaid.

"The yelling was me." He went out to the kitchen, poured mugs of coffee for himself and Jamie, and added sugar and half-and-half. "The phone was our fine attorney general."

"Thanks," Jamie said, taking the mug of coffee with both hands and settling onto the sofa. "Why were you yelling?"

Coffin held up the copy of *Overcoming Male Infertility: Understanding Its Causes and Treatments*. "Rudy gave me the wrong box," he said.

"Wrong book, too," Jamie said. "You're doing great in the sperm department. That makes you one for two."

"Hey!" Coffin said.

Jamie smiled and batted her eyelashes. "Care to give it another shot?"

Coffin looked at his watch. "I can't," he said.

Jamie set her coffee down and leaned back on the couch. The flannel shirt fell open—she'd only buttoned one button, just below her sternum. "You'd better," she said.

Later, Coffin climbed into the Fiesta and stuck the key in the ignition. The Fiesta started, for once, on the first try. Coffin put the transmission in DRIVE, turned the radio on, and pulled away from the curb. There was no clear signal on the dial except for WOMR, Provincetown's locally owned, volunteer-run FM station. *Bob's Bluegrass Hour* was just getting revved up: Men with hillbilly accents were singing a song about trains. A banjo jangled furiously. Coffin turned it off; banjo music made his jaw tighten and his head hurt. Something stirred in the backseat. A haggard face appeared in the rearview mirror.

"Jesus fucking *Christ*," Coffin said, swerving, almost clipping an oncoming car. The driver honked furiously and gave Coffin the finger.

"How anybody can listen to that banjo shit is beyond me," his mother said.

Coffin took a deep breath, then another, his heart galloping in his chest.

His mother cackled. "What's the matter? Scare you?"

Coffin turned around. "How long have you been back there, Ma?"

His mother frowned. "I don't know," she said. "Jesus, I'm losing my frickin' mind."

"Where's Mr. Taveres?"

"Who?"

"Mr. Taveres, Ma. Your boyfriend."

"Oh, *him*. No idea. I think he went back to the home."

Coffin turned right on Standish Street. It was early; a cluster of mourning doves whistled out of his way. "Which is where I'm taking you," he said.

"I'll jump out," his mother said. She opened the door.

"Ma," Coffin said. "Shut the door, please." He pulled over.

His mother's eyes glistened in the rearview mirror. "Don't make me go back there, Eddie," she said. "All they do is sit around and wait to die."

"I'm Frankie, Ma," Coffin said. "Ed's in Vietnam, remember?"

"You're *Frankie*?" his mother said. She turned her head and spat out the open door. "You're not fit to kiss your big brother's ass. Eddie's a frickin' war hero, you know. If he was around, he'd have busted me out of that dump years ago."

"You're probably right, Ma," Coffin said. He unbuckled his seat belt, got out of the car, closed his mother's door, and got back in. "But you're stuck with me, I'm afraid, and you and I both agreed that Valley View's the best place for you right now, remember?" He put the Fiesta in DRIVE and pulled out, then took the little left-right jog onto Alden Street, which passed between the town cemetery and the Catholic cemetery. Valley View was just ahead, perched on its hill, overlooking the green valley of the dead.

"I can't remember shit anymore," his mother said. "This fucking Alzheimer's eats your brain, is what it does."

Coffin said nothing. A coven of crows stood in a loose circle beside a tilting gravestone.

His mother stirred. "Frankie," she said.

"Yeah, Ma."

"Kill me."

"What?"

"You're a cop. You carry a gun. Shoot me."

"I don't carry a gun, and I'm not going to shoot you."

"*Buceta*," his mother said. "What kind of faggot doesn't carry a gun?" She sat back in her seat. "What kind of faggot won't even kill his own mother?"

NINETEEN

Coffin's cousin Tony lived in a big 1970s refurb in Eastham, about twenty-four miles from Provincetown center. He'd sold his modest Provincetown house for well over a million dollars during the height of the housing frenzy in 2006. The new house had granite countertops, a water view, and a Jacuzzi in the master suite. It was a palace compared to Tony's old place, which had been cramped, run-down, and dark. The developers who bought it immediately tore it down and built a duplex on the narrow lot, selling it for almost three times what they'd paid.

"Lemme get you a drink, Frankie," Tony said, standing with Coffin on the broad back deck, which overlooked First Encounter Beach. It was Tony's day off.

"A drink?" Coffin said, checking his watch. "It's 10:00 A.M. on a Tuesday."

"Tuesday's the new Saturday," Tony said, patting his big belly. He wore a silk camp shirt that made him look like one of the Mafiosi on *The Sopranos*. "You want a Bloody Mary or not?"

"Oh, what the hell," Coffin said, following Tony into the kitchen. It was a big kitchen, full of sunlight, stainless steel, and polished white granite. You could see the living room fireplace and the deep blue water of Cape Cod Bay from the sink. "What can it hurt?"

"That's my cousin," Tony said, filling two tall glasses with ice from the big built-in fridge, then pouring triple shots of vodka into each of them. He added V8, Worcestershire, Tabasco, black pepper, olives, and celery, stirred them, then handed one to Coffin.

Coffin sipped. It was very good.

"So where's Lola?" Tony said, shuffling back outside in his flip-flops and settling onto a wooden deck chair. "You two been joined at the hip all week. I'm surprised to see you without her."

"She's taking a half day off," Coffin said. "Her apartment got trashed—she's trying to clean up a little, put her life back together."

Tony sipped his drink and shook his head. "Bummer."

Coffin nodded. The view was very nice. A couple of dispirited fishing boats puttered along, a mile or so offshore. A gull floated by, riding a thermal.

Tony turned and looked at Coffin. "All I'm sayin' is, as much time as you spend together, wouldn't surprise me if you were boinkin' her."

"I can't keep up with the one I've got," Coffin said. "Besides, I'm not Lola's type."

"I don't know," Tony said. "I see you lookin, ha? Ha? If you're lookin', you're thinkin', that's what I always say."

"The only looking I'm doing right now is for Rudy," Coffin said. "He was driving your truck last night. Any idea where I can find him?"

"You're lookin' for Pops, huh?" Tony said. He shook his big head. "I ain't seen him since last night. He borrowed my truck and hasn't brought it back."

"Is that a problem? Not having your truck, I mean?"

"Nah," Tony said. "I'll just drive Darlene's car if I need to go anywhere. He'll bring it back, probably."

Darlene was Tony's wife. She worked in Orleans three days a week as a dental hygienist. She drove a slate gray Audi convertible.

"Any idea where he might be hanging out?"

Tony nodded. He took a pack of Marlboros from the pocket of his cargo shorts and offered one to Coffin.

"Thanks," Coffin said as Tony lit the cigarette for him. It tasted good with the Bloody Mary.

"He's got a girlfriend," Tony said, "the freakin' old goat. Back in P'town. Girl named Gemma something-or-other. I ain't met her."

"Any idea where she works? Or where she's staying?"

"She's some kind of artist. She rents one of the studios over the post office, Rudy said. I have no idea where she lives."

"Gemma, over the post office," Coffin said.

"Correctamundo."

"How's your kids?"

"Fun. Gettin' big. I don't know what I'm going to do when they get old enough to be embarrassed by me. I kind of like being their hero, you know?"

"Of course you do," Coffin said, watching the fishing boats head back to Provincetown, high in the water. "Who wouldn't?"

Cecil Duckworth climbed out of his rented car and stretched. His back was a little sore. He had spent most of the morning hunched over in his motel room, trying to get Bobby Cavalo's blood off his best shoes. Next time, he thought, he'd have to remember to bring a pair of galoshes along, just in case.

He had found the cop's address by looking in the phone book. That was detective work, most of the time—90 percent of what you needed was just lying around in plain view. The trick was putting it all together in a way that made sense. The cop's house made sense: It was small, unimpressive—what a cop could afford. The paint on the windowsills was peeling; the cop was too busy to fix it himself, too cheap to pay someone else. The cop—Coffin, his name was, believe it or not—was probably divorced, probably drank too much, maybe had psychological problems: depression or rage. Although maybe in a small town like this, you'd mostly be fine.

Duckworth climbed the two wooden stairs and knocked on the screen door. There was music coming from inside, something Indian sounding, with sitars. No one came to the door. It seemed unlikely that anyone inside the house would have heard him, what with the music playing. He opened the screen door, walked four steps across the porch, and rapped on what he would have considered the front door, which had a good-sized glass pane in it. After about ten seconds a woman came down the stairs, saw him standing on the porch, and said, "Yes? Can I help you?" through the glass. Cautious. Keeping her distance—still a good six feet from the door. *Giving herself a head start in case I kick the door in,* Duckworth thought—*but why so nervous?* He took his badge from his pocket and flipped it open. "State Police, ma'am," he said. He smiled. "I'm looking for your husband. Official business."

One of the odd things about living in a resort town, Coffin thought, was that one was always aware of the state of the tourists in pretty much the same way that people who lived in the Midwest, say, were aware of the weather, or the way in which the men of his father's, grandfather's, and great-grandfather's generations had been aware of the tides. After the Fourth of July the tourists were always up—way up. In the fall they started to recede. In midwinter they were all but invisible, and as Memorial Day weekend approached—it was now just two days away—the tourists were slowly beginning to trickle in. It was palpable, Coffin thought, as he walked down Commercial Street from Town Hall parking lot to the post office: the slight but observable diminishing of one's personal space in public; the small knots of tourists gathered outside restaurants, perusing the posted menus. A group of young men walked by, shirtless, wearing shorts and sandals, their chests smooth and glistening, already tanned. It was starting: The tourists were coming in.

In the post office lobby, Coffin jumped the line, said hello to the clerk—a woman named Carole who'd been a postal clerk in Provincetown for almost twenty years—and asked to speak to Lloyd Oates, the postmaster. Carole disappeared into the back room and came back a minute later with Lloyd in tow.

"How can I help you today, Frank?" Lloyd said, breathing a little heavily. He was a short man and very fat. He had a perpetual sheen of sweat on his upper lip. Like many very fat men, his feet seemed too small for his body.

"Have you got a renter upstairs named Gemma something?" Coffin said, keeping his voice down. All five of the patrons waiting in line were trying to look like they weren't eavesdropping. The post office was a notorious vector for gossip.

"Gemma Skolnick," Lloyd said. "Nice lady. She in trouble?"

Coffin shook his head. "Nope. Just need to talk to her. Which studio?"

"Two-oh-four."

"Any idea if she's up there now?"

Lloyd waved Carole over. "Seen Gemma yet today?" he asked.

"Yep," Carole said. She wore bifocals and kept her hair in a thick gray ponytail. "She came in about twenty minutes ago. She had a big latte, it looked like—you're not supposed to bring drinks in, but I let it go—and she said hi and checked her box. Then it looked like she was headed upstairs. Had her keys in her hand when she left."

"Great," Coffin said. "Thanks."

"She in trouble?" Carole said. She seemed hopeful.

"No," Coffin said. "No trouble. Thanks again for your help."

"I'm sorry," the cop's wife said, still not opening the door. "I don't know where he is. You might try his office."

She was pretty, Duckworth thought—if you liked skinny white girls—and she wasn't wearing a lot of clothes. A midlength bathrobe made of mango-colored silk, a little gold ankle bracelet. Was that it? Clearly no bra—too much nipple for that—and no telltale panty lines. Her hair was wet: She'd probably just gotten out of the shower. Duckworth liked skinny white girls well enough, but they did not really engage his interest—or activate his libido—in the way that Latina ladies did; no doubt it had something to do with his mother, who had been from Argentina.

"I'll do that, yes, ma'am," he said. He put his hand on the doorknob, thought better of it, took his hand away. There was something about the way she was standing—weight shifted a bit, right hand concealed behind her hip—that gave him pause. "What about his partner, Officer . . ."

"Sergeant Winters," the woman said, watching him very closely. "You might try her, yes."

He smiled again. "Thank you, ma'am," he said. "I'll give her a try." He touched his fist to his chest twice then pointed a thick finger at Jamie. "You have a lovely day, now," he said. "Y'hear?"

Coffin trudged up two flights of green-linoleum-covered stairs to the second floor of the post office where a half-dozen local artists rented studios. To Coffin's way of thinking, the best of the studio spaces were at the far end of the hallway, directly overlooking the harbor—though he understood that for most artists the southwesterly light would not be ideal.

Room 204 was halfway down the hall; the door had a frosted glass pane and stood an inch or two ajar. Music drifted out: Jimi Hendrix, playing the spooky intro to "Red House." Coffin couldn't resist: He peeked in. A woman a few years younger than Jamie was lying on her back on a large sheet of brown kraft paper, which she'd spread out on the floor. She was naked and appeared to be trying to trace around herself with a stick of charcoal. Big-breasted and very tan, she had long blond dreadlocks and a dark pubic ruff. Her clothes hung on a paint-splattered chair. She had at least two brightly colored tattoos that Coffin could see: a blue fish on her deltoid muscle and a green sea horse on her lower belly. Coffin wondered if there were others, and what colors they might be. The bottoms of her feet were very dirty. She was, Coffin thought, an extraordinarily attractive woman.

Coffin stopped peeking and knocked. "Hello?" he said. "Sorry—don't mean to disturb you."

"Just a minute!" the woman said. "Who is it?"

Coffin heard the rattling of kraft paper, imagined it sticking a little to the soles of her feet as she stepped into her jeans. "Frank Coffin," he said. "Rudy's nephew."

"Well, well," she said, pulling the door open, offering Coffin a charcoal-smeared hand. "Gemma Skolnick. To what do I owe this honor?" She'd pulled on jeans and a black Mötley Crüe T-shirt.

"I've lost an uncle," Coffin said, shaking her hand. Her grip was strong, her fingers almost as sandpapery as a cat's tongue. "I need to find him ASAP. Any idea where he might be?"

Gemma shrugged. She wore hardly any makeup. "He might still be at my place," she said. "He was when I left—snoring away. You boys were out late last night, I guess."

"He told you we were together?"

"Mm-hm. Said you were at the Old Colony, whooping it up. I didn't believe him."

"No? Why not?"

"You've been in the OC, right?"

Coffin nodded.

"So you know how it smells."

"Right," he said. "I forget about the stink test."

"What can I say?" Gemma said. "Women will smell you. Come on in."

The studio was spacious and high-ceilinged, with tall windows running its entire length, facing east, toward Fishermen's Bank. There was the usual artist's collection of driftwood and seashells on the windowsills, the usual artist's ashtray overflowing with butts. A small refrigerator hummed in the corner; a row of empty beer bottles stood on a rack of metal shelves, along with a variety of paint cans, bottles, tubes, brushes, and other art supplies. A big roll of kraft paper lay on the floor. Much of the wall space was covered in large, unstretched canvases—big, florid nudes, mostly, rendered in bright oranges and pinks. The studio smelled like marijuana smoke; a joint smoldered briefly on the edge of the table and then went out.

"So Rudy came home when?" Coffin said, not quite knowing what to do with himself. A black lace bra hung from the only chair; a bright red G-string lay on the floor beside it.

"About three," Gemma said. "Maybe a few minutes after."

"Went straight to bed?" Coffin said.

Gemma looked at Coffin and smiled. Her eyes were green. "Well," she said, "more or less. Rudy believes it's his moral obligation to screw my brains out at least once a night, no matter what. We probably got to sleep around four."

"He said that? About it being a moral obligation?"

"He didn't have to."

"He's got something that belongs to me," Coffin said, feeling slightly overwhelmed. "It looks like a hard drive, kind of."

"Oh," Gemma said. "Of course—this is about the DVR. I was wondering what was up with all the questions."

"Sorry," Coffin said. "It's a cop thing."

Gemma frowned. "You know anything about art?"

"One of my best friends is an artist, and I never know what the hell he's talking about," Coffin said. "So no, not really."

"Well, at least you're honest about it," Gemma said. She picked up the piece of charcoal, put it back down. "I'm supposed to have a couple of pieces in the erotica show at the Art League this weekend, and I wanted to do a self-portrait—but something kind of unexpected."

Coffin pursed his lips and nodded. "Unexpected," he said. "Absolutely."

"This charcoal thing isn't really working out the way I thought it would, though. It's just kind of *lifeless*, you know?"

"Ah," Coffin said. "Lifeless. Right."

"So I was thinking I'd paint myself all over with tempera—'cause it's nontoxic, right?—and then lie down on the paper. Sort of make a life-size print of myself." Gemma walked over to the metal shelves and selected three large plastic squeeze bottles of tempera: blue, yellow, and red.

"Great!" Coffin said. "Sounds good."

"It would have to be really a lot of paint to make a bold image, though," Gemma said. She tore another big sheet of kraft paper off the roll and spread it out on the floor. "And tempera dries really fast. I'd probably have to have someone help me slather it on. Like an assistant."

"An assistant," Coffin said. "Good idea. So there *was* a DVR? That's what you said, right?"

"How about you?" Gemma said, smiling brightly. "You busy right now?"

"Well," Coffin said, looking at his watch, "I really should go find Rudy."

"You help me, I'll help you," Gemma said, pulling off her T-shirt. "Fair enough?"

Her breasts were spectacular. Coffin wondered if she'd had them done. He tried not to stare. "Fair enough," he said.

Jamie sat down on the couch, Frank's World War II–vintage Colt .45 still in her hand. She felt a little shaky. There had been something about the man in the pink jacket that was wrong—she saw it from the upstairs window as he'd gotten out of his car, saw it again in the

yellowed whites of his eyes as he'd taken off his tinted
glasses to gaze in at her from the screen porch. Something avid and wolfish—it was hard to find a word for
it. She was not sure why she'd grabbed Frank's gun
from the nightstand before trotting downstairs, but she
was glad she did, glad she'd decided to keep it there
and not in the box in the closet where it had lived until
the incident two years ago. She took a deep breath. She
was glad Duckworth had not tried to open the door;
if he had, she would have shot him. She set the pistol
on the coffee table and called Frank's office. No one
answered. He refused to carry a cell phone—his Luddite streak was one of the things she liked about him,
but now it was aggravating. Where would he be? She
thought for a minute, then called Lola's apartment.

Gemma Skolnick lived in a converted barn on Pearl
Street, just where it kinked to the right and joined with
Brewster Street, which connected Bradford and Harry
Kemp Way. The barn was one of two similar structures
that stood barely a hundred yards apart; the other belonged to the Fine Art Center complex and was divided
into three "rustic" apartments. Gemma's barn had recently been rehabbed and was now a single, open studio structure with a half loft: kitchen and living/studio
space downstairs, large bedroom/office/bath upstairs.
Coffin wondered how she was able to afford it but
thought it better not to ask.

"This is my humble abode," Gemma said, tossing her
leather backpack onto the couch and spreading her arms.
"Pretty great, huh?"

"No kidding," Coffin said. "This place looked like it
was about to fall down a couple of years ago. From the
outside, anyway."

"Come on upstairs," Gemma said. "Rudy's probably gone by now, but let's see if we can find your gadget."

Coffin followed her up the wide staircase. The loft was a good-sized open space with windows overlooking Pearl Street to the south and Harry Kemp Way to the north. A big antique Persian rug covered much of the floor, and an unmade king-sized bed stood diagonally in one corner. The bath was not physically divided from the sleeping area. A big tub/Jacuzzi and shower stall stood out in the open; only the toilet was hidden in a little alcove. Everything was done in weathered wood, polished to a warm semigloss. Four big north-facing skylights provided most of the light. To Coffin it felt a bit like the interior of a Berkshires resort from the fifties or early sixties.

"Let's see," Gemma said, poking around her desk. "Here we go. One gadget." She held up the DVR, which was still connected to a white iMac flat-screen.

"Oh my God," Coffin said. "Hooray. You're a lifesaver."

"But you can't have it."

"I can't? It's important evidence in a murder case, Gemma."

"Are you kidding me? Without Rudy's permission?" She shook her head. "I don't think so, Frank. You can watch what's on it if you want to, though. That's some funny shit, I don't mind telling you." She peeled off her T-shirt again, wiggled out of her jeans, and tossed them at the hamper; her bra and panties were downstairs, stuffed into her backpack. She'd cleaned off most of the tempera with wet paper towels back in her studio, but her pubic hair was crusted with dried green paint, and she was still multicolored in a few hard-to-reach places. "You do what you want. I'm getting in the shower."

What I want, Coffin thought, *would get me in a lot of trouble.* "Somebody likes to be naked," he said, sitting at the desk and turning on the computer.

Gemma laughed, reached into the shower, and turned on the hot water. "I used to be an exotic dancer," she said. "I guess it's kind of my accustomed state." She stepped into the big glass-and-granite shower stall. "It's nice in here," she said, water streaming down her belly. She looked out at Coffin. "You can join me if you like."

I like, Coffin thought. *Jesus. I like.* "I would," he said. "Really. But there's Rudy to think about. And I've got a nice girlfriend."

"If your girlfriend's so nice," Gemma said, "why are you sitting in my bedroom, watching me take a shower?" She slid the shower door shut, steam already forming on the glass.

Coffin unplugged the DVR from the power strip on the floor, then unhooked it from the computer.

"You know," Gemma said, her back to Coffin as she soaped her breasts, "if you were still here when I got out, I wouldn't be responsible for what happened."

"You're right about that, Gemma," Coffin said softly, tiptoeing down the stairs. "You are right about that."

Duckworth parked his beige rental car in the parking lot beside the girl-cop's apartment and climbed out. She was taking a half day off, the PPD day officer had told him—very accommodating, giving out information like that over the phone. He'd found her address in the phone book. It was that kind of town.

He hitched up his pants, took a handkerchief out of his jacket pocket, and flicked a bit of dust from his shoes. *Not so lucky, those alligators.* The thought made him smile.

As he climbed the stairs, he realized he wasn't entirely sure what he was hoping to accomplish here. Find the girl-cop, who would tell him where to find Coffin, the detective, who would tell him where to find Rudy, the cop gone bad, who would tell him where the DVR was? It was a lot of finding and telling, but that, too, was detective work.

Duckworth paused on the landing. It was a very pretty place, this Provincetown. He liked the little boats in the harbor, the slightly forlorn drag queens standing in front of the Crown and Anchor, passing out flyers for that night's drag show. It was, he thought, a fine place to visit—though he preferred the vibrant nightlife of his neighborhood in East Boston, where the girls were, for the most part, actual girls.

Duckworth raised his hand to knock on the door, then noted the splintered jamb where someone had very recently broken in. "My, my," he said. "Murders, break-ins, blackmail—it's not such a nice little town, after all, is it, Lucille?" He pushed the door open silently and stepped inside.

Lola had all but finished sweeping up the kitchen; she'd bought a big pushbroom and a wide metal dustpan and brought her regular assortment of mops, brooms, Swiffers, and dustpans out of their kitchen cabinet. A green Rubbermaid trash can sat in the middle of the room, full of broken glass and crockery shards. For the last hour or so she'd been working in the bedroom, hanging up shirts, pants, and her few skirts and dresses, putting T-shirts, socks, and underwear back in the drawers. She'd ordered a new mattress, tossed the remains of her nightstand into the apartment complex Dumpster, and called a carpenter to fix and reinforce her front door. Call waiting had bleeped when she was on the phone, but she'd let the call go through to voice mail. In all, not a bad half-day's work. She folded a half-dozen T-shirts and a couple of pairs of gym shorts, put them in their drawers, then decided to call it quits and get dressed for work. She was buttoning up her uniform shirt when she heard a small sound. She looked up. Something moved in the living room, just at the edge of her peripheral vision.

"Frank?" she said. "Is that you?"

Coffin walked the half mile or so from Gemma's barn back to Town Hall with the DVR tucked under his arm. He wouldn't have felt more conspicuous, he thought, if he'd been walking around Provincetown in broad daylight with a dead body thrown over his shoulder. Town was getting busier by the minute: He passed a pair of large, outrageously muscled men dressed in black leather jackets, boots, chaps, and hats. One of the men was walking a tiny, fluffy Pekingese on a pink leash. It was a kind of Provincetown inverse corollary, Coffin thought: The more pierced, tattooed, and muscular the leather-daddy, the smaller, prissier, and more beribboned the dog was likely to be.

When he got to the parking lot, Coffin put the DVR gently onto the Fiesta's passenger seat and then climbed in, the springs emitting a rusty groan as they absorbed his weight. He turned the key, and the engine roared to life, a cloud of black exhaust erupting from the tailpipe. He put the transmission in drive and pressed the gas gently. The Fiesta bucked twice and stalled.

"Oh, for Christ's sake," Coffin said. He put the Fiesta in PARK and turned the key. The engine sputtered, then caught, but it stalled when Coffin put his hand on the gear shifter.

"*Fuck*," he said. "Come on now—be a good little car,

you piece of shit." He turned the key, and for a second nothing happened; then the engine cranked, caught, and ran smoothly. "Okay," Coffin said, hand poised above the shifter. "Don't stall."

No, ma'am," Duckworth said. He stood just outside the bedroom door, smiling brightly. "It's not Frank. It's just little old me."

Lola's stomach lurched. Duckworth's pink jacket was unbuttoned. She caught a glimpse of emerald green lining and the stag-handled hunting knife in its sheath. "Trooper Duckworth," she said. She wiped her palms on her jeans. Her off-duty pistol was resting on the kitchen counter in its clip holster, about twelve feet away. "What brings you here?"

"Well," Duckworth said, "it's a funny thing. I was looking for Detective Coffin's uncle, and when I couldn't find him I tried to find Detective Coffin, and when I couldn't find *him* I came looking for you, and here you are."

"Yes," Lola said. "Sounds like you've had a busy day."

"Well, maybe not quite as busy as you," Duckworth said. "Quite the little mess you've got here."

"I had a break-in." Lola took two steps toward the kitchen and picked up a broken cup handle that had bounced onto the carpet. Now her gun was only seven feet away.

"I saw your doorjamb," Duckworth said. He shook his big head. "They sure did a number on your place."

"Yes," Lola said, taking a step into the kitchen and dropping the cup handle into the big green trash can. "They sure did."

Duckworth had his knife out of the sheath almost before she saw him move. "I had some neighborhood boys break into my place a few years back," he said.

He smiled; his teeth were very white. "Me and Lucille carved our initials in one of their backsides, and we never had any trouble after that."

Jesus, Lola thought. *Another whacko with a knife.*

Coffin turned left out of the parking lot, then right on Commercial, past Poochie's—the bakery for dogs— and past the Crown and Anchor, where two slender drag queens in green sequined minidresses, giant bee-hive wigs, and six-inch platforms passed out flyers for that night's drag show. The Fiesta gargled and burped but didn't stall. Traffic on Commercial Street was surprisingly heavy ahead of the holiday weekend; Coffin was stuck behind a huge Winnebago as it waddled past the Unitarian Church at four miles per hour.

"Come *on,*" Coffin said. He wanted to roll down the window and give the retiree driving the Winnebago the finger. RVs had been banned from the town center some years ago. Their elderly drivers had trouble navigating the narrow streets; they'd rammed parked cars, clipped telephone poles, injured pedestrians and cyclists, gotten wedged going around tight corners, driven on sidewalks and crashed into buildings. *Where the hell is a cop when you need one?* Coffin thought. He leaned on the Fiesta's horn. At first it did nothing; then, after a second or two, it produced a weak, warbly bleat. "Oh my *God,*" Coffin said. "Even the *horn* is a piece of shit."

"Are you thirsty?" Duckworth said, sliding his knife back into its sheath. "I know I am. I mean, I could definitely use a cool drink of *some*thing. This has been one thirsty day of work for me, I don't mind telling you.

Lola watched his face. She tried to stay calm. "Would you like some water?" she said. "I'm afraid that's all I've got at the moment. I think I have one intact mug."

"A cool drink of water would be fine, yes, thank you very much." Duckworth smiled. He took off his glasses and put them in his inside pocket. His eyes were bright and flat, without emotion—like the eyes of a ventriloquist's dummy. "So, these fellas who broke into your place. What was it they were after? Any idea?"

Lola's one unbroken mug stood on the counter, two feet from her holstered pistol. "Just your basic robbery, I guess," she said, rinsing the mug under the tap, then filling it with water. "Probably junkies, looking for cash."

She held out the cup of water. Duckworth advanced a couple of steps and took it.

"We thank you, ma'am," he said. He raised the mug in a mock toast and took a drink. "You get a lot of that out here, do you?" he said. "Junkies breaking into people's houses, looking for cash?"

"Not a lot," Lola said, "but it happens."

"Funny it would happen to you," Duckworth said. "You being a cop and all. Funny strange, I mean."

"Junkies aren't exactly known for their judgment," Lola said. Duckworth was too close now; if he could move his feet as fast as his hands, he'd be on her before she could get the gun out of its holster.

"No," Duckworth said. He sipped his water, sipped again, set the mug down on the counter, took another step toward Lola—sliding his bulk between her and the gun. "I don't suppose they are."

There was a long silence. Duckworth smiled, his gaze intense, unblinking.

Jesus, Lola thought. *I'm going to have to kill this fucking freak, aren't I?* She looked at her watch. "I should be going," she said. "My shift's about to start."

The knife was in Duckworth's hand again, held low, glinting in the harbor light. "Let's not be in a hurry," he said. "We've got some things to talk about, you and Lucille and me."

Lola took a step back, then another. Away from the knife, and her gun. "I don't talk to people who pull knives on me," she said.

Duckworth chuckled. "Oh, don't mind Lucille," he said. "She's just going to help you remember the details."

He moved like a dancer—a kind of muscular glide across the floor, hips slightly forward, shoulders back. Faster than Lola thought he'd move, faster than a man his size *should* be able to move in a tight space. She was out of room—nothing behind her but wall and window, nothing between her and Duckworth but six feet of blue linoleum and a broom, leaning against the counter. She could not, she thought, get to the broom without being cut.

"Come on now, Sergeant Lola," Duckworth said, still smiling, taking another sliding step. "As long as you tell us the truth, you've got nothing to worry about."

"I'm not worried," Lola said.

"Your eyes look worried," Duckworth said. "Your eyes look *scared*. What color are they? Blue or gray?"

Something moved in the living room. The door swinging silently open. Lola held her breath, tried not to look. "Blue," she said.

Coffin stepped into the kitchen and dropped into a shooter's half-crouch, both arms extended. "Drop the knife, motherfucker!" he said.

Duckworth turned his head, started to raise his hands, then saw that Coffin wasn't armed. He smiled. "Nice little piece of acting there, Detective," he said. "You almost had me." Then Lola hit him in the face hard, with the working end of the broom.

Duckworth stumbled back a half step and Coffin

vas on him, gripping his thick wrist with both hands,
smashing it against the kitchen counter once and then
again until the knife sprang from Duckworth's grip
and skittered across the linoleum. Lola took two quick
steps forward, kicked Duckworth in the kneecap, then
drove the end of the broom handle into his belly.

Duckworth grunted, cuffed Coffin on the side of the
head with his open hand, hard enough to make Coffin's
vision darken and his ears ring, then drew back his
hand and punched Coffin twice in the face. Coffin felt
the cartilage in his nose crunch, then searing pain. His
knees wobbled and a spurt of blood splashed onto the
floor, but he clung to Duckworth's wrist, trying to keep
him from getting at the gun in his shoulder holster, trying to give Lola a chance to get to her weapon.

Duckworth roared, tried to shake Coffin off, dug for
his gun awkwardly with his left hand as Lola lunged
for hers, grabbed it, ripped it from its holster, thumbed
off the safety, and leveled the barrel at Duckworth's
head.

"Down on your face!" she said. "Now!"

Duckworth looked up, smiled, shook the bleeding
Coffin off like a dog shaking itself after a swim, and
bolted for the door in a half crouch. Lola fired once
and Duckworth shrieked in pain, then he was out the
door and gone.

"Shit!" Lola said, chasing after him. "*Fuck!* Why didn't
I just *kill* the motherfucker?"

"Seriously," Coffin said, kneeling on the kitchen
floor. "Why didn't you?" He touched his crushed nose
with the fingertips of both hands, sending fat, electric
jolts of pain through his face and down his arms. His
shirt was soaked with blood. He felt like he might
throw up. He stood and wobbled to the door. Lola was
running across the parking lot toward the street. In the

distance, and pulling away, Coffin could see Duckworth riding a stolen bike into the flow of traffic, a
forlorn tourist picking himself up off the pavement in
Duckworth's wake. *"Why didn't you kill him?"* Coffin
yelled.

"Because," Lola yelled back, over her shoulder, *"I've
never killed* any*body."*

"Neither have I," Coffin said, limping down the
stairs, nose still bubbling blood, "but there's always a
first time." He pulled out his shield and waved it at two
rubbernecking tourists standing across the street from
the parking lot, holding their bikes. "Police," he said,
"Need your bikes."

"Was that a gunshot?" one of the young men said,
handing over his bike.

"Are you o*kay*?" the other one said, giving his bike
to Lola.

"Yes. No," Coffin said, climbing onto his bike. It was
a dark green mountain bike—the seat seemed very low.
Lola was already pedaling after Duckworth at high
speed.

"Will we get our bikes back?"

"Go to Town Hall, second floor," Coffin yelled as he
pedaled away. "They'll give you a form to fill out!"

For automobile traffic, Commercial Street was one-way,
running east to west along its entire length. Bicycle
traffic, though, ran freely in both directions, adding
significantly to the traffic chaos, especially during the
height of summer and on busy holiday weekends.

Provincetown natives and year-rounders were used
to sharing Commercial Street's narrow channel with
the stream of wrong-way bicycle traffic, while tourists
often were not. Afoot, tourists wandered off sidewalks,
stood in bovine clusters in the middle of the street, and

rossed from one side to the other midblock, blindly,
s though pulled by invisible strings—attracted by
osted restaurant menus or racks of postcards depict-
ng the Pilgrim Monument or window displays of ge-
eric CAPE COD T-shirts or maritime souvenirs—painted
wooden lighthouses made in China. In motor vehicles,
he tourists opened doors without looking, turned ag-
ressively into pedestrian and bike traffic at intersec-
ions, and crowded the left/harbor side of the street,
which was the natural lane for bicyclists returning
rom Herring Cove or the Boatslip or other locations
in Provincetown's lively West End.

Coffin knew all of this in theory, but in practice it
was harrowing indeed. He veered around ambling pedestrians, narrowly missed a telephone pole that
seemed to have erupted randomly from the pavement
n front of Monty's leather goods store, and was almost
clipped twice by the sideview mirrors of hulking SUVs.
His thighs burned and he was already thoroughly out
f breath, but he kept riding as fast as he could, Lola
ust visible a hundred yards ahead. Duckworth was out
f sight most of the time, his pink jacket popping into
iew when traffic cleared for a moment or two, maybe
hree hundred yards up the street and gradually pulling
way.

Christ, Coffin thought, sucking air through his mouth,
is face throbbing, shirt soaked with blood. *We need a
miracle.*

Duckworth looked over his shoulder and laughed out
oud. The lady cop was falling behind—she'd gotten
angled up with a group of pedestrians outside the Fish
Palace, the tourist restaurant with the big neon lobster
n the window, and now she appeared to be running
ut of gas. Duckworth himself was bleeding a good bit

from his left ear; the lady cop had, as far as he coul
tell without looking in a mirror, shot his earlobe of
His neck felt sticky and his shirt collar was wet, but i
was a superficial wound, nothing to worry about. H
certainly wasn't going to go all squeamish over a bit c
blood, no, *sir*. He was fresh as a daisy, fit as a fiddl
fine as frog's hair—they could try to catch him, bu
Duckworth rode bikes as part of his fitness regimen,
hundred miles a week, at least. Once he'd stretched th
distance a bit he'd circle back, pick up his car, and he'
be gone, like a ghost walking through a closed doo
But he'd come back to haunt them again. Oh, m
yes—he surely would.

There was an opening in traffic, so Duckworth shifte
to a higher gear and pumped even faster. He glance
over his shoulder, and at first he thought the lady co
was gone. Had she wrecked? Had a heart attack? Th
thought made Duckworth chuckle. He looked agai
No—there she was, swerving around a gray miniva
squeezing between the line of traffic and the row c
parked cars on the right-hand side of the street. Sh
was *gaining*. Gaining! "*Fuck*," Duckworth said. The
he ran into something very, very hard.

TWENTY

At first, it seemed to Lola that Duckworth had simply disappeared—his pink jacket vanishing from sight as though a crevasse had opened up in the street and swallowed it, bike, Duckworth, and all. Then Lola saw that a small crowd had begun to gather beside a parked car just outside Spank Yo Mama, Provincetown's combination head shop and adult toy store, the exterior of which was decorated with florid nude murals. The car's driver's side door was open and even from a distance of seventy yards or so appeared to be considerably dented. Still pedaling, Lola looked back, trying to spot Coffin. Duckworth might be down, but she expected him to pop back up any second, and it would be good to have backup for the foot chase that was likely to ensue. She would have called for backup on her police radio, but it was back in her condo along with her gun belt and the rest of her gear.

At thirty yards, there was a sudden shout from the crowd of onlookers, and Duckworth's pink jacket reappeared—just as Lola had imagined it would. He struggled to his feet, a bit wobbly at first. His pants were torn, and there was a lot of blood on his shirt and jacket. He appeared to have a gun in his right hand. Finding himself surrounded, he pushed his way through

the crowd—growing denser by the second—and bolted
into Spank Yo Mama.

"Everybody back!" Lola yelled, pulling her own
pistol from her waistband. "Everybody get back! He's
got a gun!"

The crowd parted as though a small bomb had deto-
nated at its center, onlookers retreating as quickly as
they could.

"Call 911!" Coffin shouted, still fifty yards away. "Police emergency! Call 911!" A flurry of gawkers pulled
out their cell phones and dutifully dialed 911. Coffin
looked terrible, winded and pale on his too-small bike,
both eyes already starting to blacken.

Lola dropped her bike and ran up Spank Yo Mama's
three broad front steps, past the bronze Indian statuette
holding its smoldering bundle of sage, and into the
store's dim interior—big rack of cheap sunglasses to
her left, lots of tie-dye, bumper stickers, T-shirts, hip-
pie skirts, biker wallets, skull rings, rolling papers,
glass pipes and hookahs, knit hats with fake dreadlocks attached, and, on the right, a glass display case
that housed a pair of very large albino pythons. The
two Eastern European girls at the cash register were
pointing toward the rear of the store. "He's in the back
room," they said.

"Is there a back door?" Lola said. "Windows?"

"Back door is locked," the taller of the two girls said.
"With big lock. No windows. He can't get out."

"Any customers back there?"

The girls looked at each other and shrugged. "Maybe,"
the shorter girl said.

Coffin climbed off his bike, rubber-legged and out of
breath, and pushed his way through the small crowd
that had gathered outside Spank Yo Mama, beneath the

big pink and purple mural that depicted three chubby
ladies cavorting nude with a centaur.

"He's in the back room," Lola said. "No back door,
no windows. Maybe one or more customers back there."

Coffin took a deep breath. His face throbbed. "Okay,"
he said. "Let's go."

"Shouldn't we wait for backup?" Lola said.

"Fine," Coffin said. He looked at Lola. Her eyes were
blue-gray in the dim light. A second passed. Then another. "Okay," he said. "We waited."

Spank Yo Mama's back room was known in Provincetown, for good reason, as "the dildo room." There
were shelves full of dildos, a big oak display case full
of dildos, rotating wire racks festooned with dildos,
hundreds—if not thousands—of very large dildos
hanging from the ceiling like lewd stalactites. There
were dildos of all shapes and sizes, from the overtly
phallic to the sleekly functional to the fanciful—dildos
shaped like dolphins or, for God knew what reason, ears
of corn—dildos in every color of the rainbow, dildos
made of hard plastic, dildos made of silicon gel, dildos
made of a substance that almost—but not quite—
looked like lifeless human skin. There were dildos that
vibrated, dildos that squirmed, dildos that jackham-
mered, jiggled, jittered, or squirted; there were two-
headed dildos; there were dildos as thick as thermoses,
dildos three feet long. There were butt plugs, ben wah
balls, blow-up dolls of both genders; there were pasties
and garters and edible panties, not to mention porn
magazines (gay and straight) and DVDs (ditto). The
smell of latex permeated the room, mixed with a lin-
gering stink of patchouli. There was no sign of Duckworth.

Coffin held a finger to his lips and took cover behind

a rack of S&M magazines. Lola crouch-walked across the floor, service weapon up and ready, and was about to hunker down behind a display of male blow-up dolls when Duckworth popped up from behind the oak display case and shot her in the chest.

The shot was very loud. Lola went down hard, a smoking hole in the center of her uniform shirt. Her left foot twitched; then she lay still.

Duckworth giggled and disappeared again behind the display case. It was crowded with fancy Japanese vibrators: clear plastic penises full of colorful beads.

Coffin shivered, a big rush of adrenaline surging through his veins like a drug. His ears were ringing, the room smelled like cordite.

"Are you dead, Officer Lola?" Duckworth said. "You're being *very* quiet."

Lola lay on the floor, not moving. Coffin could hear the faint, thin wail of sirens in the distance—police and rescue vehicles rolling up Bradford Street, headed their way.

"Better make sure!" Duckworth said. He stood up and pointed his weapon at Lola.

Coffin charged, shouting.

Duckworth only had time to feel a flash of surprise before the cop was on him. He hadn't spotted Coffin on the bike chase or in the store—had assumed he was down for the count after taking those two short, hard shots to the face. Now the man had him by the right arm again, was *biting his wrist*, stomping on his feet—his good shoes!—trying to separate him from his weapon. Duckworth shrieked in pain—Coffin fought like a damn *girl,* but a vicious one. Duckworth did a quick, awkward spin move, but Coffin stayed with him teeth crunching on the bones in Duckworth's wrist breaking the skin, drawing blood. The sound of sirens was getting closer. Duckworth punched Coffin again, which made him gasp, then kneed him as hard as he could in the balls. Coffin grunted and dropped like a dead cat. Duckworth turned the gun on him, leveling the barrel at Coffin's face. "You *bit* me, you son of a bitch," he said. "You scuffed my *good shoes*." There was a very loud sound then, but Duckworth scarcely heard it. He felt a hot, hard blow to the side of his head. Then he felt nothing at all.

Holy shit," Coffin said when he could speak. "Holy fucking shit. I think he broke my balls."

"Well," Lola said, standing, tucking her .38 into her waistband. "At least he didn't shoot you." She poked a finger into the hole in her shirt. "Man, am I gonna have a freakin' bruise."

"You're not dead," Coffin said.

Lola unbuttoned two shirt buttons and showed Coffin her vest. "Kevlar," she said.

"You hate wearing Kevlar," Coffin said.

"Not anymore," Lola said. "Kevlar is my new best friend."

"So this one time, out of the blue, you thought you'd wear a vest?"

Lola poked Duckworth with her boot. He was dead, the left side of his head blown off. "Kate made me promise I'd wear it," she said. "My other new best friend."

There was yelling in the front room, and the clanking, clomping sound of cops running.

"Frank! Lola! You okay?" It was Jeff Skillings and Tony, both a little red-faced and out of breath.

"No," Coffin said, still holding his balls.

"I'm okay," Lola said. She touched her chest. "I'm bruising up already, but I think I'm fine."

Skillings nodded at Duckworth. "This guy's not fine,"
he said.

"No," Lola said. "He's not." She looked pale; her hand
shook a little as she brushed a strand of hair from her
eyes.

"Oh, man," Tony said. "Are you gonna have some paperwork to fill out, or what?"

TWENTY-ONE

"Okay," Coffin said, sitting on Lola's ruined couch and drinking scotch. "*This* is interesting."

"Who's that guy?" Lola said. Coffin had skipped to the end of the DVR. They were watching the next-to-the-last scene. "That, my friend, is the attorney general of the Commonwealth of Massachusetts."

"That's Poblano?" Lola sipped her drink. "Huh. He looks different naked."

"Most people do," Coffin said.

"Most people look naked naked. He looks *different*."

"Different how?"

"I don't know—smaller. Less *commanding*. It's like seeing Dick Cheney naked, sort of."

"Now there's a hideous thought," Coffin said.

"Sorry."

Kenji Sole had tied Poblano to the bed and was applying the Ping-Pong paddle to his backside with considerable gusto.

"Holy shit," Lola said. "The suspense is killing me. This is it, right?"

"I think so," Coffin said. "Maybe there's one more scene."

"Does he kill her? Is it Poblano?"

"Why would he? He doesn't pop up as someone with

motive. He didn't even get one of Cavalo's letters until after she was dead."

"Wait a minute," Lola said. "She's getting the strap-on ready."

Coffin leaned forward in his seat. "Nope. She's stopping. She's shushing him. She hears something."

"Oh my God."

"Well, there you go."

Lola shook her head. A little green monkey had skittered into Kenji Sole's bedroom and climbed onto the nightstand. "It's Gracie."

Gracie picked up a glass of red wine and drank from it, then dropped it on the floor. Kenji whacked at her with the strap-on and Gracie bared her fangs, then leaped off the nightstand and ran from the room. Kenji stormed out after her, white nightgown flapping.

"Oh my God," Lola said. "This is it. It's Priestess Maiya."

"What I wouldn't give for sound," Coffin said.

"Or a camera in the living room," Lola said.

Coffin downed his scotch and poured another shot from the bottle on the floor. "Check out Poblano." The attorney general was struggling to untie the scarf that bound his wrists. "He must be crapping himself about now."

"No kidding," Lola said. "Wow. Looks like Kenji was pretty handy with a knot."

Poblano seemed almost hysterical, writhing, tugging at the knotted scarf with his teeth. Then his head popped up, and he lay very still for a long moment, apparently listening.

"What's he hear? Kenji screaming?" Coffin said.

"Must be," Lola said. "What else?"

After a second or two Poblano went back to work on

the scarf, genuinely frantic now, gnawing at the fabric, tugging with both arms.

"What does he do when he gets loose?" Lola said. "Go check on Kenji or hide in the closet?"

"First he puts his pants on, then he hides in the closet. Betcha five bucks."

"Pants first?"

"Yep. It's a guy thing."

"I can't argue. If he was the kind of guy who'd check, he'd also call the cops when he found her dead."

"Bingo."

Poblano finally worked his right hand free, then, quickly, the left. He stood, stepped into his slacks, then hid in the closet. He stayed in the closet long enough that the camera's motion sensor shut down, putting the DVR to sleep. The screen went dark. When it lightened again after a few seconds, Poblano was out of the closet, still shirtless, tiptoeing into the hallway. He was back almost immediately. He tugged his T-shirt on, buttoned his dress shirt, pulled on his socks, tied his shoes, put on his watch, grabbed his tie and stuffed it into his pocket, felt for his wallet, then fled. After a couple of minutes, the screen went dark again.

"There's more, right?" Lola said.

Coffin nodded. "Whoever took the computer should be on it."

"Any bets?"

"Could be anybody," Coffin said. He shrugged. "McCurry? Ramos?"

The screen lightened. A man was in Kenji Sole's bedroom, peering at the clock radio. His back was to the camera. He set the radio down, stared closely at the thermostat, then shook his head. He turned and approached the camera. His face filled the screen, huge and distorted by the wide-angle lens.

"Oh my *God*," Lola said. "It's *Boyle*."

The picture tilted and yawed; for a moment the camera focused on the floor. Then the screen went dark.

"Wow," Coffin said. He set his drink down, picked it up again, and took a large swallow.

"Boyle's toast," Lola said.

Coffin nodded. "Yep," he said. "He sure is."

TWENTY-TWO

The meeting with Priestess Maiya and her lawyer took place in an interrogation room at the Suffolk County Jail on Nashua Street. The jail was relatively new and stood near the banks of the Charles River, a stone's throw from Boston's Science Museum and a few short blocks from Massachusetts General Hospital and Beacon Hill.

Priestess Maiya looked small and plain in her prison jumpsuit: She wore no makeup, and her hair was pulled back into a loose bun. She seemed bored. Mancini and Priestess Maiya's lawyer did most of the talking.

"That could have been anybody's monkey," the lawyer said. "The fact that there's a monkey in the video doesn't prove anything."

"We'll see what CSS comes up with," Mancini said. "It may take a few weeks, but if there's any of your client's DNA at the scene—I mean so much as a flake of dandruff—we're going to trial for murder one."

The lawyer shook his head. He was tall and thin and had enormous hands and feet. "You've got nothing," he said. "No prints, no witnesses, no timeline. My client was at home with her companion at the time of the murder, to which he will testify. No deal. Trial it is."

"J. Hedrick Sole?" Mancini said. "That companion?"

The lawyer nodded. "An unimpeachable witness."

"I'm glad you think so," Mancini said. "Because he's changed his story. He says he doesn't know where she was at the time of the murder. He says she didn't come home until almost 4:00 A.M."

The lawyer wrote something on a pad of paper and slid it in front of Priestess Maiya. She read it, then looked up, eyes flashing. "I don't deserve this," she said. She stood, her chair tipping over backward. She pulled the top of her jumpsuit open with both hands, snaps popping like a tiny string of firecrackers. She wasn't wearing a bra. Her breasts were small and pert, the nipples erect in the air-conditioned room.

"She threatened to cut Priestess Maiya's *tits* off," Priestess Maiya said, shaking her breasts in Mancini's face. "Cut. Them. Off. That's what she said. She tried to hire someone to hurt me, did you know that?"

The lawyer was tugging at her jumpsuit, trying to get her attention. "Well, nobody hurts Priestess Maiya," she said, brushing his hand aside. She set her chair upright and sat back down. "Nobody."

The room was silent. Everyone was looking at Priestess Maiya's breasts. The lawyer whispered in her ear, and she smiled, then slowly snapped up the top of the jumpsuit.

"My client will agree to manslaughter two," he said. "No more than eight years. She was suffering from diminished capacity at the time of Ms. Sole's death. At the very least."

"Ten," Mancini said.

The lawyer pursed his lips. "With the possibility of early parole."

"Done," Mancini said.

The lawyer closed his briefcase. "A pleasure doing business with you. Good day, gentlemen."

*   *   *

'Spit it out, Coffin," Mancini said. "What's eating you? Balls still sore, or what?" They were driving through downtown Boston in Mancini's Lexus.

"Ten years?" Coffin said. "That's really the best you could do?"

Mancini shrugged. "All we had was the monkey," he said. "You know how many monkeys there are in Massachusetts?"

"What about J. Hedrick changing his story?"

"The testimony of a crazy, senile meth head? Maybe the jury buys it, maybe they don't."

Coffin shook his head. "You heard her. It was cold-blooded murder. She drove three hours from Boston to Provincetown to settle a score."

Mancini smiled and looked out the window. "What do you think would happen," he said, "if she flashed her tits like that in a courtroom? On the witness stand, say."

Coffin sighed. "Chaos. Mistrial. Insanity plea. She'd get sent to Tewksbury for a couple of years and then released as 'cured.' Then she'd write a memoir about getting away with murder and sell it for millions."

Mancini nodded. "Sometimes you take what you can get in this business," he said.

Coffin said nothing for a while. They were crossing the Zakim/Bunker Hill suspension bridge with its tall concrete pylons and angled array of steel cables. It was a beautiful bridge, Coffin thought, even though it looked like a strong wind could knock it down.

"What about Poblano?"

"He's changed his story once or twice," Mancini said. 'First he said what he told you—that Duckworth was in P'town investigating cyber crime. Then we told him we knew about the blackmail notes, and he said he sent Duckworth to look into it, but with strict instructions that no one would get hurt."

"Any background on Duckworth?"

"About what you'd expect. Ex–Special Forces, Iraq vet, possible PTSD. A couple of suspensions for inappropriate behavior. On the verge of getting shit-canned when Poblano scooped him up and put him on the cy-crime task force."

"What about the two goons that tossed Lola's place?" Coffin said. "Who sent *them*?"

Mancini fiddled with the radio, settling on a classic rock station—Aerosmith singing "Janie's Got a Gun." "I have no idea what you're talking about, Coffin," he said. "Absolutely no idea."

Coffin sat in his mother's room at Valley View, watching her big TV. "C'mon, Ma," he said. "You have to talk to me *sometime*."

She glared at him, arms crossed over her chest, black eyes full of feral rage.

"We haven't talked to anyone in three days," the plump nurse said. "We're just so mad at everybody, aren't we, Sarah?"

"Thanks, Natalie," Coffin said. He couldn't stand her. "I'd be mad, too," he said, "if I had to stay here."

Natalie looked at him for a moment, as though she were about to say something. Then she picked up the untouched breakfast tray and left the room.

"I hate that fat bitch," Coffin's mother said after a minute had passed. "All that *we* shit all the time, makes me want to kill her."

Three days later, Mancini called Coffin at home. "How's your balls, Coffin?" he said.

"Better," Coffin said. "Thanks for asking."

"That's not really why I called," Mancini said. "I've got some news about Bobby Cavalo."

Coffin sat on a kitchen stool. Talking on the phone made him want a cigarette, but he'd promised Jamie he'd quit. Again. "Okay. Let's have it."

"We found his body in the trunk of an abandoned rent-a-car in Hyannis. Your pal Duckworth did some pretty fancy carving on him."

"Can't say I'm surprised," Coffin said. "So what's it look like for Poblano?"

"Don't know yet," Mancini said. "The Worcester office is talking accessory, but I'm guessing they'll cut a deal. It's too bad—I liked Poblano. I figured he'd probably be governor some day."

"Less competition for you if he's out of the picture."

"You make a good point, Coffin," Mancini said. "Hey—one question for you."

"Shoot."

"How come you and Winters didn't wait for backup before you went into the dildo room? You trying to get yourselves killed?"

"It was a calculated risk. We were afraid there might be civilians back there."

"Sure you were," Mancini said. "Lucky for you Winters was wearing her vest. Otherwise I'd have you up on charges."

"That would be the least of my worries."

"I'll keep you posted on the Poblano thing. Odds are pretty good he's going down."

Coffin hung up. Jamie was upstairs putting on her makeup. In a few minutes, they'd walk over to the Art League to check out the opening of the annual erotic art show, where Kotowski had a piece on display. There would be grapes and cheese cubes and white wine, but Coffin needed something stronger. He took a glass from the cabinet, pried a couple of ice cubes from the tray in the freezer, dropped them in, and poured a double shot of Johnnie Walker. Then he walked out to the screen porch, sat in the swing, and lit a cigarette His eyes were still badly bruised, and he couldn't breathe through his nose: He'd probably need surgery the doctor had said.

"Frank?" It was Jamie. She was beautiful, Coffin thought—long skirt, tank top, sandals, a short neck lace made of red coral from Ecuador. "What's up? How are you?"

"I'm still trying to sort the whole thing out," he said "Not so much the murder—murder I can understand It's Poblano and Boyle I can't figure out."

Jamie nodded. "I read somewhere that men fear public humiliation more than death," she said. "Maybe it's true."

"How do *two* people just step over the body of some one they've been intimate with, without so much as calling 911? Not one—two! It's un-fucking-believable." Coffin swirled his drink and set the glass down.

"Things get weird when people start to make bad choices," Jamie said. She took a sip from Coffin's glass then another.

"Usually all it takes is a whole lot of stupid," Coffin said. "One stupid action leads to another, and next thing you know, out come the guns. This was different. Maybe too much weird sex makes people crazy."

Jamie smiled and kissed the top of Coffin's head. "Maybe too much. Maybe not enough," she said. "Come on, Frank. Let's go look at some erotic art. It might take your mind off things."

Coffin laughed. "You're kidding, right?"

Jamie took his hand, pulled him to his feet, and kissed him on the mouth. "Sort of," she said.

"Ow," Coffin said.

* * *

The Provincetown Art League was an odd architectural hodgepodge, part old Provincetown sea captain's house in white clapboard, part hypermodern new construction: boxy and fortresslike from the outside; big, vaulted gallery spaces inside, with skylights and climate control. It was an awkward marriage, Coffin thought, of the old and new—an apt metaphor for Provincetown and its blind stumble into the future.

The show was pretty much what Coffin had expected, lots of paintings, photographs, and sculptures of naked men: naked men alone, naked men together, naked man eating a sandwich. There were naked women, too— naked women in combat boots, naked women with shaved heads, naked women lifting weights. Gemma's piece was there, as was Gemma herself, resplendent in cowboy boots, sequined hot pants, and a see-through top. She waved; Coffin waved back.

Some of the images were funny: a photo of little army men rappelling down a giant breast; a velvet painting of dogs dressed up in S&M gear. The most disturbing piece was Kotowski's: a large, dark painting of a woman in a black leather bustier and plumed black leather mask, violating a balding, hairy man with a big strap-on dildo. The man wore a ball gag and seemed to be crying out in ecstasy, or pain, or both. He looked very much like former Provincetown police chief Preston Boyle.

Kotowski was there, drinking a beer and admiring his own piece. "God," he said. "Is this embarrassing, or what? Have you ever seen so much godawful crap in your life?"

"Oh, look," Jamie said. "It's Lola." She waved. "Who's that pretty girl she's with?"

"Her name's Kate something," Coffin said. "I haven't really met her."

Jamie poked him in the bicep. "Are we a little bit jealous?"

"We are not," Coffin said. "We are a *lot* jealous."

"Now I'm all curious. I think I'll go over and say hi."

When she was gone, Coffin turned to Kotowski. "You really think it's that bad?" he said.

"It's a catastrophe," Kotowski said. He sipped his beer. "At least there's no anthropomorphic driftwood this year."

"I don't know," Coffin said. "I kind of liked the bald ladies."

"Photography," Kotowski sneered. "Instant art for the literal-minded."

"Don't be such a snob," Coffin said. "Not everything has to be an oil painting. What about that sculpture of two women kissing? That wasn't too bad, right?"

"The good news," Kotowski said, "is that it's probably breakable." He sipped his beer. "Say, your uncle came by last night, trying to sell me his Bollock."

"His what?"

"That painting he thinks is a Pollock. Where'd he find that thing, anyway?"

"Wait a minute—are you saying it's not a real Pollock?"

Kotowski snorted. "Of course it's not. It's a Bollock. One of several I painted in the seventies, as a joke. Damned if they don't keep turning up."

"A *Bollock*?"

"Yep. That's how I signed them. Funny, huh?"

Coffin laughed. "Poor Rudy," he said. "He must be devastated."

"Well, it's not worth what he'd get for a real Pollock," Kotowski said, "but it *is* an authentic Kotowski."

"You and your mystery collector," Coffin said. He

nodded at the painting of Boyle. "I take it you're over your block."

"Well, this one was a no-brainer," Kotowski said. "I'm still working on the title, though."

"How about *Lawsuit Pending*," Coffin said.

"He can't sue," Kotowski said. "It's satire."

"If you say so," Coffin said.

"So," Kotowski said. "How goes the spawn?"

"Still swimming upstream," Coffin said.

"You breeders fascinate me," Kotowski said. "Months of humiliation, thousands of dollars down the drain, and if it works, what do you get out of the deal? A squalling brat, that's what—a noisy little crap machine. What the fuck are you going to do with a baby at your age? Do you know how *old* you'll be when the kid gets out of high school?"

Jamie stood across the gallery, elegant in her long skirt, hair up, backlit and golden. She was smiling, animated, talking to Lola and Kate.

Coffin shrugged. "You're right," he said. "I'll be ancient. But it's what Jamie wants. *Really* wants. What am I going to tell her? No?"

"I see your point," Kotowski said, looking at Jamie. "She's way out of your league. Anyplace else, I doubt she'd have anything to do with you."

"Exactly," Coffin said.

Kotowski stared, then squinted. "Wait a minute," he said. He looked at Coffin, then pointed at Jamie. "She's knocked up, isn't she? She's got that freaking *glow* you people are always babbling about."

Coffin shrugged. "She thinks she is," he said. "Too soon to tell."

Kotowski shivered and made a retching sound. "The whole business gives me the heebie-jeebies. Preggo!

Christ on a fucking cracker." He finished his beer and set it down on a pedestal next to a wood sculpture of a fat man with a gigantic erection. "What's going to happen to Boyle, do you think? And that Poblano cat—he's *really* screwed, right?"

"Boyle's probably going to plead guilty to a couple of misdemeanor charges: theft, failure to report a death. He might do a few months, pay a fine. Of course, he's done in law enforcement—outside of Wal-Mart security guard, or whatever."

"What about Poblano?"

"He says he never hired Duckworth to kill anybody—just to recover the video of him and Kenji Sole. Mancini thinks they'll cut some kind of deal. We'll see what happens."

"Why do these guys get the kid glove treatment?" Kotowski said. "What the fuck is up with that?"

"No trials, no evidence, case closed," Coffin said. "Less work for everybody, the state saves money, Boyle and Poblano do a little time, lose their jobs, their wives divorce them. Justice is served."

"Justice? You call that *justice*? Look at you—you almost got killed. Again." Kotowski frowned. "You think Mancini was sleeping with Kenji Sole? Is that what this is about?"

"He's not on the DVR," Coffin said. "More likely he's just protecting his colleagues. What goes around comes around, and all that."

"One hand washes the other, you mean," Kotowski said. He shook his head. "They're all fucking crooks—the system's rotten from top to bottom."

"That's it?" Coffin said. "That's your big insight? The system sucks?"

Kotowski waved a dismissive hand. "You're an optimist. I can't take you seriously."

"I am *not* an optimist," Coffin said.

"Of course you are," Kotowski said. "Otherwise you wouldn't be trying to have a kid. I mean, my God— you've got global warming, economic collapse, war everywhere you look, bird flu, energy shortages, food shortages, that crazy particle accelerator in France, the honeybees dying off—you know what Einstein said, right?"

"Particle accelerator? What particle accelerator?"

"He said that if the honeybees all die, humans pretty much go extinct in four years. Four years!"

"What particle accelerator?"

"But there you are—being a freaking mammal like everything's just fine. How can you say you're not an optimist?"

Coffin raised an eyebrow.

"Jesus," Kotowski said. "You're relentless—no wonder you're good at being a cop. There's a new particle accelerator under the French Alps that's seventeen fucking miles long. If the guys who are running it aren't careful, they could produce a black hole that'll destroy the planet."

"Oh," Coffin said. "Let's go outside and have a smoke."

"Oh?" Kotowski said. "*Oh?* A bunch of French physicists might accidentally generate a killer black hole under the freaking Alps and all you can say is *oh*?"

"What do you want me to say?" Coffin said, pulling Kotowski outside by his shirt.

"Well, some expression of concern would be nice," Kotowski said. They stood in the sculpture garden, in the long shadow of a tall abstract bronze.

Coffin lit a cigarette and offered the pack to Kotowski. "Okay," he said. "I'm concerned. Happy now?"

"Reasonably content," Kotowski said, puffing at his cigarette. "More or less. For the moment."

A fat skunk waddled across Commercial Street, ignoring them. The Long Point foghorn skwonked, even though there was no fog. Coffin looked up at the night sky. The stars were in sharp focus: Big Dipper, Orion's belt. A meteor blazed and then winked out above the Pilgrim Monument. A good sign, a dark omen. "Well," Coffin said, "you can't ask for more than that."

ACKNOWLEDGMENTS

Many thanks to Richard and Alice Goldin for their amazing help and enthusiasm. Thanks to the L.A. Nation for buying so many copies of the first one. Huge thanks also to Gloria Loomis for buying the new furnace. And the new screen porch. And the new Teleaster. I am grateful also to Kelley and Maria for their guidance, patience, and encouragement, and to Bill Tapply and Chris Grabenstein for blurbing *High Season*. Thanks to Richard at All Things Digital for walking me through the ins and outs of home surveillance, and to marmar at DU for the best line ever. Thanks to all at JWEC who have expressed support for the writing of these books (and enjoyment in the reading of them). Thanks to my lovely family for putting up with my weirdness and coming to visit me in book jail. Incandescent love and devotion always to Allyson: What were you thinking?